WHAT A SWELL SITUATION.

The mob was after me because they thought I stole their money. The cops were after me because they thought I either queered their bust or I was involved in the cocaine trade. I'd been smeared with toothpaste, had my shin cracked, had my place torn apart twice, been threatened with a slow death and a long imprisonment. And the only person who could straighten this out, everyone says has been dead for two years.

Other Avon Books Coming Soon by
L. A. Morse

THE BIG ENCHILADA

THE OLD DICK

L. A. MORSE

AVON
PUBLISHERS OF BARD, CAMELOT, DISCUS AND FLARE BOOKS

THE OLD DICK is an original publication of Avon Books. This work has never before appeared in book form.

AVON BOOKS
A division of
The Hearst Corporation
959 Eighth Avenue
New York, New York 10019

First Avon Printing, August, 1981

AVON TRADEMARK REG. U.S. PAT. OFF. AND IN
OTHER COUNTRIES, MARCA REGISTRADA, HECHO EN
U.S.A.

Printed in the U.S.A.

10 9 8 7 6 5 4 3 2 1

For Sheila

THE
OLD DICK

CHAPTER ONE

Duke Pachinko lay propped against the wall, a dripping red sponge where his face used to be. He wouldn't bother anyone again.

The blonde looked at the body, and then she looked back at me. Her eyes narrowed and her lips parted. Her tongue darted out of her mouth and moistened her lips. She reached out and took the gun from my hand. Her fingers closed around the barrel and moved up and down its length, caressing it slowly. Her skin looked very white against the blue-black metal. She raised the gun to her mouth. Her tongue came out again, and she ran the tip of it lightly along the barrel. Her mouth formed a moist circle and closed over the end of the gun. She kept her eyes locked on mine the whole time. Her eyes were slightly slanted and blue like those of a Siamese cat. Her breathing deepened.

She tossed the gun aside. She put her hands around my wrists. She slowly raised my hands and placed them on her breasts. At my touch, a brief cry escaped from her throat. Her breasts were firm and heavy beneath the thin silk of her dress. She wore no bra, and I could feel the temperature of her flesh rising behind the cool fabric as her breasts seemed to swell. She pressed herself against my hands. Her nipples grew hard in my palms.

Her breath was coming in deep shuddering gasps. I put my hands at the neck of her dress. A quick pull, and the silk tore apart with slithery ripping sound. The blonde moaned low as her dress fell around her ankles.

I stepped back to look at her. She was something to see. In a few years all that beautiful flesh would begin to sag,

9

*but right now she was as firm as a marble statue and as
juicy as an overripe peach.*

*She stepped out of the remnants of her dress and
walked across to me, moving like she was hypnotized, her
eyes fastened on the bulge in my trousers. She undid the
button at the waist and pulled down the zipper. She put
her hand inside my pants. She gave a long sigh when she
found me. I was huge and hard and burning hot. I . . .*

Shit.

I closed the book and put it down on the bench beside
me. I really didn't need to read stuff like that. It wasn't
that sex offended me; it was just that I couldn't see the
point. After all, I was nearly seventy-eight years old, and
I hadn't had an erection for five years. Hell, if my own
fantasies couldn't get me up, I couldn't very well expect
results from those of some pseudonymous hack.

I thought about the blonde fellating the gun and I
smiled. If the detective had just finished emptying it into
the face of Duke Pachinko, the barrel probably would
have been uncomfortably hot to touch, not to mention the
coating of machine oil that would have been on it. A
mouthful of blisters and four-in-one wasn't my idea of an
erotic sensation, but maybe the blonde knew something I
didn't.

I turned to face the sun. I unbuttoned my shirt, revealing a seventy-eight-year-old chest with scraggly gray hairs
covering half a dozen ugly scars—not a pleasant sight, but
I didn't care. One of the few advantages of getting really
old is that people don't talk to you. They cluck and they
say, "Look at that. Isn't that disgusting? That old fart
should be put away." But unless you go around waving
your schlong at school kids, they keep away from you.
They're probably afraid that old age is contagious.

A fair number of women had once liked my chest, scars
and all, but that was a long time ago. It must have been
three decades since I'd received a compliment. At least I
wasn't fat. When you got old, you either went soft or you
got dry. Fortunately, I had gotten dry.

Actually, considering that I was seventy-eight, slightly
arthritic, and often insomniac, I wasn't in too bad shape.
My health was pretty good, no major problems. My stomach acted up from time to time. My doctor at the clinic—a

thirty-five-year-old with a weight problem, ulcers, fallen arches, a smoker's cough, and dandruff—told me to stop eating spicy food. Since that was one of my few remaining real pleasures, I usually ignored the advice. I also often regretted having done so, but what the hell. If I were going to go, a lethal *chile verde* seemed as good a way as any. "J. Spanner: Suddenly, in the night, from an exploding burrito." I could go along with that.

I exercised a fair amount, mostly walking, and I lifted some weights to keep up the strength in my arms. My muscles had shrunk, but they still almost worked, which was more than you could say for most of the people waddling around. Christ, a trip to the beach revealed so much excess weight that I was surprised the country didn't overbalance and tip into the sea.

Oh, I was a tough old bird, all right, as I once overheard someone say about me. Since I had just told that person to fuck off, I'm not sure it was meant as a compliment, but I took it as one. In fact, however, except for my nose, which is prominent and rather beaky, I thought of myself much more as a lizard. My skin was dry, and a lot of time in the sun had given it the color of old leather. Like a lizard, I thrived in the sun—the hotter, the better —and I didn't feel very good if the day turned cool or damp. I'd sit for hours, my shirt open, hardly moving, soaking up that warmth. I didn't even sweat any more, no matter how hot it was. Yes, I was very definitely saurian.

I always liked hot climates, and the older I got, the more I found I needed the heat. Summers in L.A. were fine, with the temperature often getting over a hundred in the sun, but the winters were starting to give me trouble. Even when the weather was good, it would feel too cold. I'd have liked to be able to move to Mexico or somewhere tropical, but my finances didn't permit it.

Finances. Shit. The ever-increasing erosion of my little bit of capital could hardly be dignified by that word. I was still managing to get by okay—at least I wasn't yet shoplifting or eating cat food—but nothing more than that, and I didn't know how much longer it would last. Somehow or other, I had gotten myself into the position that if I didn't die soon, I'd be broke. Well, I'd worry about it later . . . which was probably the attitude that had gotten me into this situation in the first place.

I stretched my neck like an iguana and felt the sun on my forehead, which, for the last thirty years, had extended to the middle of my skull. The park I was in wasn't much more than a strip of brown grass next to and overlooking one of the huge, dry, concrete-lined canyons that are called rivers in L.A. I couldn't quite see the boxlike monolith of the May Co., but I could hear and smell the cars in the Sears and J. C. Penney parking lot. A real wilderness area.

There were some kids playing baseball across the park from me. There were white kids and black kids and Chinese and Japanese and Mexican and a couple I wasn't sure about. That was something you wouldn't have seen even ten years ago. Lots of people didn't like it; but then, lots of people are assholes.

There was a group of older kids sitting under some sad gray trees that didn't seem to be coping with exhaust fumes very well. What did? The kids were passing a joint around, and even though they were giggling, they didn't look very happy.

I watched as an immense shiny black limousine moved slowly along the road that ran next to the park. The road eventually ended up in the parking lot, and I figured the limo's owner had just come from picking up the weekly special at Thrifty Mart, spending three bucks on gas to save thirty-nine cents on razor blades. The car had those dark one-way-glass windows, and it looked more like some sleek experimental submarine than an automobile.

It glided to a stop directly opposite me and about fifty feet away. I couldn't see inside, but I had the feeling I was being watched. Maybe the chauffeur was going to get out and tell me that his employer—a wealthy elderly widow—admired the depth of my tan, and wanted to set me up in a villa in the Bahamas.

The chauffeur didn't get out, but the back door opened. A thin, very tall figure unfolded itself from the back seat. He wore a black three-piece suit, a brilliantly white shirt, a dark striped necktie, and heavy dark glasses that made his narrow face look like a death's head. It could have been a Madison Avenue version of the Grim Reaper.

When he took a couple of steps toward me, I suddenly realized that I wasn't far wrong. Instead of the benevolent dowager I had momentarily fantasized, I was seeing a ghost. A ghost who I didn't think would be especially friendly.

One of the reasons I'd made it to seventy-eight was that I usually had a good sense of when to bow out. This looked like one of those times.

He was still some distance from me, so I stood up casually, making like I hadn't really noticed him, and started to walk away. I planned to walk north through the park. The limo was pointing south, and there was no place nearby for it to turn around, so that took care of the car. If the guy followed on foot, I was going to go across to the parking lot, and then into the shopping center. If I didn't shake him, I wanted to be sure there were lots of people around when we met.

"Hey, Jake!" he called. "Wait up."

I didn't turn around, but started to walk faster.

He called my name again. I glanced over my shoulder and saw that he was starting to run. With his coat flapping behind him and his long arms and legs working, he looked like a great black stork trying to lift off the ground. I started to run.

I said I was in pretty good shape, but that was relative. Even though my body still more or less functioned, it didn't mean I was ready for a cross-country run, and I hadn't gone very far before I started to feel lousy.

I looked back. He wasn't moving any better than I was, but his legs were longer, so he gained a little with every step.

I ran by the dope-smoking kids, who laughingly shouted encouragement. We must have looked funny, all right, two old coots, gasping and flailing along. Inside, I felt like I was racing like the wind, but I knew from the outside that we must have seemed like a slow-motion pantomime.

Ordinarily, you wouldn't notice it, but there was a slight upgrade to the park. Now it felt like a forty-five degree slope, Heartbreak Hill in the Boston Marathon. My legs grew heavy and my chest burned. The air seemed viscous, resistant, like I was running through molasses. The pounding of my heart was all I could hear. It sounded like death approaching. I figured I had gone all of fifty yards. Old age sure is swell.

I turned my head to look back, my foot caught on a sprinkler, and I fell on my face. I tried to get up, but my legs were leaden jelly, so I rolled onto my back and waited.

He came up and stood over me. He put his hands on his knees, taking deep breaths. We panted at each other for about five minutes. Every so often one of us tried to say something, but nothing came out. Finally, he managed some intelligible sounds.

"What were you trying to do, Jake, give us both coronaries? You stupid son of a bitch."

"Hello, Sal," I said.

His name was Sal Piccolo. In the old days, he'd been known as Sal the Salami, because of the size of his sexual organ. I didn't know what he was called these days. I couldn't place it, but somehow I had the idea that he was supposed to be dead. On the other hand, at my age you naturally tended to assume that most of your contemporaries were dead, so maybe that was how I'd gotten the idea. In any case, I wasn't exactly pleased to be wrong.

"What'd you run for?" Sal said.

"You know very well why I ran."

"What? You don't mean that—"

"Yeah. I mean exactly that."

"But that was—what?—forty-two, forty-three years ago?"

"About that."

"Come on, Jake. I'm seventy-five now."

"So?"

"So you think I still hold that grudge?"

"Why not? You always were a vindictive bastard."

Forty-something years ago, Sal Piccolo was a hell of a lot more than a vindictive bastard. He was very nearly The Man. He'd managed to get a pretty good-sized piece of most of the rackets in town. There was very little he didn't have a finger in, and even less that he didn't know about. He had a good thing going for himself, but—naturally—he wanted more, and eventually he wanted too much. He tried to muscle his way into a large interest in one of the studios. The studio boss was an old-time New York street fighter who wasn't about to put up with any shit like that, and he hired me to muscle Sal back out. Not only did I get him out of the studio, but I got him into prison for a good long stretch. Obviously, Sal wasn't very happy about that turn of events, and—in true Hollywood fashion—swore he'd get me.

He very nearly kept his promise. One of his boys, an eight-foot-tall monster named Dinky O'Grady, came after me with a meat cleaver. Dinky had arms like a gorilla and a brain the size of a walnut. He gave me two of the worst scars I carry, and I gave him a third eye in the center of his forehead.

That's the kind of stuff that's known as the good old days. Shit.

Sal had been strictly an independent, and when he went up, his organization didn't last very long. Some well-connected boys from back East came out, divided up his action, and that was that. None of the new guys had anything against me, so I was able to stop ducking for cover every time I heard a car backfire. In the last forty years, I probably hadn't thought about Sal Piccolo more than a handful of times. But I figured he'd thought about me a lot more. He'd certainly had plenty of time for reflection. And now there he was, smiling over me like a grinning skull.

"If you're going to do it, do it," I said. "I'm not going to beg or squeal or whimper. I'm too old and too tired. I want to live as much as anybody, but if the last few years have been any indication of what the next few will be like, you won't be taking anything very valuable from me."

"Not like you took from me, you mean?"

"That's right."

Sal smiled and shook his head. "Same old Jake Spanner. Hard as nails, and never give an inch."

"This is the old Jake Spanner, not the same one. But why don't you just get it over with, okay?"

I wasn't quite as bored as I sounded. In fact, I was scared, but I was also damned if I was going to play mouse to his cat. Given the choice, I'd always tried never to give any satisfaction to assholes. A few years earlier I might have been able to perform some nifty physical move to get myself out of this situation, like kicking him in the crotch and then stomping on his face, but now that was out of the question. About all I could still do was to diminish his pleasure by acting cooler than I felt.

Sal shook his head again. "You really think I came here to kill you?"

"It wouldn't be the first stupid thing you've done."

A spasm of anger contorted his face, but he quickly regained control. In the old days, Sal, like most people who usually got their own way, had had a short fuse. He still seemed to, but now there was also more control than I remembered.

"Thirty years is a long time," he said.

"That how long you did?"

"Yeah."

"That's a long time." I looked up at him standing over me. "But maybe not long enough."

"It was long enough, Jake. For the first ten years, I thought about you all the time. I hated you more than I ever hated anyone or anything. Each night I went to sleep thinking about what I would do when I finally caught up with you. My hatred was the thing that kept me going. I wanted to make you suffer the way you made me suffer."

"I didn't do it to you, Sal. You did it to yourself."

Even as I said it, I groaned inside. Shit. Sal had made an honest expression of what he had thought and felt, I had made an honest reply, and we both sounded like we were mouthing dialogue from some hideously bad movie. I could hear the hoots of laughter coming from the darkened theater. That was the problem with trash: not only was it awful in itself, but it also made perfectly legitimate ideas and feelings seem ridiculous.

Sal, however, seemed untroubled by the aesthetics of the scene, as he slowly nodded his head. "It took me ten years to realize that."

"Oh?"

"You're right. I'd been stupid—stupid and greedy. I finally saw that you weren't to blame. I was."

"You got religion?"

"No, not religion. You might say I got . . ."

He paused, searching for the right word, and I was certain he was going to say "self-knowledge."

". . . I got self-knowledge," he said with absolute seriousness.

Under the circumstances, I thought it best not to laugh. Instead, I said, "Oh?"

"Yeah. I had a lot of time, and I used it. I changed,

Jake. . . . What's the matter? You look like you don't believe me. Don't you think a man can change?"

I looked up at Sal. He seemed sincere, but he had always been a good actor when he kept his temper under control. He'd also always been one of the most devious sons of bitches I'd ever met. Did I believe him? Did I think a man could change? I answered honestly. "I don't know," I said.

"What about you, Jake? It's been over forty years, more than half your life. Haven't you changed in that time?"

I shrugged. I really didn't know. Oh, I could look in the mirror and see the wrinkles and the sags, and I could feel everything slowing down, but inside I felt the same. I could remember being sixteen and putting my hand on a woman's breast for the first time, and I was still that same kid. I was the same twenty-five-year-old who was in Paris when Paris was the place to be. I still knew how I felt the first time I shot a man, and the first time I was shot. But even more than specific memories, I was still looking at things with the same eyes, responding with the same brain. Maybe I knew some more stuff, and maybe I understood some things a little better, and maybe a few ideas had changed, but the basics were still the same. Inside, I was still essentially the young, sharp, tough kid I'd always been. That was maybe the greatest humiliation of growing old—the discrepancy between the internal reality and the exterior one. Even though I'd had a lot of practice by now, I still had trouble reconciling them. I've heard that's what happens to athletes at the end of their careers. In their heads they still have all the moves, they still think their bodies are the perfectly conditioned, superbly functioning, completely responsive machines they were when they were twenty. But they're not twenty anymore, and their reactions are fractionally slower, and that fraction is enough for failure. It must be a little bit sad to be a fine athlete, because you grow old twice.

Shit. I wasn't usually so introspective. Sal was going to get his revenge by making me maudlin. What a way to go. "J. Spanner: Finally, after a lingering bout of morbid solemnity."

"So you came here to tell me I could stop worrying about you, is that it?" I said.

"No, Jake, that's not it." He seemed to grow more serious. He looked around. The dope smokers were still watching us, though without much interest. "But this isn't a very dignified position for two old men to have a conversation in."

He held out his hand. I took it and got to my feet, but not before I had almost pulled him down on top of me. The line between dignity and slapstick can be very fine.

We went over and sat down on opposite sides of a dusty picnic table next to the chain link fence that guarded the river.

"Every time I see this," I said, pointing into the concrete gully, "I keep expecting to see giant ants."

"What?"

"You know, from the movie *Them*. Giant mutant ants that lived in the storm drains."

"Never heard of it."

"Sure, you must've. About twenty-five years ago. Starred James Whitmore, I think."

"I was in the joint then."

"That's right, of course. Well, you didn't miss much . . . the movie, I mean."

"Hmm," Sal said, not really paying much attention. He seemed kind of uneasy. He glanced around at the limo, which was gleaming darkly in the sun. The driver was leaning against it, smoking a cigarette.

"Looks like you're doing okay," I said.

"What?" He turned back around. "Oh, yeah. I'm all right. I may have been stupid, but I wasn't a jerk."

"What do you mean?"

"I was putting dough away, banking it, buying things, investing a little. Not a lot, but some. So when I got out, I had something waiting for me. Not like most of the punks inside, who have to start pulling jobs the moment they're released. Thirty years' of compound interest adds up."

"I guess it does."

"How about yourself?"

I couldn't see his eyes behind his dark glasses, but I didn't need to. I could imagine the expression in them. I was wearing a loose-fitting fifties Hawaiian floral print shirt in some shiny fabric, baggy trousers of the same vintage, and much-repaired sandals, without socks. I would've been a hot number on Skid Row, but as it was, I looked like a senile beachcomber who had misplaced the ocean. I had better clothes. I just didn't bother to wear them very often.

"Today's board of directors' meeting for General Motors was canceled, so I decided to take it easy," I said.

"No, really. How are things?"

I looked at him for a long minute. "I wasn't stupid, but I was a jerk."

Sal nodded. "I see. . . . Rough?"

I shrugged. "It could be worse. It probably will be."

"This'll sound dumb, but today I'd trade places with you."

He was right: it sounded dumb, and I laughed. "Okay I'll give you this swell shirt, and you give me your limo."

He tried a smile, and then looked down at the long line of ants that were traversing the picnic table. I watched him watch the ants for a while. Fascinating.

"Sal, what're you doing here?" I finally said.

He looked to each side, and then over his shoulder, and then at me. He took off his glasses. His eyes were tired and strained. "I need help, Jake."

"In what?"

He paused. "You got a family?"

"Not really."

I had a daughter in Kansas—Kansas!—who wrote me a note every few years, and a couple of grandkids I'd never seen. It was to be expected. After my wife left me to go home to her folks, I didn't see my daughter for nearly twenty years. Now she didn't see any reason to see me, and I couldn't blame her. Besides, she didn't approve of me, and that was only natural, since she supported Ronald Reagan, Anita Bryant, and any repressive, fascistic causes that came along. Imagine having a child like that! It just shows how little influence heredity has on personality. But maybe these things skip a generation, like diabetes, and her kids'll get back on track.

"Too bad," Sal said. "I've got a grandson. Seventeen. He's a great kid. Going to be a doctor."

"That's really nice, Sal. I'm happy for you."

He looked down at the table. He put a bony finger across the line of ants and watched as they panicked, regrouped, and then went around the obstruction. He looked up.

"He's been grabbed," he said.

"What! Kidnapped?"

"Yeah. A week ago."

"Shit, Sal. You go to the police?"

He gave me a look that said it was a stupid question.

"Why not?" I said. "You're not still connected with anything, are you?"

"No. I've been clean since I got out."

"Then why not tell the cops? This is their kind of thing."

"Hell, Jake, I can't do that. Habit, for one thing. I never went to the cops for a problem. I can't start now. For another, I'm an old villain. What kind of attention would they give me?"

"You might be surprised."

"I doubt it. Anyway, I couldn't trust them not to screw up."

I thought Sal was wrong, but I wasn't going to argue with him about it. "So what are you going to do?"

"Give those bastards exactly what they want."

"Which is?"

"Money."

"How much?"

"Three-quarters of a million."

"Jesus Christ! You got that much?"

"Just. By getting rid of everything I have, I can just make it."

"Shit. You won't have anything left."

"I'll have my grandson."

"Maybe."

Sal's fist hit the table. "I'll have my grandson," he repeated, as though saying it again would make it true.

I didn't share his confidence; but then, it wasn't my grandson's neck on the line. Sal had no choice but to believe it would work.

"What about the boy's parents?" I said.

"His father's dead. His mother—my daughter—is a cheap tramp screwing her way around Europe, trying to pretend she's not pushing fifty."

"At least she's not a neo-fascist."

"What?"

"Nothing. Go on."

"Even if I knew where to reach her—which I don't—she wouldn't be any help. Tommy's been my responsibility since his father died. I've looked after him, sent him to the best schools. He's going to go to Harvard. Think about that. A grandson of mine at Harvard. And now . . ."

He turned his head away. This was all very strange. A guy I had sent to prison forty years before was sitting across from me, spilling his guts out. Sal Piccolo was nothing to me, one way or the other, just another ghost. But I felt sorry for him, or at least for his predicament. There aren't many things that are uglier than kidnapping, and I understood why Sal had said he'd trade places with me today. Under the circumstances, I wouldn't have accepted. The way it looked, Sal would probably lose his money and the kid. Fucking ugly. But why come to me?

That's what I asked him.

"I've got the money," Sal said, "and I'm going to make the drop tonight. I want you to come along."

What! The man was clearly unraveled. "You're crazy," I said.

"No, I mean it."

"Why?"

"The usual reasons. Back-up. Moral support. Whatever."

"No—I meant, why me?"

"Why not you?"

"Sal, you're not only crazy, you're blind. Maybe you haven't noticed, but I'm about a million years old. I just ran fifty yards in around two minutes, and nearly killed myself in the process. What the hell good would I be if there was any trouble? Come on, Sal, don't play this thing any dumber than necessary."

"I don't think I'm being dumb. What do you think I should do?"

"I think you should go to the cops. But since you won't do that, get somebody young, somebody strong, somebody whose body still works, for Christ sake. It shouldn't be that hard. If you don't know anyone—hell—the phone book is full of P.I.s and security agencies who are professionals at being bodyguards."

Sal shook his head. "No good."

"Why not?"

"You know as well as I do, Jake. You must run into it all the time. We're old men, and nobody takes old men very seriously. We're just easy marks—to be played with or ripped off or fucked around. . . . Look. A while back I hired an investigator for something. He was young and strong and tough, just like you said. He was highly recommended. Well, when the dust cleared, he had taken me for about ten grand. When I called him on it, he laughed. It was a joke. As far as he was concerned, I was old, and therefore I didn't count. I wasn't there, I wasn't a man, I could be fucked around with."

"So you were unlucky. Not everyone's like that."

"Oh?" he said, his thin lips curling in disgust.

I knew what he meant. Every day, I was treated to the feeling that I was invisible, or useless, or taking up space —that I was senile, or feeble, or incompetent, or stupid. It wasn't necessarily in big things, it was just a general attitude, and it took a lot of effort to overcome it. Mostly, it was too much trouble to try, so you lived up to people's preconceptions and eventually their preconceptions became valid. You became feeble and stupid; you took up space. People have always divided the world into "us" and "them," but when you're old, you never fit in, so you're always "them." You can never be sure about, never really trust anyone a lot younger; the gulf in attitude is too great.

I looked at Sal and shook my head. I was being maneuvered into some place I didn't want to be, and I didn't like it.

"Jake," he said, "there's nothing between us. No love, no friendship, nothing except maybe some understanding. You're the guy that sent me up. Okay, so what? Maybe that's why I can come to you. You were a son of a bitch, but you were a straight son of a bitch. I need someone who I know won't fuck me."

"Sal, I—"

"Jake, I'm scared. This is my grandson, my life. Put yourself in my place."

Shit. He had touched all the bases, pulled all the strings. The old times, fraternity, pride, guilt, and now straight-out sentiment. He was still pretty good. What the hell could I say?

"All right, Sal. I think you're making a real big mistake, but if you want me to go along, I will. I don't see how I can be any help, but if you want company, you've got it."

Sal looked at me and nodded. "Thanks, Jake." He reached in his jacket and took out a slender wallet. Alligator, I thought.

"What are you doing?" I said.

"I'm going to pay you."

"I don't want your money."

"I'm not some asshole who asks for favors and doesn't give anything in return. I never worked like that. I pay my way."

"Look, I—"

"Don't be a schmuck, Jake. You told me to hire someone. That's what I'm doing. Does five hundred dollars seem fair for the evening?"

"I'm not doing this for money."

Why the hell was I doing it? Certainly not out of friendship. Maybe I felt sorry for him? Maybe it sounded like fun, a last bit of action? Shit, I didn't know. But I did realize that Sal was the kind of person who had to pay. If he hadn't bought you, he didn't feel right about it, in control. There are a lot of people like that, who don't trust relationships unless they can be clarified by cash.

"Five hundred okay?" he asked, pushing five crisp bills across to me.

I looked down at the money. If that was the way he wanted it, why not? It would put off cat food for a little while longer.

"Yeah, five hundred's fine."

I shook my head and laughed. It was actually kind of funny. After fifteen years, I was working again. For one night, I would be the world's oldest private eye.

Take that, Duke Pachinko.

Shit.

CHAPTER TWO

"Yoo-hoo, Mr. Spanner!"

Damn.

I had been thinking about my meeting with Sal, not paying attention to what I was doing, and I had automatically taken the most direct route from the park back to my house. Usually, I walked the long way around and approached my house from the other direction, so as to avoid just this occurrence.

Mrs. Bernstein was a sweet lady, getting on a bit, in her late sixties, who lived a couple of doors up from me. Her husband had died about five years before, and for four years she'd been making a play for me. She always seemed to be on her small front porch, washing the window or repotting begonias or something, and she always called out to me with some sort of invitation, usually to eat. I didn't like constantly refusing, and since there was no sneaking by, I mostly played the coward and went around the block.

There wasn't anything wrong with Mrs. Bernstein. Quite the contrary. She was a genuinely friendly, considerate, sympathetic, concerned, unselfish woman—who could reduce me to snarling, loutish nastiness inside of five minutes. The problem was, she was too nice, the image of Everybody's Grandmother. She was one of those women who had a compulsion to mother you, who wasn't happy unless she could wear herself to a frazzle, caring for you. There were lots of men who liked that, even needed it. If she could find one of those, everything would be great, because their personality kinks would complement one another. But I haven't wanted mothering since

24

I was eight, so Mrs. Bernstein tended to drive me crazy. She was also the worst cook I've ever known.

Still, you could turn down somebody for only so long, before you became a complete schmuck, and two years ago I finally accepted one of Mrs. Bernstein's invitations. To mark the occasion, she pulled out all the stops and made me what she called her "world-famous" cabbage rolls.

Wonderful. I've hated cabbage rolls for probably my entire life. In fact, one of my very earliest memories was hating my own grandmother's "world-famous" cabbage rolls. For seventy-five years I'd never been able to figure if people were sincere in their enthusiasm for them, or if that was the first example of gross hypocrisy that the young Jacob Spanovic was exposed to.

The evening, in fact, turned out to be a lot worse than I thought it would be. Mrs. Bernstein's cooking made my grandmother's seem three-star. Two years later, and the recollection of that meal still made me queasy. I had been polite, though, and dutifully gave the cabbage rolls the praise that had been expected. That was my big mistake, because now, every time Mrs. Bernstein spotted me, I got invited for my "favorite dish."

I should have known better. The late Mr. Bernstein (when he was still early) used to come over to my place for a drink every once in a while. No matter what we started talking about—the weather, the Dodgers, or that asshole Richard Nixon—the subject always became his wife's cooking.

It seemed that, when they were married, the first meal the new Mrs. Bernstein fixed was cabbage rolls, the recipe for which had been passed from mother to daughter for generations. Not wanting to upset his young bride, Bernstein said the cabbage rolls were wonderful. He repeated that judgment the next three or four times they were served, and by then it was too late. After lying, out of love and kindness, there was no way he could suddenly start to tell the truth, and for the next forty years, he was given cabbage rolls twice a week. Naturally, they acquired a significance far out of proportion to their reality, and came to symbolize everything that had gone wrong with his life.

"I figure I've eaten fifteen thousand cabbage rolls," he

used to say after he'd had a couple of shots of whisky, "and I've hated every fucking one of them."

"Well, why don't you say so?"

He'd look wistful for a minute, and then shake his head. "Too late. It'd kill her." He'd knock back another shot. "But you know, Jake, there are times when I think I'd rather die than eat another fucking cabbage roll."

I thought about that when Bernstein was run over by a cement truck, on his way home to dinner, and I wondered what was going to be on the table that night.

Shit.

Everybody tries to be nice and decent and polite. No one wants to be unnecessarily nasty or to cause anyone else needless pain. So we keep our real feelings to ourselves, and little annoyances grow into great festering wounds. Hell, for all Bernstein knew, his wife hated making the damn things as much as he hated eating them, but neither of them could say anything.

Well, Jake Spanner was on record: cabbage rolls stunk. Too bad the record wasn't public.

"Yoo-hoo, Mr. Spanner!" Mrs. Bernstein called again, waving a plastic spray bottle of Windex. Outside of the television screen, Mrs. Bernstein was the only person I'd ever known who said "yoo-hoo," but the expression seemed to fit her, just like the faded print dresses she always wore.

It didn't look like I'd be able to fake a sudden onset of deafness or senility.

"Oh!" I said, trying to look surprised. "Hello, Mrs. Bernstein. I didn't notice you there."

"I haven't seen you for a while, Mr. Spanner."

For a long time I tried to get her to call me Jake, then gave up on it.

"I've been busy, Mrs. Bernstein."

Yeah, I had to get over to the park every day to sit in the sun and read sleazy detective stories. The fate of the Republic depended on it.

"Oh, that's nice. I thought maybe you've been avoiding me."

"Of course not. Why would I do that, Mrs. Bernstein?"

"I don't know. Maybe you don't like my cooking?"

"Don't be silly. I love your cooking. It's just that I've been busy lately."

We were nearly yelling at each other across her front yard. I figured I had better stay on the sidewalk or else she'd ask me in for some of her homemade coffeecake.

"So why are we shouting, Mr. Spanner? Why don't you come in for some nice lemon tea and homemade coffeecake?"

"Gee, Mrs. Bernstein, I'd love to, but I'm expecting an important phone call."

"Then how about dinner tonight? I made your favorite cabbage rolls, and I've got plenty."

"Golly, I'm sorry, but I can't. I'm meeting an old friend."

"Oh, I see."

She struck just the right note of hurt disappointment to make me feel like a real shit, and I almost said, "Look, I really am. I'm keeping an ex-gangster company when he delivers three-quarters of a million dollars to ransom back his kidnapped grandson." But I didn't think it would help. Instead, I said, "Maybe another time?"

"Next week?"

"Maybe," I said uncertainly.

"Friday?"

Shit. For the second time in an hour I'd been suckered. And I used to be pretty fast on my feet. Was this a sign that all those little blood vessels in my brain were starting to dry up?

"Yeah, Friday'll be swell."

Mrs. Bernstein brightened considerably. "And don't worry. I'll make another batch of your favorite."

"That'll be great."

"You know, they were my husband's favorite, too."

"Yeah, I heard." I almost added that I liked them in just the same way, but only a complete asshole would be ironic at the expense of a kindly, if pushy, old lady.

"I'll never forget that I made them on the night he was killed."

"Oh, yeah? Well, I hope I'll have better luck."

"I hope so too . . . Jake." She smiled tentatively.

I smiled back, waved, and walked off.

"Don't forget," she called. "Friday."

I shook my head and waved again.

Nice going, Spanner. Another victory for honesty and forthrightness.

Swell.

Well, it was still a week and a half off. Maybe by then I'd have a bad cold and be unable to smell or taste anything.

Yeah, maybe.

I went up my driveway, trying not to look at the disaster that was my front lawn. The grass was mostly gone, and small piles of petrifying dog turds dotted the area like ornamental displays in a coprophiliac's rock garden. Years of fertilizing, reseeding, resodding, and a generation of Japanese gardeners hadn't been able to do anything with it. Now, old and broke, I had yielded to the inevitable. Even the crab grass was dying.

My house, like all the other ones in the neighborhood, was a tiny two-bedroom box built right after the war. I was only the second occupant of the house—the first lost everything in one of the phony-oil-well swindles that swept California in the late forties—and I had been there about thirty years. When I moved in, I had my choice of buying or renting. At the time, I had been doing pretty well, and could have plunked down the seven grand they were asking and owned the place outright. Needless to say, I didn't.

What the hell. Rents were cheap and there was no reason to think things would ever be different. More important, even though I was old enough to have known better, I still had the feeling that big changes were imminent, that something was about to happen. When it did, I wanted to be able to move fast and light, unburdened by things like houses and mortages. That attitude was one of the reasons my wife had packed up a couple of years earlier, thereby disencumbering me of herself and our kid.

So for twenty years, just like the twenty years that had preceded them, I went on feeling like I was a transient, that this arrangement was only temporary until something better came along, that there was still plenty of time to make a decision. Until the day that, with the clarity of vision that can only come with hindsight, I woke up and realized I had blown it. I was old and retired. The real value of the dough I had so carefully put away was decreasing by the minute. There was no P.I. pension plan, no annuity for old gumshoes. And the dumpy little tract house I had been renting for a quarter of my life was suddenly worth sixty-five grand, way out of reach of an ancient private eye whose string had long since been played out.

Like I told Sal, I had been a jerk.

The only thing that was keeping me even half afloat was the fact that over the years I had become good friends with Hank Cheney, the present owner of the house and my landlord. He didn't need the money, and I had once done him a favor, gotten his kid out of a jam, so he let me have the place cheap, way below what he could get for it.

Now it looked like that arrangement, too, might be about over. Hank was involved in litigation with his kid, the same one I had helped. The kid, now a hot-shot thirty-seven-year-old accountant, was trying to use Hank's gesture of friendship and generosity as evidence of mental incompetence. The idea was to get his father institutionalized so he could take control of his affairs. If Hank's failure to maximize profits was accepted as a sign of feeblemindedness, I was in big trouble.

Shit.

I should have dumped the kid in the river when I had the chance.

Mrs. Bernstein, on the other hand, had been letting me know for years that her house was completely paid for. The unspoken suggestion was that it could easily become my house as well, if I were interested. At moments, the idea was not without appeal . . . until I thought about her yoo-hoos, and her print dresses, and her mothering, and her revolting grandchildren, and her cabbage rolls. Put that way, an East L. A. welfare hotel and Tender Vittles didn't look too bad.

Sure, it didn't. Who was I kidding?

Well, something might turn up.

I went in the back door, through the kitchen that was filling up with dirty dishes, and into the living room. I sank down on the big floral-patterned maroon davenport that was far too large for the small area. I sat on something that I supposed was a giant gardenia, and the cushion exhaled a tired sigh that echoed my own. The furniture had belonged to the previous occupant. I had never especially liked it, but had never gotten around to

changing it. Now it was like me, faded, with very little
bounce left it it. And I still didn't like it.

I put my feet up on a dark wood coffee table that bore
the circle marks of ten thousand glasses, and leaned back,
closing my eyes. I thought about Sal and the night ahead.
Bah. Madness. Insanity. I could only hope it wouldn't be
a giant mistake. I tried not to think about what could
happen. I tried not to think about my possible eviction. I
tried not to think about my dirty dishes.

No luck.

I knew I should get some rest, for the night, but even
though I was tired from my run in the park and starting
to ache, I was too keyed up. Hell, crazy though I thought
it was, I had to admit I was excited about the prospect of
a little activity.

I stood up with a groan and got an enamel metal box
out of the corner cabinet. I pulled the venetian blinds
shut, making the room even drearier than usual, and sat
back down. I filled the tiny clay bowl of my long-
stemmed Moroccan pipe with some good home-grown
stuff, lit it, and sucked the harsh smoke deep into my
lungs. Almost immediately I felt it going to work. As
those kids in the park might have said, it was dynamite
weed.

Those same kids also probably wouldn't have believed
what I was doing. Since every new generation seems to
think that they invented the wheel, be it sex or dope or
talking dirty, they'd have trouble accepting the fact that
I'd been smoking marijuana since before their parents
were born.

I smiled. The memory of the first time was still vivid,
coming back to me now nearly every time I lit up.

It was in the twenties, and I had come down from Paris
to Tangier. In those days, surprisingly enough, Tangier
really did resemble the fantasies that Hollywood would
create during the thirties and forties about North Africa.
It *was* mysterious, alien, wide-open, sinister; as a young
would-be writer who thought he should put away experi-
ences like preserves for a long winter, I loved it all.

Not an hour off the boat, I was wandering around the
medina, negotiating narrow alleys, inhaling the street
smells of saffron and rotting garbage and piss, and I went
—naturally—into the most mysterious, sinister-looking

café I could find. I eventually realized that they all looked sinister and mysterious, but in fact were not any more so than a neighborhood bar or soda fountain. It was a great disappointment. But there were compensations.

There were only men in the café, some sitting around small rickety tables, others squatting on mats on the floor, playing a card game that seemed to involve nothing except throwing each card down as hard as possible while voicing some Arabic expletive.

Immediately after I sat down, the waiter brought me a steaming glass of mint tea and an odd, small-bowled pipe. Since other men were smoking similar pipes, I figured it was some kind of local custom. I didn't especially want to smoke, but to refuse would have been unfriendly and impolite. At that point, I'd never heard of *kif*.

Imagine my surprise.

The waiter kept bringing me fresh glasses of the hot sweet tea and freshly filled pipes. I later learned that his name was Habib and he'd worked at the café since he was a small boy. His head was narrow, and his hair was cut so short I could see the moles on his scalp. He had a four-day stubble of beard on his sunken cheeks. His breath smelled of cardamom when he bent close to me, smiling, asking earnestly, *"Etes-vous bien fumé? Etes-vous bien fumé?"*

After a couple of pipes, my French disappeared. After a couple more, my English did, too.

"Etes-vous bien fumé?"

I could only nod my head and grin like an idiot, trying to keep my tongue tucked inside my mouth. Yeah, thanks. I was very well smoked. Indeed.

Back home it was easy to get dope if you wanted it, even during the great marijuana scare of the thirties. If my work didn't put me in contact with someone who could provide it, the after-hours joints where musicians hung out were always a sure bet.

It was never a big deal with me, just something without which my life would have been a little less pleasant. And now, the older I got, the worse things would be without it.

At my age, alcohol could have really bad effects. The same with all those pills—tranks, barbiturates, mood elevators—the doctors were so anxious to hand out in order

to get you out of the office so they could treat patients
who had something more curable than old age. My lungs
were still okay, though, so I figured smoke was a better,
safer way to relax, sleep, feel good. And I sure as hell
wasn't concerned about possible long-term side effects.

It was also cheap. Liquor and unnecessary medicine
were too expensive for nonexistent incomes, but marijuana didn't cost anything if you grew it yourself. Even I,
who couldn't do shit with my front lawn, had a couple of
great little bushes out by the back fence, that provided
enough to keep me happy through the year.

From what I gathered, I wasn't the only decrepit degenerate doing this. Besides those of us who'd been smoking since it was known as boo or tea, there were lots,
maybe introduced to it by their grandkids, who were
starting to indulge. It made too much sense not to.

But it was kept kind of quiet. There were too many
tight-assed prigs around who believed it was utterly disgusting and unnatural for people beyond a certain age to
want to have any fun. You were just supposed to sit
quietly, not to make a fuss, and wait for the big D to bring
you blessed relief. The idea of groups of old coots sitting
in the TV rooms of their Senior Centers, smoking themselves silly, would be almost too shocking for words. I
could see the headlines in the tabloids next to the supermarket checkout:

GOLDEN-AGE DOPE FIENDS
Retirement-Village Pot Orgies
Superannuated Hophead Tells All!

I laughed.

Oh, yes. Once again I seemed to be pretty well smoked.

I got up, put the enameled box back in the cabinet, and
opened the blinds. Hazy light streamed in, making the
thick layer of dust beneath the furniture very evident. I
stretched out full length on the couch, my feet resting on
the stamen of a giant tulip, the backs of my knees caressing a nearly obscene orchid, and my butt again settling on
the welcoming gardenia. I felt like a stoned pixie.

I reached behind my head and got a paperback from
the lamp table. The saga of Duke Pachinko and the

granite-faced private eye with the permanently engorged member had been left behind in the park. Not much of a loss. The new one was something called *Red Vengeance*, featuring, the back cover assured me, "a detective who made Mickey Spillane look like a Boy Scout." Dandy.

Whatever happened to that intense, solemn young man who had gone to Paris a couple of centuries ago? The would-be intellectual, the college graduate, the student of literature. He'd sat around cafés, discussing Art and Life as though he'd known something about both of them, talking about obscure poetry with even more obscure poets, impressing impressionable young ladies with his high seriousness, in an effort to get inside their knickers. Jesus. He, along with a hundred thousand equally earnest young Americans in Paris at that time, was going to be a writer.

So what happened?

He finally had the honesty to admit that even though he wanted to be A Writer, there was no way in the world he was going to write.

Then he went home.

And fifty years later he was lying on an unbelievably ugly couch, reading about a guy named Al Tracker who could shatter other guys jaws without ever hurting his own hand, and who had beautiful women lining up to give him blow jobs.

Tempus fugit.

Forty pages into the book, there had been a garroting, a defenestration, a dismemberment, and a gang rape. Al was out for vengeance (red, I supposed), and a malignant dwarf with a steel hand was out to rip Al's balls off.

I dozed off.

CHAPTER THREE

It was dark when a pair of dogs, arguing about who got to go where on my front yard, woke me up. As usual when I went to sleep on the couch, my neck had cramped in an awkward position, and it took a couple of minutes to un-kink myself.

I got up, grabbed a plate of cold chicken from the fridge, and sat down at the kitchen table. After a couple of bites, I knew I wouldn't be able to eat. My stomach was churning, acidy, like I had just eaten some of Mrs. Bernstein's kugel. It was the feeling I'd always gotten before an important operation. Pregame jitters, I supposed; the uncertainty before action. I couldn't remember the last time I'd felt like that. Even though it wasn't especially pleasant, I was surprised to realize I had missed it. You felt lousy, but you did know you were alive, that something was on the line. Christ. If I felt this way, what the hell was Sal going through? Poor son of a bitch.

A hot shower and a careful shave filled up twenty minutes. Dressing, another ten.

I didn't know what to expect, but in situations like this I'd always figured you wanted to be as unobtrusive as possible, nothing bright or flashy, so I put on the darkest clothes I had. A chocolate-brown shirt buttoned at the neck and wrists, navy-blue trousers, and black canvas high-tops. Quite elegant. I looked like a seedy cat-burglar. Or one of those old guys who hung around playgrounds with deep baggy pockets filled with jangling change. Great. I'd become a model for *Molester's Monthly*. But at least I'd be able to blend into the shadows if I had to.

If I had to. Shit.

For obvious reasons I usually didn't spend much time in front of mirrors, but I did that evening. I wanted to see if there were any signs, any visible indications, of the man I had once been, the tough, competent operator who could be relied on in a pinch to come through. Did any of that still remain to be seen? Or was it only inside? Or there at all? I couldn't tell. Maybe in the eyes, maybe something in the jaw. The angle of the head. I just couldn't tell.

I shook my head. Something was happening to me. Sal had shaken loose a lot of stuff I generally tried not to think about, and I didn't like it. "J. Spanner: Disappeared while gazing upon his reflection; presumed drowned."

Come on, Sal. Hurry up. Let's get going. Let's get it over with.

I tried to read, but even the malignant dwarf being thrown into a threshing machine failed to hold my attention.

I turned on the television. It filled up the silence in the room, but I couldn't focus on it. Trying to think of unknown possibilities, what-ifs, made me antsy, and I kept getting up, because I felt like I had to piss. I didn't. I wondered if I was getting kidney stones. Maybe cancer of the bladder. Maybe . . .

I was stewing so much that I nearly jumped when the doorbell finally rang.

Under the dim yellow porch light Sal's eyes were completely in shadow and he looked even more cadaverous than he had that afternoon. I unhooked the screen door and he came in.

He was wearing the same clothes. He carried a black leather attaché case with two half-inch stripes of red leather running around it about a third of the way in. It probably came from Rodeo Drive and was probably worth more than all of my living room furniture. Sal's knuckles were white as he gripped the handle.

His eyes ran quickly over my nifty outfit. He didn't say anything. When he glanced around the living room, it looked as though he smelled something that was slightly off but he couldn't figure out what it was.

"This is just my summer place," I said. "The main house is at Malibu, but I come here to avoid the crowds."

Sal grunted. "At least you've got something."

"But I don't. That's the problem."

He grunted again. I didn't think he was hearing me.

He looked at the couch, trying to decide which grotesque flower to sit on. He picked the tulip. I turned off the sound on the TV and sat on the gardenia again.

He put the case across his bony knees and lay his forearms across it. His spine was completely straight, and he was leaning slightly forward. His eyes were watching the movement on the TV screen, without seeing it. Even though he was trying to keep it in check, I could see the strain was really getting to him. His tension, though, instead of feeding my own, had just the reverse effect. My nervousness and anxiety vanished. One of us had to stay calm, and I figured that that—if anything—was what I was being paid for.

"It's all in there?" I said, nodding at the attaché case.

Obviously, it was all in there, but there were times when even fatuous remarks were preferable to nothing.

"Yeah," Sal said.

"Hmm."

I found it very bizarre to be one cushion away from so much money. I couldn't relate to it. It seemed somehow unreal that an amount that could buy so many big things would take up so small a volume. On the other hand, I remembered pictures from Germany in the early twenties, when money became worthless, and even a suitcase full of the stuff couldn't buy a box of matches. More and more, at least in the supermarket, it seemed as though we were moving in that direction. But inflation wasn't the issue here. The issue was whether one attaché case of dollars could still buy one teenage boy.

"I didn't hear the car pull up," I said, in order to say something.

"I had Eric leave me at the corner."

"Eric?"

"My driver."

"Oh." How nice to have a driver called Eric. Most chauffeurs used to be named Fritz, but I supposed styles had changed.

"I didn't want him to know where I was going."

"Right."

That afternoon we had decided to use my car for the drop. Neither of us felt up to pushing that monster of a limo around, and we certainly didn't want to involve any-one else in this thing. Besides, my car would be much less conspicuous. I had offered to pick Sal up, but he thought it'd be better if he got out of his house, rather than sit around. Considering what I had been feeling earlier, it made sense.

"You're sure you want to do it this way?" I said.

"I'm sure."

"It's not too late. We can still bring in the cops. I can call them now and they'll cover us."

Sal shook his head, not turning to face me, keeping his eyes on the television.

I'd had to ask him because I still thought it was the smarter thing to do. At the same time, though, in a funny kind of way, I was glad we were going through with it. That reaction had nothing to do with the best interests of Sal and his grandson, Tommy, only with me. A last dream of action, I supposed. I wasn't exactly pleased about feel-ing that way, but there it was, all the same.

"Why don't we get going?"

Sal looked at his watch. "Not yet."

"Come on. We're both going crazy here. Believe me, it won't matter if we're a few minutes early."

"No!" For the first time since he'd sat down, he looked at me. His lips were bloodless, a thin white line pulled taut against his teeth. His eyes were hot. It seemed like he was on the verge of uncoiling in all directions at once, like those spring snakes that leap out of trick boxes of candy. "No!"

Okay. Okay. I held my hands up. I wasn't going to argue. It was his money, and his grandson, and I was his P.I. for the evening. If he thought that twenty minutes made a difference, it made a difference.

As quickly as he flared up, he relaxed. He shrugged, helplessly.

I nodded and smiled. "Don't worry. It'll all be okay." I hoped I sounded more confident to Sal than I did to my-self.

He turned back to the television, keeping his eyes fixed on the images of sanitized mayhem that raced across the screen. At frequent intervals he raised his wrist and glanced at his watch, trying to will time to speed up. I didn't know why he was so concerned about the time.

Hell, I was sure the kidnappers would be happy if we were a little early. They'd probably been in position for hours already, looking at their watches as often as Sal did, and wishing it was over. Still, I knew that victims of kidnappings tend to follow instructions—however unimportant or meaningless—very precisely, like it was a magic ritual, every step of which had to be perfectly performed or else there'd be failure. If they'd told Sal to spit over his shoulder three times and recite "Jingle Bells," he'd have done it.

Instead, we waited. All the time, Sal resolutely avoided looking at me. He was nervous and tense, all right, but there was something else in his manner that I couldn't quite place. Before I had it pinned down, he gave a sigh, stood up, and nodded.

From the back of a chair, I grabbed the suit jacket that went with my trousers and started to put it on.

"Aren't you taking a gun?"

"Come on, Sal."

"You have one, don't you?"

Yeah, I still had one, but I didn't know why. Maybe because it was one of the few tangible things I had left from the major part of my life. Like a carpenter keeping the tools he knew he'd never use again. I should've gotten rid of it a long time ago, but it was in a box on a shelf in the closet. I got it down once in a while to clean and oil it. And, knowing it was stupid, put it back on the shelf again.

"Take it, Jake."

"What for?"

Sal jiggled the attaché case.

"So what am I supposed to do if there's trouble?" I said. "Shoot off a few of my toes? Or maybe put a bullet in your hip? Believe me, it's much better if we don't have it."

"Take it. Please."

"This is already crazy, Sal; let's not make it ridiculous."

But even as I said it, I knew I'd do it. I felt the same curious kind of ambivalence I'd had all day about this whole thing. I knew it was a mistake, but at the same time it excited me. I shouldn't have been doing it at all, but since I was going to, I thought I might as well do it right. Or to put it another way, why be a partial fool, when I could be a complete one?

I got down the gun, a 9mm Browning, and slipped on the shoulder holster. Christ, it felt strange, seemingly much heavier than its two pounds. Strangest of all though, was the way that putting it on catapulted me back to a time when I wore it almost as a matter of course. Images, more recollections from the body than the mind, momentarily welled up, and I felt myself back in dark alleys and damp warehouses, waiting for goniffs like Joey Samosa or Pig Galway to show.

Ah, back in the saddle again.

Shit.

I put on my coat, and Sal and I went out through the back to the garage.

Outside, the air felt damp, heavy, gritty, like a towel in an Istanbul bathhouse, as the detective Al Tracker might have said. Down the street someone was having a late-night party in his swimming pool.

My car was a twenty-year-old Chevy. Had it been in better shape, it might have soon become a minor classic. As it was, it was just an old car. With the price of gas, and everything, I used it as little as possible, but I was still glad that I had it. It didn't run too badly, once it got started, though every year it was harder and harder to get the engine to turn over. I knew the feeling.

"You're sure this'll get us there?" Sal said, fingering the peeling leatherette of the dashboard.

"No problem."

To my surprise, the engine caught the first time. I said a silent thanks to whatever deity looked after the internal combustion engine. It would've looked real good if I'd had to call the kid at the garage for a start in order to make the ransom drop. Real professional. Real encouraging.

I headed over to the freeway. I didn't go on it that often anymore. My night vision wasn't as good as it used to be, and the car sometimes stalled when I accelerated. I figured, though, that if I could act like I was twenty years younger, maybe the old Bel Air could as well.

The breeze coming in through the wind-wing was warm and heavy. I was starting to stick to the seat.

"This feels more like an East Coast night," I said.

"Yeah, it does. This was the kind of night when kids'd play stickball in the street and all the men'd sit on the stoops in their undershirts and drink beer."

"Right." I nodded. And tempers got short, and minor differences of opinion about John J. McGraw and the Giants ended up being resolved with broken beer bottles and kitchen knives.

"I really liked those nights when I was a kid. You got to stay up late because it was too hot to sleep."

"Yeah. Or you took your mattress up to the roof or out on the fire escape."

Sal turned to me, smiling for the first time that night. "Of course! Shit, I haven't thought about that for years. I used to love to do that, go up and sleep next to the pigeon coop. You had to listen to that fucking cooing all night long, but it was about the only time you ever got to be by yourself."

Sal's momentary brightness faded and he fell silent again, staring out the window and tapping his fingers on the attaché case resting on his lap.

I got up the on ramp and headed west along the Ventura Freeway. The freeway always felt like a new thing to me. Every time I got on it, I had to remind myself I'd been riding it for nearly twenty-five years. To me, it sure didn't seem that long ago that there hadn't been a freeway. Or much longer still since the Valley had been empty except for some orange groves, chicken ranches, and small vegetable farms. Passing the shopping malls and the thousands of tract houses, it seemed incredible that I could still remember when a lot of this had been wasteland covered with tumbleweeds. Now you had to drive almost as far to see a tumbleweed as you did to get a fresh egg.

We had just passed the Woodman Avenue exit, when Sal slapped the case with his palm and said, "Angela Della Rossa!"

"What?"

"That's who it was."

"Who what was?"

"You got me thinking about going up to the roof in the summer, and I remembered how it was up there that I got my first hand job."

"From Angela Della Rossa?"

"Yeah."

"Oh."

Great. I was concentrating as hard as I could, so that my aging reflexes didn't put us into the back end of some jerk who was about to cut us off at fifty-five miles an hour, and Sal was telling me some sixty-year-old sexual reminiscence. Did I need that?

"Jesus! Did she ever have great tits. Big, but really firm, you know." Sal closed his eyes and clicked his tongue in appreciation. "You know, I never plugged her, but even after I started making it regular, Angela Della Rossa was still the dame I thought about when I beat off. Funny."

Come on, Sal, give me a break. We're out to ransom back your grandson and you're talking about some Brooklyn bimbo from the Stone Age. What the hell's going on here?

"I wonder whatever happened to her."

"Well, Sal, she probably got married and had a bunch of kids and got fat. And if she's still alive now, those great tits are hanging down to her waist."

"Shit." Sal sadly shook her head.

"And her only regret," I said, "in a long and successful life is that she never let Sal the Salami stick it to her."

Sal looked at me, maybe a little pissed, and then gave a brief laugh. "Okay, Jake." He turned back to the window and started drumming his fingers again.

I got to the Topanga Canyon exit and started up into the hills. Time was, when the only people in the canyon were a few gaga old codgers in scrapwood shacks, and the land was almost being given away. Now it was filled with millionaire rock musicians who got back to nature surrounded by electrified fences and guard dogs.

We finally got to the coast highway, and I headed north.

"Now, where are we supposed to turn?" I said.

"It should be a little bit farther."

The turning was just past the Soak 'n' Sip, a redwood-sided building that announced itself as L.A.'s first hot-tub wine bar. It must have been too late for soaking, if not sipping, because the place was dark.

The road we were on started out paved, and then became gravel. When it turned to dirt, I stopped the car. Except for the beam from my headlights, it was completely dark. Gulls cawed in the distance and there were some small animals rustling around in invisible bushes. Otherwise, nothing but heavy silence. It was the kind of place where bandits waited to stick up the midnight stage.

"Hey, Sal, this is feeling really bad. I don't like the looks of this at all."

"Come on, Jake, let's go." He rapidly tapped the case with his knuckles.

"No, I mean it. I think we better talk about this."

"No time, Jake. We'll talk later. Get going." Sal was twitching, looking at his watch, and bouncing a little on the seat. "Come on."

"If this is a set-up, we're better off pulling back and making other arrangements. Don't worry. They want the money. They'll get in touch."

"And if they don't? I don't know who the fuck these creeps are or what they'll do. This is Tommy's life we're talking about, you son of a bitch. If you don't feel up to it, I'll go ahead by myself. Get out."

"Hold on, Sal. Calm down. What'd they say? How much farther we supposed to go?"

"They said, about a mile after the dirt started. There'd be one of those flashing emergency highway lights. We leave the money there and go back. I'll get a phone call later, telling me where to get Tommy."

"Wonderful. We're already way the hell in the middle of nowhere, and we're supposed to go a mile farther. It stinks."

Actually, from the kidnapper's point of view it was nearly perfect. There was no chance of anyone coming along by mistake. They could see or hear anyone that did come along, and they'd have plenty of warning if we weren't alone. And even if we tried to do something fancy, set up some kind of trap or surveillance, all they had to do was climb over a couple of hills, get to a fire road, and come out ten miles away. They obviously knew what they were doing.

"You shouldn't have agreed to these arrangements," I said rather lamely. Of course he shouldn't have. And he shouldn't have let his grandson be nabbed.

"But I did. And I'm going through with it, right by the book, just the way they said. Now, get out. I'll pick you up on the way back."

I looked at Sal but I couldn't see his face in the darkness.

Shit.

One of the few things I really believed in—and that

was constantly reconfirmed for me—was that people got themselves into jams because they couldn't anticipate the possible consequences inherent in a situation. They didn't understand cause and effect, or they lacked imagination, and so they were surprised when they found themselves neck-deep in shit and sinking.

Even if nothing else was functioning terribly well, my imagination still was, and I sure didn't like the possibilities I saw down that dirt road.

But I'd been hired to do a job, to help out Sal. I'd walked from jobs before, but even if I knew I was right, doing so had never made me feel real swell about myself. Damn.

I put the car into drive and moved down the road. If I couldn't keep Sal from being an ass, maybe I could keep him from paying the price.

I heard Sal exhale slowly, as though in relief. "Thanks, Jake."

"Yeah, sure."

We'd covered about half of the mile, when my headlights picked up the yellow and black stripes of a barrier across the road, the kind of heavy sawhorse that highway crews used.

"What the fuck's that?" I said.

"Oh, yeah. They said the road'd be blocked. We just have to pull it aside."

"Swell."

Sal started to open his door, but I told him to stay put. I shifted to neutral and got out.

Except for the idling of the engine, there were no sounds. The night was oppressively still, not even a breeze. I smelled dust and dried brush.

As I walked to the barrier, I had the feeling that this situation somehow seemed familiar, struck a chord. I almost laughed when I realized it was something out of one of those thousands of books I'd read. A Chandler novel. *Farewell, My Lovely,* I thought. Marlowe and his client were delivering a pay-off, and the drop was in one of the deserted canyons off the coast road.

I tried to move the barrier, but something was holding one of the legs. As I bent down to free it, I remembered that in the book Marlowe gets knocked out. At the same instant, I heard a sound behind me; then Sal called my name. He might have said more, but I never heard it.

I was trying to stand up and get out my gun, when the back of my skull cracked like the San Andreas Fault and my vision exploded into Fourth of July sparklers.

They looked real pretty before they flared out and left me in blackness.

CHAPTER FOUR

I hadn't been hit on the head since 1952, and I had forgotten just how shitty it could be. My entire body felt like
it had been steam-rollered, my skull had been replaced
with a decomposing grapefruit, and I heard a horrible
sound, like a cat trying to get rid of a hairball.

That was me. I was on my elbows and knees, dry-
heaving my guts out. I had tried to stand up too abruptly
and everything, including my stomach, had flipped upside
down. I'd dropped back to the ground even more
abruptly, where I'd been repeatedly and unpleasantly
sick.

I made the mistake of looking at the awful little puddle
beneath me, and heaved a couple more times. Still no
hairball.

Somehow, I managed to roll myself away and things
began to settle down a little. After a few minutes I started
to feel well enough to wonder where the hell I was and
what the fuck had happened.

At first I thought I must have slipped in my bathroom
and cracked my head on the tub, one of the things that
they warn happen to old people all the time. But that
didn't account for the fact that I was lying on dirt, not my
nice sea-green tiles. I knew I wasn't a very good house-
keeper, but I'd never let things get this bad.

Then I thought I'd been mugged in the park. But that
didn't explain how Sears and the rest of the shopping center had turned into a mountain. And why was everything
so quiet and so dark? There was a little bit of light behind
me, but nothing else.

I rolled over to see where the light was coming from. It

was the headlights of the Chevy. For a second, I couldn't figure what my car was doing in the bathroom, and then everything came back with a dizzying rush that almost made me sick again.

The car's engine was off. Both doors were open. Beneath the one on the passenger side, a dark shape was sprawled on the ground.

I tried to call Sal's name, but my throat was raw and it came out more like a growl.

Slowly, slowly, I thought. I wanted to get over to Sal, but I wouldn't do either of us any good if I was sick again.

I got up to a sitting position. The damage didn't seem too bad. I had a lump at the base of my skull, but whoever had hit me had known what he was doing. The blow had gone mostly onto my neck, and it didn't seem that anything was broken. He'd just wanted to put me out temporarily, not cause permanent damage. How considerate.

Everything else seemed to be okay as well, even though I was stiff and sore all over. I had a bruise on my left side, under my arm, where I'd fallen on my gun. Lot of good that had done. Jesus.

From the way my knees hurt, I figured I must have dropped onto them as I went down, but they moved, so I guessed they'd be all right. In fact, nothing seemed to be too bad, which was kind of a pleasant surprise, since I knew very well that seventy-eight-year-old bones had a tendency to snap like matchsticks. Shit. A broken hip on a dirt road in the middle of nowhere was not my idea of a classy exit. I didn't even want to think about an obit for that one. A little too close. A little too real.

Also a little too real was Sal Piccolo lying in the dirt, unmoving, next to my car.

Using the barrier, I pulled myself up to my feet. For a second I thought I was going to go over again, but I held on until the dizziness passed.

Pain shooting up and down from my knees with every slow step, I crossed the twenty feet to where Sal lay. It felt a hell of a lot farther, and part of me wished that it was. Even though I had to get to him, I wasn't at all anxious to find what I knew would be there.

I thought I probably felt worse than I'd ever felt in my life. Christ, what an asshole I'd been to think this was going to be fun. What a schmuck. Why didn't I just stick to my memories and my paperbacks and my park bench, like every other fucking old fart.

I turned Sal over, expecting to see a bloody hole, or something. Instead, his eyelids fluttered open.

"Oh, shit," he said, and then groaned.

All the stuff I'd been feeling burst out in a barking laugh. It was relief. I realized I'd been thinking things would continue on just like in the book, where Marlowe got up and found his client dead. So much for life imitating art.

"What's so fucking funny?" Sal said hoarsely.

"Nothing." I shook my head, which was a mistake, because it felt like things were still loose inside. "You okay?"

"Yeah, I think so." He groaned again as he tried to sit up.

"Careful. Take it easy."

"I'm okay. Just help me up."

Easier said than done. For the second time that day, we flailed around like a pair of Skid Row drunks whose motor coordination had been wiped out by too much Sterno and shoe polish. However, I finally got Sal sitting on a corner of the front seat, with his feet resting on the ground. He was leaning forward, holding his head in his hands. It looked like it might be too heavy for them. I sort of draped myself over the open door, breathing heavily.

"I assume the money's gone?" I asked.

"Yeah."

"What happened?"

Sal closed his eyes and put his fingers up to his temples, concentrating. After a minute he opened his eyes and raised his head. He swiveled around so that one foot was inside the car, and he leaned heavily against the back of the seat. Under the dim courtesy light his skin was gray. His expensive black suit was covered with dust and dirt. He looked beaten, exhausted. I could only imagine what I looked like. I didn't want to know.

"Let's see," Sal said. "You bent down, didn't you?"

"Yeah. The barrier was caught, or fastened, or something."

"Well, as you did, this guy came out of the bushes

over there." Sal pointed off to the right. The scrub was
thick and outside the range of the headlights. A platoon
could've waited there unseen.

"What'd he look like?"

Sal shook his head, wincing a little at the movement.
"Don't know. He had one of those ski-mask things on. He
was big. Moved fast. By the time I saw him, he was almost up to you. I tried to warn you, but—"

"Yeah. I heard you call my name, just before I got hit."

"Yeah, shit. I was too slow. By the time I realized what
was happening, you were going down."

"What was I hit with? Could you see?"

Sal shrugged. "I think it was a sap of some kind. It
didn't look like it was the first time he'd used it."

"That was what I thought. He could've cracked my
head like an egg, but he hit me in just the right spot. Either I was lucky, or he knew what he was doing."

"I've seen enough of those guys at work. I'd say he
knew what he was doing."

I carefully touched the lump I had. It hurt like a son of
a bitch. "I suppose I should be thankful. What next?"

Sal shook his head, his mouth twisting into an expression of disgust. "Jesus, Jake, I froze. Like some goddamn
greenhorn who's never seen any action. I couldn't decide
if I should get out and help you or get behind the wheel
and get the hell out of here."

No question. He should've gotten away. Whatever
had happened to me, had happened. Nothing Sal could've
done would've changed it, but the issue about himself and
the dough hadn't been decided yet. Still, it was kind of
nice that he'd even thought about helping me. Stupid, but
nice.

"You should've driven away," I said.

"I guess. What gets me is that I didn't do anything. Just
sat there like a farm boy, with my mouth open and my
dick hanging out, saying, 'Huh? Huh?' Shit, I know better
than that."

"Maybe you *knew* better, Sal. Face it, it's been a long
time since either of us has been street-fast."

"Yeah, but still . . . Shit!"

"We're both old and slow—okay?—so give it a rest.
What happened next?"

Sal looked like he wasn't convinced that being old and

slow was a satisfactory explanation. I usually felt the same way, but it didn't change anything.

He nodded a little. "Actually, it wouldn't have made any difference even if I had done something."

"What do you mean?"

"Well, almost as soon as you went down, a car pulled out from behind and blocked the road."

"From behind? You mean, it came up the road behind us, or that it had been parked, and pulled out from the side?"

"From the side. About fifteen, twenty yards back."

Shit. A nice setup, and we walked into it like a couple of pigeons.

"So even if you'd jumped right behind the wheel, you wouldn't have been able to go anywhere. You'd've been stuck between the barrier and the car, right?"

"Right. But the point is, I didn't think fast enough to even try."

My head was getting worse by the minute, and I didn't need any more of Sal's self-recriminations. "The point is, we shouldn't have been here in the first place. But we were. So go on."

"Okay," he sighed. "A guy got out of the car. Fast. Ran over to me, waving a gun. He had a mask on, too, but he was a lot smaller than the other guy. Couldn't have been more than five-three, four."

"Anything else about him?"

"Yeah. He had a real funny voice."

"Funny? How?"

"I don't know. Sort of high-pitched, squeaky. Like, maybe, a record that's being played too fast. I'm not sure, but I got the idea he was pretty young."

"How young? A kid?"

"Not that young. Twenties, I'd guess, but I don't know. I have trouble with age. Below forty or so, they all seem the same to me."

"I know what you mean."

"But I still think he was young."

"Okay. That's something."

That's something. What the hell did I think I was going to do with it? Listening to myself, I couldn't believe what I was doing, that I was carrying out an interrogation like it was routine, like it hadn't been more than fifteen years since I had last done it, and like I was going to do something with the answers. Christ! Like I wasn't some decrepit old dick with a bump on his head who hurt all over, and who should have been in bed hours ago with a glass of warm milk and a plate of graham crackers.

"So he told me to get out of the car," Sal went on. "I got out. He told me to hand over the money. I said I didn't have any money, but he just repeated I should hand it over. I asked him if he had Tommy, if Tommy was all right. He didn't say anything, just said to give him the dough, in that high squeaky voice of his. It sounded like he was getting real pissed off, you know. And I got the idea that maybe he wasn't quite right." Sal tapped his temple with a forefinger. "The other guy, the one who'd hit you, had come over by then. The little one told me to turn around. I said he didn't have to do that, that the money was in the briefcase. I said he could have it, but to just let me have Tommy back. He kind of laughed then, a real strange sound that almost made me shiver, and I got the idea that maybe I had a real crazy one there, like, uh, Eddie Peanuts. You remember him?"

Yeah, I remembered Eddie Peanuts. Few people that had heard of him were ever liable to forget. His real name was Eddie Patterson or Peterson, something like that, but he was known as Eddie Peanuts, because he always carried a pocketful of them that he cracked with one hand, usually while the other one held a razor-sharp six-inch blade. He was also called Mad Eddie, but only by people who were pretty sure he'd never hear about it.

For a couple of years, '31—'32, maybe '32—'3, Eddie was very much in demand by anyone who wanted to scare anybody else—or worse. He loved hurting people, a true sadistic psychopath. He probably would've worked for nothing, but everybody made sure Eddie was well paid.

With somebody like Mad Eddie, you could never be certain which stories were true and which were just stories, but the fact that they were told at all was usually enough. He'd been known to reduce big tough numbers to quivering aspic just by sitting in the same room with them, cracking his peanuts, one after the other. Eddie's type, though, had a tendency to flame very brightly but also very briefly. It wasn't long before the people who employed him decided he was more of a liability than an asset. One dark April night, Eddie was helped off the Santa Monica pier, with enough lead inside him to make sure he'd sink. Even so, it was a long time before a lot of people could see peanuts without feeling an uncomfortable twinge. If Sal was right, and the guy that had gotten us was anything at all like Mad Eddie, things didn't look encouraging for our side.

"What happened next?" I said.

"Well, when I heard that laugh, I figured that wasn't anyone I was going to fuck around with. He looked up at me and said real quiet that I should turn around. I knew what was coming but I didn't say anything, and I turned around. Shit, I can't remember ever doing anything like that—saying, okay, here I am, I'm all yours, slug me."

"That you did is probably the only reason you still have a head to ache. So you were hit then?"

"Yeah. Down and out. I figure it must've been the big one. He's really good. I've hardly got a bump." Sal shrugged. "That's it. What do you think?"

I felt like telling him that things had worked out just the way he deserved for being so stupid and stubborn, but I didn't. The temptation was always great, but I've never yet encountered a situation that was improved by saying I told you so. Anyway, I recognized that part of the responsibility was mine.

I looked at Sal for a while. I was still hanging onto the door. I badly wanted to sit down, but I wasn't sure I could get up again if I did.

"Well," I said, "there are two possibilities. The pair that hit us are the same ones that grabbed Tommy, and for whatever reason, they decided to change the arrangements."

"You think it could be that?"

I shrugged. I kind of doubted it, but I really didn't know one way or the other.

Sal nodded sadly. "And if not . . ."

I shrugged again. "Then a joker entered the scene. Somebody ripped off both you and the kidnappers."

Sal and I looked at each other. There was no need to say anything more. He didn't exactly seem to shrink; it was more that he went hollow, that there was nothing but a thin gray shell around a terrible, terrifying emptiness.

"What do you think?" he finally said, sounding tired, very tired. "Should we go on to the drop?"

I looked at my watch. We were twenty minutes late. Christ, only twenty minutes. It felt a lot longer, years longer. Amazing how time flies when you're having fun.

I shook my head. "No, there'd be no point. If the kidnappers were the ones that hit us, they were never at the drop. If it wasn't them, they must have figured something went wrong and cleared out. And even if they are still there, I doubt they'd come out and talk. No, you can figure they'll be in touch."

"Then we're going back?" Sal sounded completely defeated.

"It looks the best thing. We don't know what the situation is. I mean, you might be getting a phone call telling you to pick up Tommy."

Sal gave me a look—half hopeful, half hopeless—that made me wish I hadn't said that. Especially since I didn't really believe it. Real smart, Spanner.

With a groan I launched myself from the door. I reached in the car, got a flashlight from the glove compartment, and started hobbling, stiff-legged, down the road. My knees were now so sore I could hardly bend them, and I began to wonder if something hadn't cracked after all.

"What are you doing?" Sal called, but I waved my hand without turning around.

What I was doing was continuing to play the damn stupid game I had been playing all night, acting out the role I'd been hired for. After having fucked up all the way down the line, I was now going right by the book. Questioning Sal. Getting the story down. Taking in all the information there was to get. Just like I was still in business, and not an ancient fool. Now I was going to check out the place where the car had been parked.

The old dick looks for clues.

Swell.

Moving with all the grace of a rusting mechanical toy, I staggered over to the spot, a thirty-foot-deep break in the manzanita scrub that lined the road. I didn't know what I thought I might find. Or what I'd do with it if I did find something. Make a plaster cast of tire tracks? A fragment of fiber from a ski mask, to be analyzed and then traced in turn to the manufacturer, the sporting goods store, and the crook who bought it? Maybe a discarded matchbook that would lead me to Flo's Cantina, where the gang hung out? Sure.

In any event, I didn't find anything. Nothing. It had been months since there was any rain, so the ground was as hard as concrete and there were no tracks. Nor were there any matchbooks, or butts from a rare brand of Egyptian cigarette sold by only one tobacconist in a hundred-mile radius. In fact, there was no sign that anyone or anything had ever waited in ambush. Which, I supposed, was exactly what one would expect. In all the cases I'd worked on, the number of times that the discovery of an obscure bit of physical evidence had led to a solution could be counted on one hand. And you'd still have fingers free to scratch your head and pick your nose. It just didn't happen. Maybe to Al Tracker, but not to me. Still, you never knew. So you went through the motions, which was what I did.

On the way back to the car I paused and looked at the area from the road. I tried to remember if I'd noticed the opening on the way in, but I couldn't recall. Probably not. My attention had been directed ahead, and it was just about at that point that I first saw the barricade. Was missing the gap one more lapse, or had it been unavoidable? I couldn't tell. The area was in pretty heavy darkness. Perhaps a car parked back as far as it could go wouldn't be noticed in passing unless you happened to turn to look right at it. Maybe not even then, I tried to tell myself, if it was dark-colored.

Shit.

I realized that for all my careful questioning, I had failed to ask Sal what was probably the only meaningful thing. Like a has-been ham, I was playing a familiar role but I kept forgetting my lines.

I got back to the car and climbed behind the wheel. My legs still hurt like crazy, and it was a relief to sit down. Sal was slumped in the seat, leaning back, eyes closed. When I pulled the door shut, he turned and looked at me.

"Anything?" he asked, not really sounding interested.

"No. Look, I'm a jerk. What the hell kind of car was it?"

"I don't know."

"Come on. Think."

"I said I don't know. What difference does it make?"

"Maybe nothing. Maybe plenty. Just don't give up yet. Things might still work out."

"Sure."

"Look, asshole, this has been your thing all the way. You want to pack it in now? Fine. You can let them take your grandkid and your dough and hit you, and you can just roll over. I didn't want in this at all, and if that's the way you want it, be my guest."

I turned the key in the ignition. It would've spoiled the effect of my pep talk a little if the engine had sputtered and died, but the Chevy once again rose to the occasion.

Sal sat up, some life showing in his eyes. "Okay."

"Okay." I smiled and put my hand on his arm. "Hold on, pal. What kind of car was it?"

"I really don't know. You know, they all kind of look the same now, not like it used to be."

"Yeah, I know. Does that mean it was new?"

"I think so. Fairly big."

"Color?"

"Dark." Sal closed his eyes, thinking. "No, I can't do better than that. Just dark. Maybe black, maybe blue. Even brown or green. Shit, I don't know. Big help."

"Nothing else? Come on, concentrate, think back. Go through the whole thing again."

Sal shook his head, slumped back, and then suddenly sat up straight. "Wait a second. There was something."

"What?"

"When I turned around, just before I was slugged, I was looking right at the car, and I can remember thinking, 'I've got to remember that.'"

"What?"

Sal pressed his eyelids with his fingertips, then looked up and shrugged helplessly. "No idea. I hadn't even remembered that there was something, until you made me think back. Being hit must've knocked it out of me. Damn!" He hit the dashboard with his hand. "What was it?"

"Relax. Don't force it."

"Shit. It's strange. I have this idea that just before I was hit I kept saying to myself, 'I'm seventy-five; I am seventy-five.' "

"You are seventy-five, right?"

"Yeah, but why would I tell myself that? What does that have to do with whatever I saw? Damn it. What is it?"

"Take it easy. It probably just means you were thinking you're too old for this kind of stuff. Don't fight it. You know something's there now. Let it come up on its own."

I backed up to the place where the other car had waited. I didn't know what I was looking for. Maybe something to convince me that I hadn't screwed up there as well. I didn't find it. Maybe it hadn't been my fault, but I couldn't help thinking that I should've noticed something, maybe even seen the car, if I'd had even half my wits working, if I'd been able to do the job instead of just playing at it. If I'd been able to cut it.

Dammit.

I got the car turned around and went back to the highway.

The ride back to the city wasn't exactly a triumphal return. Except for Sal giving me directions to his house in Beverly Hills, I doubt if we exchanged half a dozen words.

Sal stared out the window, grimacing and drumming his fingers, trying to remember whatever he'd thought was so important. I tried to concentrate on my driving, but my thoughts kept going around and around the same futile circle—what I did, what I didn't do, what I should've done, what I could've done. And over everything, uncertainty about the whole situation hung like the pall of a bad cigar.

No, it wasn't a cheerful journey. I was glad when I finally pulled up at the driveway to Sal's house.

From what I could see of it, I was impressed. It was Spanish style, white, with a red tile roof, exactly what I'd always thought of as the best kind of Southern California architecture. Not especially big for Beverly Hills, it had the solid quality and quiet class that they put into houses fifty years ago that made them age beautifully. Inside, I knew there'd be dark pegged-wood floors and lots of leather furniture, worn soft and golden over the years. Just the kind of place I'd always seen myself in, living out an elegant old age.

Did anyone still insist that crime didn't pay? Of course, Sal had done thirty years in prison. I couldn't work out the equation between the time and the house. Only Sal could know if they balanced in any way. Probably not, unless he saw prison as inevitable, which maybe it had been. In that case, it was obviously better to have the house at the end than not to. Then I remembered that Sal said it had taken everything he had to raise the ransom. I supposed that meant the house as well. Shit.

No way the equation could balance then. And we still didn't know about his grandson. I couldn't tell which was worse, the awful uncertainty or the sense of complete powerlessness. Sitting in the dark with Sal, it was all so bad I could hardly believe it. My worst fears for the evening had come to pass. And then some.

I didn't want to think about what must be going on in Sal's head. In mine I was flipping from depression to frustration to anger. I wanted to do something, but there was nothing, unless I chose to howl at the moon. I didn't know whether I was angrier at the sons of bitches who were causing all this pain or at myself.

Looking at Sal slumped, beaten, on the seat, I felt the weight of my responsibility in this. Even though I've always believed that everyone had the right to go to hell in his own way, I shouldn't have been such a goddamn willing accessory to Sal's madness. And I certainly shouldn't have agreed unless I'd been sure I could do what was required. Damn. It was a little bit late to be thinking about those things.

Sal turned and we looked at one another. There was nothing to say. We both knew how things stood. Suddenly, all the night's shit seemed to descend on me. I felt more tired than I could ever remember.

I offered to go in and wait with Sal until he heard something, but I was relieved when he turned me down. He must've figured that as bad as it was to be alone at a time like this, there were some things that were just too bad to be shared. I made him agree to call me as soon as there was any word.

Before he got out Sal said, "Thanks anyway, Jake. I appreciate it."

I supposed he'd meant well, but if his goal had been to leave me feeling as shitty as possible, he couldn't have come up with a better exit line. Damn. He could give Mrs. Bernstein lessons.

Halfway up the drive he turned and looked back at me. I got the feeling that he didn't want to go into the house, that by not going in he thought he could put off whatever lay ahead. He seemed to sigh, then make himself turn around and continue on.

I watched him for another minute before I pulled away.

Two hours later, lying on my bed, I was still seeing that sad figure moving slowly up the drive. Tired and aching as I was, sleep wouldn't come. And sleep was all I wanted, so I could stop replaying in my mind the day's events. The more I went over them, round and round, the more unreal the whole thing seemed. From a beginning just like every other day for years, there had been a gradual but inevitable descent into some kind of terrible nightmare that might have seemed comic if it wasn't so damn black. As in a nightmare, things had happened to me, but I didn't feel quite connected to them. They seemed somehow distant, arbitrary. A ghost from the past. A kidnapped grandson. Unseen assailants. All hidden shadows playing strange death games off-stage. It felt like I had been dropped into one of those books I read all the time, and a heavy-handed writer was moving me about to fit the requirements of his absurd plot.

But it wasn't a book, and even if I went to sleep, the nightmare wouldn't be over when I woke up. At least Sal's wouldn't be. I again saw the image of him reluctantly trudging up to his empty house.

Shit. I was an old man, too fucking old for this kind of stuff.

I got up and put some ice cubes in a plastic bag and wrapped it in a towel. If it wouldn't cool down my brain, maybe it would ease the throbbing at the back of my head, every beat of which kept repeating, "You blew it, you blew it, you old fool, you old fool."

CHAPTER FIVE

Unh.

I woke up to the telephone ringing. I couldn't remember falling asleep but the clock said six-thirty, so I must've finally managed to for a little while. My pillow was cold and soaking wet from the melted ice pack. Swell. That was all I needed, pneumonia on top of everything else. "J. Spanner: Tried to numb his skull; succeeded."

Apparently, I was feeling better. The swelling had gone way down on my head, and so, it seemed, had my sense of self-pity. There's nothing quite like being knocked unconscious, to diminish your self-esteem and to make you feel like batshit.

"All right!" I called to the phone as it rang for the twelfth time.

I figured I had been through enough. I wasn't about to leap out of bed in order to fall on my face. Careful prodding and bending, though, seemed to indicate that standing up was within the realm of possibility. I swung my legs out of bed and slowly got to my feet. At the eighteenth ring I took my first step. Not bad, not bad at all. While it still felt like I'd been run over by a truck, the treadmarks were fading. I might need to use a walker for only the next six or seven years.

"All right, you son of a bitch! I'm coming!" I yelled at the telephone, and by the twenty-third ring I was there. Surprisingly enough, the caller still was as well. It was Sal.

"Jake, what took so long? You okay?"

"Yeah, I guess I am. A little stiff, but that's all. What is it, Sal?"

"I heard, Jake."

"From who? The kidnappers?"

"Yeah. One of them called about half an hour ago."

"And?" I said, when Sal didn't go on.

I heard a long sigh in my ear. "It wasn't them, Jake. They weren't the ones who knocked us over."

Shit. Shit. Shit. Even when you expected the worst, it was still a blow when the ax actually fell.

"That's rough, Sal. What'd you tell him?"

"Just what happened. Exactly as it went down."

"And what'd he say?"

" 'Tough shit.' Those were his words—'Tough shit, old man.' They weren't interested, didn't care. That was strictly my problem, he said, and it didn't change anything. They still want the money. I told him I don't have any more, and he said I'd better find some. Fast. I tried to explain, but he wouldn't listen. Gave me until next week to come up with the dough. If I don't, he said they're going to start sending me Tommy through the mail. Piece by piece."

"Jesus, Sal!"

"They put Tommy on for a minute. He said he was okay, but he sounded real scared. Kept saying, 'I want to come home, Grandpa, I want to come home.' Then those assholes did something to him and he screamed and then they hung up."

The nightmare was continuing, all right. Listening to Sal, I forgot all my aches and soreness as I felt the anger rising in me, churning my gut. I wanted to smash those scum, inflict pain, make them feel some of the suffering they were causing. Fuck. The righteous anger of the impotent. I looked down and saw my leg twitching with tension. Calm down, Spanner, before you have a cerebral hemorrhage. I took a couple of deep breaths, exhaling slowly.

"So what are you going to do?" I tried to make it sound like it was solely his problem but I knew it wasn't, not after last night, not after that phone call.

"I suppose you think I should go to the cops."

"Yeah, I think it's about time for that."

"Well, I don't, and I'll tell you why." He started talking very hard and fast, as though it were vital that he convince me, too. "If I wanted to catch those bastards, I'd go to the cops, but that's not what I want. Oh, yeah, I'd love to get those shits and tear their cocks off and feed 'em to them. But that's for later. Right now the only really important thing is to get Tommy back. And it still looks to me that the only chance I have to do that is to come up with the money they want."

"I thought—"

"Yeah, you thought right. I'm pretty well tapped out, busted. I've got a couple of possibilities out of town, though, that might pay off—old debts, maybe a hustle or two—and I'm going to have to give them a shot."

"And if they don't come through?"

Sal paused for so long I thought we'd lost the connection. "Are you still willing to help me?" he finally said.

"To do what?" As I said it, I knew what he wanted. I wasn't quite so sure what my answer would be.

"Try to get a line on the guys that hit us."

I was right. "Sal—"

"Look, I realize it's probably impossible, but if you did manage to find them and we could get the dough back, then . . ." He didn't need to finish it. Then he'd be right back where he was before last night's fuck-up.

"Sal, that's the kind of thing the police should handle."

"Listen, Jake, I've been up all night thinking this through, and I know I'm right. Let's say we bring in the cops. And let's say they find those guys. And let's say they recover the money. Do you think they're just going to hand it back to me, with no questions, with smiles and good wishes, and a suggestion that it's not such a hot idea to carry that much dough around in a briefcase late at night?"

"They might if you explained the situation."

"Yeah, they might, but only if they were involved in the pay-off, and I can't have that. Look, you saw what the setup was last night. We're dealing with smart cookies who know how to cover their asses, who'll be able to spot any funny stuff a long way off. They know what they're doing. No, Jake, I can't bring the cops in for one part without having them in for the whole thing. And I can't risk that. I couldn't last night and I can't now. You didn't hear that guy on the phone. You didn't hear Tommy. Man, these people are serious."

Sal had a point. In fact, lying awake this morning I had reached all the same conclusions. The only hope for

Tommy was to deliver the ransom, and the only way to do that was to get it back from whoever ripped us off. If the cops were involved at all, they'd be in all the way, and that could well be it for Tommy. I figured the kid's chances, no matter what happened, were piss poor. However, he was still alive, for the time being, and maybe the kidnappers would play it straight. It had happened before. If that was your only hope, you damn well hung onto it. I realized I had reversed my position from the previous day, but the situation seemed different to me now, or at least clearer. No, there was only one of Sal's conclusions that I had real doubts about.

"Sal, what good do you think I could be? You saw how well I handled things last night. Shit, that's what created this problem."

"That wasn't your fault, Jake. I don't blame you."

"Thanks anyway, but the hell it wasn't. I walked us right into a sucker trap and never noticed anything was wrong."

"Nobody would have."

"I'm not so sure about that. I keep thinking that if I'd been able to do the job, if I hadn't been so damn old, I'd have spotted a dozen things to alert me that there was trouble, and you'd still have your money. But I didn't."

"You're full of shit. You know that, Jake?"

"Yeah? I also keep thinking that of all the mistakes I made last night, the biggest one was agreeing to go along in the first place. Sal, this time, be smart. Get someone who can do it right."

"Cut the crap, huh? I want you. Will you help me?"

"Sal, this is too important."

"I think it's important to you, too."

I sighed. "It is."

"Okay, then."

"Sal—"

" 'Sal, Sal,' " he mimicked, a harsh whine in my ear. "What's this bullshit? Who are you thinking about? Me or you?"

Good question. I didn't know.

"If you don't want to help me," he went on, "just say so. But don't give me this number about you're too old, you're no good, you can't make it. If that's what you think, why don't you just curl up and die? That's what you told me last night. Remember? I think you can do it. Too much is at stake here. I wouldn't be asking you if I didn't. And I think you think so, too." He laughed, not especially warmly. "You're like the virgin who keeps saying no while she nods her head yes. What do you want, Jake? Me to say I love you?"

Damn.

Sal was pretty sharp. That was exactly what I was doing. Nearly all of me badly wanted to go ahead, but I didn't want the responsibility for the decision. I wanted to be swept off my feet. Sal was right—that was bullshit. I couldn't have it both ways. Either I did it or I didn't, but whichever way I went, I had to accept the consequences.

Sal was also right about the fact that I thought I could handle the job. Despite all the evidence to the contrary, and despite what I had tried to tell both Sal and myself, I really did feel that, if it could be done, I'd be able to do it. Deep down, I felt it. Or maybe I wasn't so sure, but wanted the chance to prove it—to myself, to anyone—to show that Jake Spanner still had it. Or maybe it was to redeem myself after last night, to make things right again. When I'd been working, I'd screwed things up a few times —maybe more than a few—and it had always bothered me for a long time after. Three-A.M. shakes, four-A.M. guilt. This was a load I sure didn't relish carrying around with me.

Most of all, though, I was involved; had a commitment. To Sal, who had everything in his life on the line. To his grandson, locked in some room, alone and frightened. And to myself. I'd been hired and paid to do a job, and I hadn't done it. Just like in those dumb books, that used to mean something to me. It seemed it still did.

Jesus! I couldn't believe what was going through my mind. The motives weren't all clear, maybe they weren't all smart, and they sure weren't all honorable. Motives rarely were. But all mine certainly did point in the same direction. I was saying no and shaking my head yes. The hell with it, I told myself; enough. "J. Spanner: Lost while searching his soul."

"Hey, Jake, are you still there?" A small tinny voice issued from the receiver.

"Yeah, Sal, I am. For as long as you want me."

Christ. The comedy continued. The old dick was back on the case.

I heard a sigh of relief in my ear that I felt was hardly justified under the circumstances. "Thanks, Jake."

"I wish you'd stop thanking me. Or at least wait until I do something to thank me for. Which, believe me, I think is pretty unlikely. I really don't know what the hell I'm supposed to do."

"I don't know, Jake. You been in this town a long time. You know lots of people. Start asking around, I guess. Maybe you'll get a line."

"You forget, I've also been out of circulation a long time. Most of the people I know are dead."

"Well, you'll think of something, Jake. If I remember right, you always used to."

"Not always. Not nearly always. And that was a long time ago. I'm not sure I even know how to go about this anymore."

"Oh, hell, it'll come back once you start. It's like fucking. You never forget how to do it."

Bad analogy, Sal. Real bad analogy.

"The problem is, we've got so goddamn little to go on," I said. "We've got a Mutt and Jeff pair, is all. Mutt is short, with a funny voice, maybe young, who reminds you of a psychopath who's been dead over forty years. Jeff could maybe be muscle who's a pro with a sap. Maybe they're a regular team, maybe it was a one-shot deal. Maybe they're in business locally and are known, but maybe they're imports. Maybe they're working for themselves, maybe for someone else. Maybe some cops could recognize the description, but maybe not. And anyway, I don't know any cops anymore, and even if I did, I'd have a hard time getting any info unless I explained why, which we both think isn't such a swell idea."

"Hey, Jake, you see? You're getting into it."

"Oh, yeah. Lot of progress. Nothing but maybes. So far I've got it cut down to anyone in North America. And even that's not necessarily right. What I need is something else, something to focus it a little. You haven't remembered that thing you were trying to think of?"

"No. Shit, it's been so close I've almost had it, but I can't bring it in. I keep trying to get at it, you know, but it keeps moving away."

"Well, I told you, don't fight it. Maybe—shit, another fucking maybe—it'll pop into your head when you don't expect it."

I paused, trying to figure what to ask next, trying to remember what I used to do, trying to visualize myself talking to a client, eliciting information and inspiring confidence. Oh, I was confidence-inspiring, all right, sitting in my kitchen filled with week-old dirty dishes, barefoot, in faded striped pajamas that years ago had lost the fly buttons. The scene could have served as an advertisement for euthanasia: "Before it gets this bad . . . do the thoughtful thing. They'll thank you for it."

I finally managed to come up with something. "Who knew about this?"

"No one. Only you."

"Are you sure?"

"Absolutely."

"What about Eric?"

"Who?"

"Eric. Isn't that your driver's name?"

"Jesus! What's the matter with me? Of course it is." He sounded embarrassed. "Sorry, Jake. I haven't been to sleep. I must be getting punchy."

"Aren't we all. Look, just a couple more questions, then I think you should try to get some rest."

"I'll be okay. I'll rest when I get Tommy back. Anyway, Eric couldn't be involved. He doesn't know anything, nothing. I'm positive."

"Okay. Anybody else? To put together that much money in cash must've taken a while."

"Yeah, it did."

"Well, did anyone get curious or start to ask questions or seem too interested?"

Sal gave a bitter laugh. "Yeah, nearly everyone. Fucking bank managers. Dying to know what was going on. But I was careful, moved around enough. Sorry, Jake. I really don't think anything's there. Besides, no matter what happened while I was getting the money, I was the only one who knew where the drop was to be made. I didn't tell anyone, remember, not even you until we were on the way. And whoever it was, was waiting for us, so it couldn't have happened on this end."

Damn.

He was absolutely right, of course. The joker had to come from the kidnappers' side, no question. It was completely obvious, and I'd missed it. Great. That kind of dazzling acumen really boded well for my investigation.

"I must be pretty punchy, too," I said. "So there's no help there, knowing where the connection was, since we've got no line at all on the creeps who grabbed Tommy."

"Nothing."

"No surprise." I sighed heavily. "Look, I can't think right now. I've got to get a little more rest before I can figure out what to do. Besides, I think my ear's gone numb from this damn telephone."

"Yeah, mine, too."

I told Sal I'd get back to him. He said that might be a problem, since he was going out of town as soon as possible to see if he could raise some money, but he gave me the number of an answering service where I could always get a message through to him.

"Okay, Sal," I said. "Good luck."

"Thanks, Jake. You too."

"Buddy, you're the one who needs it, especially with me working for you. You're really sure you want me to do this?"

"Don't start again. I'm sure. And look, I intend to pay you for this."

"No, you won't. You paid me last night, and I don't figure I've earned it yet."

"But—"

I hung up. It was the only way I could keep Sal from having his own way. What a goddamn stubborn, persuasive son of a bitch. I felt a little bit sorry for whoever he was going to try to screw money out of.

No, I didn't. If he succeeded, that meant it wouldn't be so disastrous when I failed. If I failed, I corrected. Be a little more positive, I tried to tell myself; there was always a chance.

Yeah, and there was always a chance I'd be wintering in the south of France.

A scalding shower, long enough to empty the hot water heater, had me feeling almost human. Not necessarily a shining example, but at least a member of the species.

I lay on top of the bed, trying not to think about what the hell I was doing. If the consequences weren't so damn grave, it'd be ludicrous. But then, the most serious things often were. The key was to act as though you didn't realize it.

The key was to act. The problem was, I couldn't see how. I wished I felt I had a better grip on this. I couldn't understand; it all still felt so vague, fuzzy, like I was seeing it from a great distance. All shadows. I had to manage somehow to give them substance.

I went over everything I knew, all I had to go on. That filled up the two minutes it took for me to go back to sleep.

Only to be awakened two hours later by another fucking phone call. Just as well. If I got too much sleep, I might start to feel good. I was limbering up, though. It only took nine rings for me to reach it this time.

"This better be good," I said.

"It is."

"Oh, Sal. Sorry. What is it? Where are you?"

"I'm still at home. Jake, I've got it."

"What?"

"What I was trying to remember. A—M—seven."

"Huh?"

"A—M—seven. That's part of the license number."

Part of the license number? Could this really be happening?

"You're kidding," I said.

"No shit, Jake."

"You're sure?"

"Yeah. Or at least I think I am. You remember how I said that when I turned around, just before they slugged me, I spotted something I wanted to remember?"

"Yeah. Go on."

"I kept trying to visualize it in my mind. Tried to see myself turning around and noticing something, but I couldn't figure out what, couldn't see it. Only knew I kept saying, 'I am seventy-five.'"

"Yeah?"

"Well, I decided, after all, that I'd better get some rest before I started. Maybe for the first time I wasn't thinking about what I couldn't remember, wasn't pulling at it, you know, and just as I was going to sleep, the whole thing popped into my head, clear as anything. I saw myself turning around and then seeing that their car was at enough of an angle that I could make out the plate. I couldn't see the whole thing. The first letter and the last two numbers were covered with dirt, or something, but I could see the center of it. A—M—7. I remember I was kind of surprised, but I knew I had to do something to remember. That's why I kept saying to myself, 'I am seventy-five.' I figured if I could remember repeating that, I'd be able to get back to the thing that made me say it in the first place. And it worked. How about that?"

How about it? A partial license. Shit.

But why not? As a cop I'd known used to say, "In the Land of the Bizarre, the improbable is to be expected." Since yesterday, I'd clearly become an inhabitant of that country.

"Was it a California plate?"

"Yeah. Yellow on black. This'll help won't it?"

"Maybe, Sal. Just one more maybe. But you put together enough maybes, and maybe you'll have something. In any event, that was smart, Sal, real quick thinking. I hope I can start to react as well. There isn't anything else, is there? No more mental itches?"

"No. I'm pretty positive that's all there is."

"Then it'll have to do." I paused. "You know the chances are that this'll come to nothing."

"I know that."

"But I'll follow it."

"I know that, too. Look, Jake, you be sure to let me know what's going on, through that answering service I gave you. Okay? Even if there's nothing, I want to know."

"Don't worry about that. I'll keep you posted. And for whatever it's worth, try not to worry about the rest of it, at least not too much. Things can still happen. The score's against us, but we're not out of it yet."

Jesus. I was surprised I didn't say, "It's always darkest before the dawn," or "Let's win one for the Gipper." My brain must've been turning to oatmeal.

"Yeah. Right." It sounded like Sal believed me about as much as I did.

I hung up. I stood staring out the window into my back yard, shaking my head.

It wasn't a matchbook from Flo's Cantina, but it was something.

Damn.

It looked like some kind of blight had hit my tomato plants.

CHAPTER SIX

When I was working, I'd known people all over, in all kinds of jobs. Newspapers, show business, real estate, investment, insurance, police, and in most departments of the city, county, and state governments. It went with being a P.I. In fact, to a large extent it was the job. You didn't so much discover anything as locate the person who already knew it. Then, for a lunch or a sawbuck or a little bit of sweet talk or maybe a favor in return, you became a hero and a genius to your client. It wasn't always that easy, but for a lot of my work, I'd figured I was never more than three or four phone calls away from getting anything I needed.

But, as I'd told Sal, that was a long time ago. All of my connections, acquaintances, and friends who'd had useful positions had long since ceased to occupy them. They'd moved or retired. Or worse.

My once-full address book had more cross-outs than a bowdlerized version of Henry Miller. Hell, whole sections of the alphabet were now nothing but deletions. At times it seemed nonstop, the dying of friends.

Still, I did know some people who weren't yet under the ground, and the principle hadn't changed. If you wanted information, you went to the people who had it. If my friends no longer had access to it, maybe they had kids who did. The strings were different, but some of them could still be pulled.

Or so I hoped, as I headed toward the west Valley for the second time in about twelve hours. This wasn't one of my favorite parts of the city. For most of my life there'd been little out here. But it had mushroomed like a boom town during the golden days of the aerospace and electronics industries, and then nearly died when the bottom fell out. Now it was just another suburb on a freeway, built at a time before the Arabs made long commutes a luxury rather than an inconvenience. Maybe it was just the association with the moon shots, but I'd always felt that it was a vaguely lunar landscape out here, desolate, arid, capable of sustaining life only in carefully contrived artificial environments.

One of those environments was a place called Sunset Grove. Treeless and without a view, Sunset Grove was a nursing home. It was a one-story building, U-shaped around a grass courtyard. With its jarringly colored doors and trim, it looked like nothing so much as a tacky motel. Which was hardly surprising, since it was owned and operated by the same corporation that ran a nationwide chain of tacky motels. It was obviously good business for them. If they didn't get you on the road, they'd get you at the end of it.

Actually, considering the horror stories that were told about nursing homes—physical abuse, drug-induced stupors to ensure tranquility for the staff, weekly showers for which the patients were all stripped and put in a room together to be literally hosed down, places where five or ten patients were made to share one set of dentures, and so on—Sunset Grove was not that bad. It wasn't the Ritz, but it wasn't Dachau either. It was reasonably well run, competently staffed, clean. You could tell it was a good home because there were displays of plastic flowers in every room.

Patrick O'Brien had been there for about four years. Statistically, that was better than average, since a third of the people entering nursing homes died within the first year, and another third within the next three. Those numbers weren't encouraging; but then, nothing about nursing homes was. The gate in the walls surrounding Sunset Grove didn't need a sign telling all who entered to abandon hope. Hope just naturally disappeared once you were inside. Before you went in, you had already given up your health, home, and nearly everything else that had ever meant anything. There was only one more thing to give up, and even relatively decent places like Sunset Grove didn't provide much reason to hold onto it. Everyone there knew this was probably to be the last stop. It couldn't have boosted the spirits to realize that this stop would be made at a place that looked like it belonged next to Route 66 in Oklahoma.

No, no one chose to go to Sunset Grove; you went there because you didn't have any choice. Patrick O'Brien hadn't. He'd known it, as did everyone else, though no one was happy about it.

His had been an almost classically bad retirement. When he left the force after his thirty years he was still only in his fifties. Before he retired, he'd looked forward to doing nothing, but he soon discovered that for some people, doing nothing was the hardest possible activity. Then, he figured he'd supplement his pension with a job, but the opportunities available weren't that great. As he got older, they got even fewer and less meaningful, and then nonexistent.

He had plenty of time on his hands and nothing to fill it with. A lot of men who retire discover that their hobbies, which were fine as hobbies when they were working, make lousy careers when they stop. That was especially true for O'Brien, whose only real hobby had been drinking.

The whole thing was as clear as it was inevitable. He drove himself crazy, then he drove his wife crazy, then they drove each other crazy. Bitterness led to anger led to depression, and then the whole thing started over again. Until Maggie, his wife, must've decided she'd had enough and broke the circle by dying of a cancer that appeared out of nowhere and killed her in six weeks.

O'Brien's steady deterioration after that was as predictable as everything else. If you felt really rotten about yourself, it eventually caught up with you. Having enjoyed ridiculously good health all his life, his body started to fall apart. Nothing really serious, just enough little things to make it increasingly difficult for him to look after himself. He knew better than to move in with his son's family. So that meant Sunset Grove, whose glossy little brochures said it was "a graceful retreat."

Yeah, and so was Dunkirk.

The only thing at all out of the ordinary in this whole sequence was that O'Brien wasn't one of those who packed it in during the first year. In fact, soon after he entered Sunset Grove he started to pick right up. I don't know what it was, but something in the place got to him. Maybe it was the essential hypocrisy of places like this. Maybe the smiling condescension offended him. Maybe the perpetual, unthinking, mindless, mirthless cheerfulness touched his dark, Irish temper. Whatever it was, Sunset Grove reawakened the outraged, bristling anger that had been the dominant emotion of his life, and with it came renewed vitality. After about fifteen years of aimlessness, he again had a purpose: to make life as difficult as possible for all the smiling, mealy-mouthed bastards who surrounded him. He was not going to take any shit. He was not going to go gentle . . . anywhere.

And he thrived, like those couples whose relationships were endless raging battles but who would be lost without the conflict. O'Brien, who had spent thirty years kicking the asses of slimy punks, had a new opponent: the world —or Sunset Grove, anyway, which was as much of it as he still had contact with.

I'd been glad to see the change, because Patrick O'Brien and I went way back, to the days when he'd had a beat in Boyle Heights and I'd had a one-and-a-half-room office behind Pershing Square that said "J. Spanner and Associates" on the door. The associates, I supposed, were the wide variety of insects and small furry creatures with whom I shared the space. Hell, I was fairly young and thought a name like that would be more impressive. Than what, I didn't know. When business got good enough so I could change offices, I left the associates— literal and figurative—behind.

O'Brien spent his whole career as a patrolman. Unlike most cops who never advanced, it wasn't owing to a lack of ability or brains. Rather, he never thought his six-two, two-forty body would fit very comfortably behind a desk, and he never wanted to do the ass-kissing he figured was necessary to get out of his uniform. For a cop, he'd had a curious dislike of authority, something he might have inherited from his Molly Maguire grandfather.

For obvious reasons, Patrick O'Brien was never known as Pat, always just O'Brien or, sometimes, O'Bee. Whereas his Hollywood namesake appeared gruff but kindly, O'Bee tended to be foul and nasty. I liked him a lot.

I parked the car, and spotted O'Brien sitting on a lawn

chair under an umbrella, apart from everyone else, glowering at the eight-foot wall that kept the world from in-
truding into Sunset Grove—or vice versa. I walked across
the grass to him. It had been several months since I'd
seen him, and as I got close, I was shocked at how bad
he looked. He'd always been fat, but it had been hard,
solid flesh, appropriate to his roaring, expansive personality. Now the tension seemed gone, and there was just soft
weight there, not strength. His full head of wavy hair—
which for years had utterly pissed me off—was no longer
an angry auburn, but more a dull brown. I didn't like
what I saw.

"Hey, O'Bee," I said, "you're looking well."

He turned and glared at me. The green eyes, at least,
still had the same sharpness.

"Yeah. And you're looking like a fucking prune, Spanner." So, it seemed, had the tongue. "Christ, don't you do
anything except sit in the sun? I've thrown away old boots
that had better complexions than yours. It's going to catch
up with you, you know. One of these days you're going
to wake up and you're not going to have any skin left, just
this gooey jelly all over your body."

"It's nice to see you too, O'Bee."

He stopped glaring and smiled. "Sit down, Jake. That's
if you can bear to sit in the shade for a while."

"I'll manage."

"You bring me something to drink?"

"You know you're not supposed to drink."

"I know that's what the doctor says, but what I know
is something different. Besides, what's that bulge I see in
your pocket? Either you brought me something or you've
started to love me."

I made a face at the old joke, pulled out the half pint,
and handed it to him, shaking my head. He unscrewed
the bottle and took a swig. He winced as it went down,
putting his hand up to his side, then sighed and smiled.

"You sure you should be drinking that?"

"It's okay, Jake. Really."

I doubted it, but he took another drink and then put
the cap back on.

"You hear about Buchanan?" he said.

"No. What?"

"Dead. Keeled over in his doctor's waiting room."

"Shit."

"He wasn't even sick. Just there to get a vitamin shot. And Nat Dawson?"

"Who's that?"

"Ex-cop. Out of Central."

"Don't know him."

"Oh. Nice guy. Decent. Well, he killed himself. Gas. Didn't find the body for two weeks. You can imagine what it was like after that time, in this hot weather."

"I'd just as soon not, thanks. You're sure full of cheerful news."

"Hell, it could be worse."

"How?"

"It could be us."

"That's true." I nodded but, seeing the way the whiskey had made red spots on O'Brien's cheeks, I thought it might well soon be one of us. "You want to get out of here for a while?"

"What, and leave all this stimulating companionship?"

He waved a large hand around the courtyard. At intervals old people were sitting, singly or in pairs, some dozing, some staring blankly, a few reading, none talking. It had the feeling of isolation and suspension of an airport transit lounge in the middle of the night, everyone waiting for his flight to be called, wondering how much longer it would be.

A woman wearing a severe hair-do, a frozen smile, and a turquoise nylon uniform that was almost identical to the outfits used in the motel chain's coffeeshops went around telling everyone what a nice day it was and how they were having such a good time. There was no disagreement. She looked over at us, frowned briefly, and then went into the office.

"She doesn't seem to approve of you," I said.

"Ah, the Iron Maiden. She and her husband are the new directors. I like to think maybe I drove the old ones away. Though I'm not sure it was a change for the better. He used to be with a mortuary. Guess they decided there was more money in bodies that were still a little warm. She thinks I'm a troublemaker."

"She's right, isn't she?"

"Oh, hell. All that means is that I wouldn't let her treat me like an infant or a vegetable. Every time she came over to me with that look that said 'Isn't everything wonderful' or 'Have you been a good little boy,' I made an obscene suggestion. I wanted to see if I could crack that goddamn smile of hers."

"Apparently, you succeeded."

"Not for a long time. No matter what I said, and I got pretty inventive, she just kept smiling. It was hard, you could see, like she was sucking on a lemon, but she kept it up. She had to. Then I finally got to her."

"What'd you do?"

"Well, she said one of those goddamn annoying things, like 'How are we today?' meaning *me,* and I said *we'd* be a hell of a lot better if she did something or other to *us.* At this point I'm not even sure what particular act it was I proposed, but it must've hit a nerve. She looked like she'd been hit with a bucket of ice water. Then she went all red. Then she spit out something, like that I was a disgusting, filthy old man who was nothing but trouble and who should've been put down a long time ago like a diseased dog."

"That was real nice."

"No, you don't see. It was great, perfect. It was the first time she ever acknowledged that she really noticed me—had ever noticed any of us, for that matter. I was here, goddammit, I was here!" O'Bee slapped his broad chest with his hand. "I tell you, Jake, it was an absolutely shocking moment. Shocking, as in electrical. We were all in the rec room, all the old wrecks, for some reason— mid-morning cookies or some shit like that—and the place just lit up like a switch had been thrown. Right away, the Iron Maiden realized what she'd done. She looked around and sputtered a bit, and then stormed out. Complete silence for a minute. Then everyone—at least everyone who wasn't totally stroked out—started clapping, and then laughing, and then—goddammit!—started talking. I don't know whether you've noticed, but no one talks around here. It's like only the Iron Maiden and the rest of the staff have the power of speech. Which is exactly what they want—no talk, no complaints, no trouble. But they sure talked that morning, like a dam bursting, and I thought, What we have here is the start of a goddamn revolution."

Talk about a dam bursting. It was good to hear

O'Brien full of fight, and he'd even started to look a little better. I guessed we all needed listeners once in a while, and he obviously didn't have many at Sunset Grove. "And did you have a revolution?"

"Of course not," O'Bee snorted. "The bastards hold all the cards, always have. Everything was back to normal the next day. Except the Iron Maiden doesn't talk to me anymore, which is fine with me, the stupid bitch. She doesn't realize it, but by avoiding me, she shows that she knows I'm here. Even more"—O'Bee turned to me, smiled, and winked—"she wishes that I wasn't."

When we reached the car, I could see the woman watching us from the office window. I couldn't tell if she was smiling. O'Brien opened the door and made a gesture of invitation to her. I don't know how he did it, but with his bland smile and that innocent wave of his arm, he somehow suggested that if she got in the car, as soon as we were outside the gates, we would perpetrate unspeakable acts upon her scrawny, tense body. The figure at the window whirled and disappeared.

O'Brien chuckled evilly as he sat down, and took another pull at the half pint.

I drove to a Mexican take-out stand I had noticed on the way over to Sunset Grove. I hadn't eaten for twenty-four hours and realized I was ravenous. O'Brien didn't want anything, saying he hadn't had much appetite lately and would just suck on the bottle. I got a couple of soft tacos piled with carnitas and chorizo and covered with a lot of hot sauce. No doubt I'd regret it in a few hours, but so what? At my age most pleasures carried a price, but there were so few of them that I was usually willing to pay it.

We sat at a table next to the stand while I ate and O'Brien drank. He shook his head and muttered predictions of intestinal disaster as he watched me put away the good greasy stuff. It kind of reminded me of the old days, when O'Brien and I would meet for lunch at some little joint downtown. He'd have a few beers and I'd have a few tamales. I also usually wanted a favor of him.

In the past I'd always been able to be straight with O'Brien, never had to dance around. I figured that still held. Besides, my request was so ridiculous, there was no way to work it into any reasonable conversation.

"I need some help," I said.

"Ah, so your visit wasn't entirely social."

"Not entirely, no. But I've been meaning to—"

"Yeah, yeah, sure," he cut me off. "You in some kind of trouble?"

"I'm not. I'm trying to help someone out of trouble."

"I think I've heard that before."

"It's possible." Indeed, it'd been one of my standard lines.

"But not for about a hundred years. What the hell are you doing?"

"O'Bee, you're not going to believe this."

"After what I just saw you shove in your face, Jake Spanner, I'd believe anything was possible from you. Spill it."

I did. I gave him a slightly edited version of the situation, sticking primarily to the facts and leaving out my feelings. I also left out Sal's name, because it didn't really make any difference to anything; because maybe O'Brien wouldn't be keen to help an old crook like Sal, no matter what; and because the fewer people that knew, the less chance there was of a leak or a screw-up. That was the way I'd always done things—no names unless absolutely necessary. I'd figured that if a client had wanted publicity, he'd have gone to a newspaper, not a P.I.

I stopped my account before Sal's final phone call and looked at O'Brien.

He shook his head. "You're right. It is hard to believe. It's fucking incredible, is what it is. Like I said, what the hell are you doing? Don't you think you're a little old for stuff like this?"

"Yeah, I think so, but I'm in it anyway."

"So I see. What do you want me to do? It looks like you're doing a pretty good job on your own, getting slugged and losing three-quarters of a million bucks. Shit!"

"Well, you see, we've got a partial license number."

"Ah, the light dawns. Might this have something to do with the lieutenant?"

I smiled. Innocently.

The lieutenant was O'Brien's youngest kid, a fast-rising star in the police department. He never referred to him by name, only by title, as though he found it amazing that any offspring of his could be so contrary as to become

one of those cops who wear suits. Actually, I knew he
was proud as anything of kid's success, and enjoyed a
pretty good relationship with him.

"You haven't changed at all, have you, Jake Spanner?
Shit! Forty years ago you were doing the same thing, always getting me to give you department information so
you could get yourself or some sleazy client out of a jam.
Always coming to O'Brien to save your bacon."

I shrugged but didn't say anything. I knew him well
enough to know that the growling and the bitching meant
he'd already decided to help. If he wasn't interested he
would've said so straight out, and that would've been that.
It had been the same way forty years ago.

"And now you want to take advantage of the fact that
I happen to have a slight connection with a member of
the force? To play upon whatever possible affection said
member might have for me, so that he will violate policy
and thereby jeopardize his standing in, and his future with,
the department? All in the name of some dubious family
tradition that says the O'Briens are duty-bound through
eternity to pull Jake Spanner's fucking fat out of the fire?"
He looked a little surprised that he'd had the wind to
get all that out.

I shrugged again. "And?" I said.

"What?"

"There must be something more."

He glared. "There is." He took a deep breath. "And
you expect me to do all this because you were such a hot-
shit big spender that you gave me a whole half pint of
whiskey? Is that what you think?"

"Something like that."

"Well, let me tell you, Jake Spanner, that I may be old,
and slow, and sick, and stupid, but I can't be bought that
cheap. No fucking way. If I am going to sacrifice my dignity and make a disgusting play on the emotions and risk
the lieutenant's career, I expect to get at least another
bottle out of it."

I sighed. "Okay."

"And something a little better this time." He held the
nearly empty bottle at arm's length and squinted at the
label. "What the hell kind of name is 'Levy's Select' for
Irish whiskey?"

"It's the liquor store's house brand. Does it make any difference?"

"Only if you're drinking it. The next bottle's got to be better—at least the house brand of an Irish liquor store. Levy's Select! Jesus Christ!"

"Okay. You got it."

"And . . ."

"And? There's more?"

"Yeah, one more thing." Suddenly he was completely serious. "I assume you're going to try to find the guys that hit you."

"Right."

"I want to help you."

I looked at O'Brien. His green eyes were no longer flashing; they were pleading. What the hell was happening? Was there some kind of virus around that was making every old coot go crazy?

"Okay," I said.

O'Brien grinned and slapped his hands. "Let's go see the lieutenant, that brown-nosed little puppy."

We got up. On the way to the car, O'Brien threw a heavy arm around my shoulders. "Just like the old days, huh? O'Brien and Spanner on the case."

I disengaged myself from him. I was having enough trouble carrying my own body around today without adding a fat Irish drunk.

"Spanner and O'Brien," I said. "Remember who's buying the whiskey."

At the station it took us a while to get in to see the lieutenant. The guy at the desk took one look at us—O'Brien in a faded flannel shirt that didn't quite close over the bottom of his pink belly, me in another dapper mid-fifties get-up—and decided we were just another pair of geezers with nothing better to do but make nuisances of ourselves. He was right, of course, but that didn't change the fact that the lieutenant might, possibly, still want to see us. He seemed incapable of understanding a word we said, like either he was deaf or we were mute. At first he tried to jolly us out of the station, then he offered us fifty cents to buy a bottle of plonk, then he tried to ignore us, then he threatened to throw us in the can. For being pains in the ass, I supposed.

I was used to stuff like that, and knew if you were patient, if you spoke real slow so they could see your lips move, they sometimes figured out that you weren't speaking a foreign language, that maybe even, all appearances to the contrary, you had something to say. O'Brien, though, acted like he'd run into the police version of the Iron Maiden. He seemed to bristle and swell up like a blowfish. Started roaring and cursing, prophesying a future for the guy which included everything from an impacted bowel to writing parking tickets in Watts. Just as I thought we were in fact going to end up in jail after all, somebody came along who recognized O'Brien.

He whispered something to the desk man, who looked at us, pissed off, and said, "Well, why didn't you say so?"

O'Bee's head reared back, his eyes opening in amazement, so wide that white showed all around the green iris. I quickly said that we had, six or eight times, but the guy just shook his head and looked disgusted.

As we were led back to the offices, a Mexican kid with long greasy hair, a torn shirt, and a mouse over one eye, who had seen the whole exchange said with some admiration, "Nice going, guys. Look, would you tell somebody back there I been waiting two hours?"

I heard the desk guy say, "Oh, shut up!" just before the swinging doors closed behind us.

"Jesus!" O'Bee said. "That son of a bitch is so dumb, he couldn't find his ass with both hands at high noon."

It had been a long time since I'd been in a police station, but nothing had changed. A few new machines, computer terminals and so on, but that's all. There were the same paper coffee cups all over, the same half-eaten sandwiches, the same stacks of forms and memos and directives that had filled up O'Brien's old station house downtown. Also the same scent of pettiness, violence, sordidness, futility, and the knowledge of the people who worked there that no matter how much muck they cleared away, there was always more. The five thousand watts of fluorescent lights didn't so much brighten the place as put the dinginess in bold relief.

The lieutenant was waiting for us in the Squad Room. I'd known him almost since he was born, had even been kind of an honorary uncle to him when he was young, but it had been quite a while since I'd seen him. He didn't look anything like his father. He was much shorter, tighter, more compact, with dark straight hair and a thick mustache that was new to me. If he'd had an eye-patch, he would've looked a little like the guy that used to advertise those shirts. Only his green eyes were the same as O'Brien's, and they looked pretty happy to see his old man.

"Hey, Pop! Jake. What are you fellas doing down here?"

O'Brien looked up and down with a scowl. "Well, if it isn't His Fucking Holiness, the lieutenant. What do you do in here, shit silver dollars, that they won't let anyone in to see you?"

"Oh, shit, that wasn't you out there, was it?"

He looked at me. I smiled and nodded.

"Christ, Pop! We heard you all the way back here. We thought the goddamn place was under siege." He looked at me. "He used to listen to you. Couldn't you have tightened his leash or something?"

"Hell, I thought he was doing pretty well."

The lieutenant shook his head, grinning. "Incorrigible. A couple of senile delinquents. Come on."

We followed him into the glass cubicle that was his office. He turned and laughed. "Don't take it personally, you know. Anderson, the officer at the desk, is supposed to get rid of all the obvious nut cases."

"Oh, thanks. That's much better," O'Bee said.

The lieutenant laughed again. "No. You see, Anderson thinks everyone is crazy. Last week he kept a city councilman waiting half an hour."

"Well, that makes sense. Anyone on city council has to be mad as a hatter."

"There's a beat-up Mexican kid out there," I said, "who's been waiting two hours to see somebody."

"Oh yeah? Anderson! Shit!" The lieutenant picked up the phone, said a few words, then hung up. "Thanks, Jake. Now, what are you boys doing?"

O'Brien looked at me, then at his kid. "We want you to run a partial license."

"You what?"

"You heard me."

"What's going on here?"

"It's nothing much. Just a little something that we want to check on."

"Jake, do I assume that you're involved with this?"

"Yeah, I—"

O'Bee cut me off. "Shut up, Jake. I'm asking this."

"Come on, Pop. You know the rules. I can't do that for you."

"You're a goddamn big-deal lieutenant. You can do whatever you want." He turned to me. "You see, Jake; what'd I tell you? You take a good, decent cop, a guy who's willing to do a favor every once in a while, without making a federal case out of it, and you take him out of uniform and you give him a desk and you put him into a glass outhouse of an office, and all of a sudden he starts acting like he's the police fucking commissioner or something. 'We can't do that. It's against the rules,'" O'Bee said, lowering his voice and wrinkling his large nose. "Shit! Give me an asshole like Anderson any time. At least you know where you stand with him."

The lieutenant rolled his eyes upward. "I let him go on like this," he said, "because it's the only exercise he gets."

But O'Brien was just hitting his stride. "And am I some asshole who comes in off the street? I'd probably be better off if I were. But I'm only the guy who put braces on his teeth so he could smile like goddamn Robert Redman, and who put him through that fancy-ass college so when he gets in the department he can move up and not walk a beat, like was good enough for his poor old dad."

"Uh, poor old Dad—"

"Shut up, you ungrateful little punk! And how does he repay his poor old dad, who sacrificed for him?" O'Brien was talking quite loudly by this point. "Why, he forces him to go into a nursing home that makes the Black Hole of Calcutta look like a summer camp, and where his poor old dad gets one bowl of oatmeal a day and has to stay awake all night because if he doesn't, the rats'll come out and eat his toes."

I looked around. All activity in the Squad Room had stopped and everyone was looking toward the office.

"Christ!" The lieutenant got up and leaned out the doorway. "Go back to work, huh?" he said, and shut the door. "You know that's not true."

"Of course it's not." Now that the audience was gone,

O'Bee was speaking normally. "But maybe they don't know it. You want 'em talking about how you mistreat your poor old dad?"

"Poor old Dad! Shit! You really are a nasty old man. I'm just glad I'm the result of an affair Mom had with the milkman."

O'Bee stared at him for a second, and then they both started to laugh. O'Brien laughed so hard he began to cough, a deep ugly sound that shook his body. I hadn't ever seen O'Brien like that, and it wasn't pleasant. The lieutenant tried to help his father but was waved off.

When the spell was finally over, O'Bee's voice was soft and hoarse. "Will you help us out? This is something I want."

A look that I couldn't read, something uncharacteristically serious, passed between O'Brien and his son.

The lieutenant sat down behind his desk and began fiddling with some papers. "You're not going to tell me what this is about, are you?" O'Brien shook his head. The lieutenant looked at me. "You know, my reluctance has nothing to do with the rules. I just don't want you guys to get into trouble."

"No trouble, Lieutenant," I said.

"I mean, you're not as young as you used to be."

"Jesus, would you listen to that?" O'Bee said.

"Shut up, Pop, for once, would you? I mean, be careful. Okay?"

"Don't worry," I said. It seemed like I'd been saying that a lot lately. Without much effect.

"I do. I will. I don't want to come in one day and see in the morning reports that my father and his oldest friend have been hauled in for something or other."

"Ah, here it comes," O'Bee said. "The first rule of command—when in doubt, cover your ass."

The lieutenant made a despairing face and then pointed a short, thick finger at me. "Jake, you're responsible."

For what? That we wouldn't make asses of ourselves? It was already too late for that but I nodded agreeably.

The lieutenant looked at me and shook his head. "This is like having a child molester babysit. Shit! Tell me what you want and then get out of here."

I gave him the information. He said it'd take a couple

of hours, and he'd leave the material with O'Brien in the morning.

"Take care, Pop," he said as we left. "And Jake, you take care of him. Other than the milkman, he's the only father I've got."

Outside the station I said, "That's a good kid."

"Yeah, he turned out okay, didn't he?"

"That's also an interesting technique you have, making yourself so objectionable that people give you what you want, to get rid of you."

He shrugged. "It works." He seemed to drift off for a moment, then returned. "Hey! How about that! We're in business!"

O'Brien clapped his hands and then slapped me on the back, almost sending me sprawling. One more reason for hoping the situation could be resolved quickly: I doubted my body could stand a long association with the lumbering Irishman.

I got O'Brien back to the nursing home and me back to my home. In the last twenty-four hours I'd done more driving than in the two previous months. I was tired.

Since it didn't look like there was anything I could do until the next day, I smoked myself to the point where the adventures of Al Tracker would seem amusing, if not intelligible. Somewhere between Al wiping out a witches' coven and being beaten to a bloody pulp by a gang of Oriental men with bamboo sticks, I got a call from Sal. He hadn't had any luck yet, so he was glad to hear that I had gotten things started. I said I was glad he was glad, but that he shouldn't count on anything. He said he wasn't, but that he had confidence in me. Rather than get into what was becoming our usual song and dance, I said goodbye.

Just as Al was about to sink himself into the lubricious body of his client's wife, I gratefully sank into deep, dark, dreamless sleep.

CHAPTER SEVEN

When I went out to Sunset Grove the next morning, I found O'Brien and the Iron Maiden standing ten feet apart in front of the office, looking like they were waiting for a bus. He was carrying two plastic shopping bags from Safeway and she had on her frozen, surgically implanted smile. Both were trying to pretend the other wasn't there.

As soon as I got out of the car, she scurried up. "I understand Mr. O'Brien will be staying with you for a few days?"

Huh? I looked at O'Bee.

"Uh, Jake, I thought it might be easier if I stayed with you until we got this taken care of." He raised his eyebrows and nodded his head encouragingly.

"Sure, okay. Yes," I said to the woman, "Mr. O'Brien will be staying with me."

Her expression didn't change. I couldn't tell if she was disappointed that I'd gone along with O'Brien's story, or relieved that he'd be away for a while.

"You be sure that he takes his medicine. We wouldn't want him to get sick, would we?" she smiled.

"No, we certainly wouldn't."

O'Brien got in the car. She bent down to the level of the window. Still smiling, and without unclenching her teeth, she said, "I hope something heavy falls on you."

Before O'Brien could reply, she executed an abrupt about-face and marched quickly away.

O'Brien smiled benignly at her retreating figure. "She's probably off to change a catheter. That always cheers her up." He turned to me. "Hey, Jake! Here we go!"

He slapped me on the leg with a thwack. I winced, certain I had a large red hand-print on my thigh. I was beginning to feel like the much-battered Al Tracker.

Back at my place, O'Brien looked around, nodding his head. He hadn't been there for years. "Nice," he said.

"Nice?"

"Yeah. It's yours, it doesn't have orange and purple fire-retarding curtains, and it doesn't smell of Lysol and mortality. Nice." He looked at the couch and then looked at it again. "I know it's been a long time, but does this look like what I think it does?" He indicated the nearly obscene orchid on the center cushion.

"Yeah."

He grinned, sat down heavily, and wriggled his large rear.

"You want a drink?" I said.

"Nah."

"No?"

"No. We got work to do. Boy! Do we ever have work!"

He reached in one of the shopping bags and pulled out a thick sheaf of computer paper.

"Shit!"

He nodded and handed it to me. It was all neat and clear. Each line had a license number, a car make, model, and color, and a name and address. It started at AAM 700 and ended with ZAM 796. They were separated by what looked to be something over twenty-two hundred entries.

"Shit."

I only glanced through it quickly, but none of the licenses seemed to be designated as belonging to armed robbers, associates of kidnappers, or short psychopaths with funny voices.

"Shit."

O'Brien laughed. "What'd you expect? A three-by-five card?"

"I didn't really think about it. If I had, I guess this is what I would've expected. Still . . . Shit."

O'Bee and I divided the list and sat on opposite sides of the kitchen table, crossing out anything that didn't fit the vague requirements of new, big, and dark. Because the line had to be drawn somewhere, I arbitrarily decided to eliminate any car older than two years.

We hadn't gone very far before we realized that we had

no idea what kind of cars belonged to names like Cordoba, Cutlass, Cougar, and a whole lot of other European cities, offensive weapons, and predatory animals. Almost no models were still around from the days when we'd been consumers, and it gave us a sort of uneasy feeling. This was the kind of thing that took you by surprise: you went along, thinking you were keeping up pretty well, when suddenly something happened and you discovered you had lost touch with whole huge areas of experience, that without being aware it had happened, you found you were standing in the middle of an alien landscape.

O'Brien offered to call his sixteen-year-old grandson, but I didn't want to involve the lieutenant any further, even indirectly. Using newspapers and magazines I had lying around, we managed to connect images with most of the names, at least enough to see how things went. If the name was something young, cute, or cuddly, it was small; something vicious was fast; and if the name felt heavy, the car probably was as well.

It took us about three hours to eliminate two-thirds of the list. Not nearly enough. Another arbitrary decision and another forty-five minutes, and we had it down to cars in the vicinity of L.A. To do so didn't strike me as unreasonable. More to the point, reasonable or not, there didn't seem to be much choice. The problem was that we were still left with around two hundred possibilities, spread between San Bernadino and Oxnard, Newport, and Newhall. That was still way too many, but I couldn't see any way to narrow it further.

"Shit," I said for about the twentieth time, as I flipped through the list. "If time wasn't a factor, we could do it."

"But it is."

"Yeah. We need help."

"You're not thinking about asking the lieutenant again?"

"No. I think we pushed our welcome about to the limit, don't you?"

"Just about. Poor old Dad might be good for a bit of computer time, but running a check on two hundred citizens is a whole other thing. Especially since you don't want to tell him why."

"Exactly."

"So what are you thinking?"

"Hell, I don't know. What about your place? Anybody there who could lend a hand?"

"You kidding? Most of 'em can't raise a hand, much less lend one. Besides, their serum porcelain levels are too high."

"Their what?"

"Nursing-home joke. They're all crocks."

"Oh."

We fell silent, trying to think of people who could help us, trying to recall who was still alive and who was living in a trailer in Florida. Then we both looked up at the same time and simultaneously said, "The Tar Pits."

"Of course!" O'Brien said. "It was too obvious."

"You think they'll go along?"

"Hell, I'd be surprised if they didn't. I heard that last month they rented two buses and went down to that nude beach."

"You're kidding. To observe?"

"What do you think? To participate."

"Jesus! That's a staggering thought."

"Isn't it? Imagine all those wrinkles exposed in one place at one time. Like a convention of raisin producers."

"Christ, what a crew. Our thing'll probably seem too tame for them."

O'Brien and I set about sorting the possibilities by area, so they could be checked out as efficiently as possible, assuming our anticipated help came through. It turned out that there were two hundred and eleven vehicles. My only hope was that a lot of them would be eliminated as soon as they were seen, because either the color was not dark enough or the owner was obviously inappropriate.

As we were working, O'Brien said, "You know this is a really thin operation."

"I know."

"Based on a lot of dubious assumptions."

"Isn't it, though?"

"It surely is." O'Bee starting counting them off on his fingers. "That the partial license we're working with was correct to begin with."

"Yep."

"That neither the car nor the plate was stolen."

"Yep."

"That the right car is one of the ones we've decided to focus on."

"Right."

"That we'll be able to figure out which is the one we want."

"Right."

"That if we find the right guy, he'll still have the money."

"Yeah."

"And that if he does, we'll be able to get it back." O'Brien was onto his sixth finger. "That's more than a handful of assumptions, Jake Spanner."

I nodded. I'd been aware of all that stuff, but laid out like that, it certainly did look, as O'Brien said, thin.

"O'Bee, you play bridge?"

"No. Crib."

"Well, in bridge sometimes you end up with tough contracts that'll be set unless the cards lay one particular way. However unlikely that might be, that's your only chance, so you play based on the assumption that the cards do, in fact, lay just that way. If you get lucky, you win. If not, well, you were going to lose anyway, and you at least gave yourself the possibility of success. This looks like the same kind of deal. All we've got are two faint, fuzzy lines, and all we can do is see if they'll intersect somewhere."

O'Brien eloquently raised his eyebrows.

I sighed and nodded. "Damn right."

CHAPTER EIGHT

The Tar Pits was a two-story apartment house built around a large patio and swimming pool. While hardly luxurious, it had been well constructed and was kept in good condition, attractive, comfortable. It was a co-op for people over sixty, kind of a geriatric version of a swinging singles building, though perhaps a little less sedate than that.

The place was cooperative in much more than the legal sense. The people there helped one another out, contributed their energies and particular abilities—legal, medical, organizational, culinary, whatever—to the common good. The goal was self-sufficiency, and as a group, having lots of different skills and backgrounds to draw on, they managed pretty well. At least they didn't need a retirement village social director to plan a jolly afternoon of pottery-making or to remind them how much fun they were having. The group was there if someone wanted it, but avoidable if someone didn't. It was called the Tar Pits because, as the residents said, it was full of fossils.

O'Brien and I each knew a couple of people who lived there, and over the years we'd met a lot more. If I hated to go to Sunset Grove because it gave me the creeps, the Tar Pits was always full of surprises. I'd go there and find that half a dozen people were planning a trek in the Himalayas. Or that after thirty-five years of marriage each, the Callahans and the Schultzes had decided to switch partners for a while. Or that Mrs. Pitman had moved in with Mr. Andrews, Mrs. Jenkins, and Miss Tucker to form some bizarre kind of *ménage à quatre,* and that Mr. Andrews strutted around like a rooster and was known as the Sultan. It all seemed to work out well for those involved, but I gathered that some of these arrangements were profoundly upsetting for the children, who found both their parents and their own children living what they considered to be, at best, highly unconventional lives.

Basically, though, these relationships merely reflected certain realities: that there was a need for companionship; that there were three times as many old women as old men; that pensions could be lost if an old widow became a new wife; that propriety somehow didn't seem so important, once you realized there might not be a tomorrow; that a person tended to regret what he didn't do, not what he did do. Yeah, when you got to your sixties, you usually had a good grip on reality, if nothing else.

Or some of us did. Others of us still played cops and robbers. Shit.

"Well, look who's here!" a voice said as we walked onto the patio.

"Our own Sam Spade!" a second voice said.

"And the fuzz. Oh, oh!" said a third.

"Jesus! The fruit salad," O'Brien said.

The voices belonged to three guys sitting under an umbrella advertising Cinzano. I had known them from way back, from one of the studios. They had been in make-up, costumes, and set design, and had been together since the days when their pleasure had been a crime. More than a couple of times I had gotten them—individually and collectively—out of some ugly little messes. Though forty years together had made them look like triplets—all neat, pink, plump, and seeming to be fifteen years younger than they were—one tended to be outgoing, always ready for action. Another complained a lot. And the third was quiet, often nervous in a protective kind of way. Obviously, everyone had always called them Itchy, Bitchy, and Twitchy. I wasn't sure if they'd been given the names because they fit, or if they'd grown to fit their names.

"Would you boys like a Margaret?" Itchy said.

"I keep telling you it's called a Marguerita, you fool," Bitchy said.

"And I keep telling *you* I only make the damn things. I never claimed to be good at languages."

"Now, now," Twitchy said.

"Shut up and drink your Margaret, and stop clucking like an old lady," Bitchy said.

O'Bee and I turned down another offer of drinks.

"You like my new eye shadow, Jake?" Itchy said.

"Oh, is that what it is? I thought maybe Bitchy'd hit you."

"If only he would. He's all talk and no action, that one. It's called 'Midnight in Paris.' What do you think?"

"I remember it well."

"I think," Bitchy said, "that it makes you look like the model of Joan Crawford in the Hollywood Wax Museum."

"Nobody asked you. You're just jealous, because you have those little pink eyes and if you wore make-up, you'd look like a queer rabbit."

"At least I don't look like an over-the-hill drag queen."

"That's not fair. *I'm* not the one with the dress what's-her-name wore in *Gone with the Wind,* hanging in *my* closet."

"Well, I don't wear it."

"Well, I hate to think what you do do with it."

"Uh, Jake—" O'Brien said, poking me hard in the ribs with his elbows

"Right." I rubbed the spot. "Is Leo around?"

"I think he's upstairs."

"Okay. O'Bee, why don't you tell these three what we want?"

"You want what they all want," Bitchy said.

"Not this time, we don't. O'Bee?"

"Thanks a whole fucking lot."

"Don't worry, Patrick," Twitchy said. "We won't bite."

"Well, maybe only a little," Itchy said.

The three of them started to giggle. As I walked away, I heard O'Brien call, "Hurry up, Jake."

I laughed. The three had been playing this routine so long, I doubted if they or anyone else knew what was an act and what was for real. Never having tried to hide anything, they forced everyone to accept them on their own terms. That some people didn't was one of the reasons I'd had to bail them out from time to time in the past. Outsiders their whole lives, they never seemed to notice the isolation of old age. If anything, it had been liberating—a new license to outrage, new preconceptions to shake. They were something, all right.

I knocked on the door to 212.

"Jacob! Come in."

Leo Kessler was the only person who called me that, but he was also the only person still around who'd known me when I was a Spanovic. We went back so far, it was scary. Back to the neighborhood, to college, and then to Paris. After that our paths split, with Leo going on to Oxford, Cambridge, and a long and distinguished academic career, while I chose to associate with a slightly different class of people, like George the Roach and Slimy Solly Wiseman.

We lost track of one another for nearly thirty years, until he came out to teach in California, and we'd kept in touch since then. It was important for both of us to maintain contact with someone who knew who we had been so long ago, a link to a past that was rapidly ceasing to be even a memory. At the same time, though, it made us kind of uncomfortable, because we each somehow represented the other's unrealized potential.

I went into the book-filled apartment. So many books that it seemed like there were no walls, only rows and rows of books in half a dozen languages, from the floor to the ceiling. I thought about my stacks of lurid paperbacks.

"Jacob, you're looking as disreputable as ever, which I take to be a good sign."

In the decades between Paris and California Leo acquired a vaguely British accent that was still with him, and that I found goddamn incredible for someone from my neighborhood.

"And as always," I said, "you're looking like you made a wrong turn thirty years and three thousand miles away from here."

"You mean I'm wearing a tie."

"Right."

Actually, if anyone ever looked like the Central Casting idea of what he should be, it was Leo Kessler, Professor Emeritus of Literature. He was short and trim, in a brown tweed jacket with leather elbow patches, a solid brown vest, a stiff, gleaming white shirt, and a carefully hand-tied dark-green and white polka-dot bow tie. Other than funeral directors, Leo must've been the only person in Southern California who wore a jacket and tie all the time.

I kidded him about it, but I couldn't imagine him any other way. With his glossy white hair, gold-rimmed glasses, and highly polished little shoes, he was as neat and precise as the sentences he wrote in the authoritative scholarly essays that earned him his reputation. He had lots of little widows working themselves into lavender frenzies over him, but as far as I knew he was no more active in that regard than I was. At least, I thought somewhat meanly, I sure as hell hoped he wasn't.

"You keep your nifty little tie on when you went to that beach?"

Leo smiled. "You heard about our excursion. Sorry to disappoint you, Jacob, but I did not participate. Living in the Tar Pits has certainly loosened me up, but, uh—"

"It hasn't entirely untied you?" I helped out.

"That's one way of putting it, yes. You know, Jacob, despite that, I sometimes wish that I knew back then"— he gestured vaguely over his shoulder with his hand— "what I've learned in the last few years."

I shook my head. "Madness lies that way."

"I know. But sometimes it's hard not to want to correct the past. Especially when it seems, more and more, much closer than the present." He made a sound of disgust. "But enough, right? You know all that."

Did I ever.

I took a deep breath. "I've got a little bit of the present that might interest some of the people here."

"Oh?"

Leo was one of the unofficial leaders in the Tar Pits, and I quickly told him what I wanted. That I needed help checking out some cars, finding out whether the color was light or dark, and who owned or drove it. I didn't tell him why, just that I needed to know. Again, I wanted to keep quiet as much of the situation as possible. If loose lips sank ships, Itchy, Bitchy, and Twitchy could put the whole Sixth Fleet on the bottom.

Leo looked a little disbelieving, then he shook his head and chuckled. "You're still at it, aren't you? You know, Jacob, you always amused—maybe even amazed—me. You were an intelligent, well-educated man, much more so than most of the tenured colleagues I've known, yet you chose to live like and with thugs. Incredible."

"Gee, and I always thought you were the aberrant one."

"And you're still doing it."

"Once a thug, always a thug."

"Forgive me, but I say this as a friend. Are you really up to it?"

"Of course not. If I were, do you think I'd be trying to enlist the aid of the old croakers who live in this place? Come on, Leo, cut it out. I didn't come for advice. Only to find out whether anyone here'd be interested."

"Are you serious? The chance to play sleuth? You'll have to beat them off with a stick."

"You know, it's not all that interesting. Basically, it's just a matter of waiting around, as inconspicuously as they can, until they spot the car, and, if it's dark colored, the person or people connected with it. Then they call in. That's all."

"Is there any danger?"

"Only if they doze off and miss their bus stop. At most they might have to use a bit of ingenuity to find out what I need. You know, go up to a house and pretend they have the wrong address, so they can get a look at whoever owns the car. That kind of thing."

"That should be no problem. We've learned to become fairly ingenious around here. How many people do you want?"

"As many as you can get. There are about two hundred cars to check out and very little time."

Leo nodded. "I'll start on it right away. I should be able to get you lots of help. I may have to somewhat enhance the way it sounds, though. A group here recently completed a class in self-defense, and some of them have been walking around with chips on their shoulders, just dying to try out what they've learned."

I groaned inwardly, seeing some wild-eyed old geezer threatening to judo-chop someone unless he came clean. "Please, Leo. The idea is to do this quietly."

Just then I heard hoots of raucous laughter coming from the courtyard, followed by O'Bee's rather desperate cry of "Jake!"

Leo and I looked at each other. "Well, as quietly as possible," I said.

I gave him the lists of license numbers and addresses,

and explained in detail what I wanted and how we'd work it.

Another cry of "Jake!" from down below.

"I'd better get going." I pulled out two of Sal's C-notes. "This'll cover bus fares, gas, whatever."

Leo stared at me, then took the bills. "Oh, Jacob," he sighed.

I got downstairs in time to rescue a grateful O'Brien from a complicated story involving a vat of Crisco and the old Hollywood Stars baseball team. As I'd expected, Itchy, Bitchy, and Twitchy were delighted to help, and said they'd get some other friends involved as well. O'Bee muttered something about every hairdresser in Hollywood being on the case. Even though we left them happily discussing where they could get summer-weight trenchcoats, I was confident that they'd be serious when it counted.

O'Brien and I took a very roundabout route back to my place, and managed to locate three of the cars on the list. One was light brown, one was a bilious green, and the third, while the right shade of red, belonged to a forty-five-year-old home economics teacher.

That left only two hundred and eight.

Progress.

CHAPTER NINE

With the aid of Leo and the merry threesome, I ended up with about thirty people spread throughout Southern California, trying to get a line on the automobiles. Damn, that was probably more agents than the local Pinkerton office had. For someone who'd run a one-man show for most of his life, it was rather an odd experience.

O'Brien stayed at my place. He manned the telephone and kept a careful record of which cars had been located and which hadn't, which could be eliminated for whatever reason and which were still in the running.

I was on the street, moving as fast as I could. Like the others, I traced down cars, but I also checked on the possibles that were phoned in. About every two hours I called O'Bee to find out any new developments.

As I'd told Leo, it was a slow, tedious procedure. Since it mostly involved nothing but waiting around, there was no way to speed it up. Fortunately, the one thing you learn—you were often compelled to learn—when you get old is how to wait. Most of my overage operatives were pretty good at it.

Another thing they proved to be good at was surveillance. It should have come as no surprise, since being old is almost as good as being invisible. Unless you mutter to yourself or make disgusting noises, nearly everyone either plain doesn't notice you or makes a point of avoiding seeing you. Either way, you can hang around for long periods of time, without attracting attention. After all, what else does an old fogey do except hang around?

Things went along pretty well. Not well enough, because I hadn't found my man, but they did keep moving. And movement was my only hope, if my long-shot gamble was to pay off. As I'd thought, most cars were eliminated as soon as they or their owners were spotted. That didn't necessarily take me any closer, but it didn't put me any further away.

I was also happy that there were very few incidents. The unbelievable Mr. Andrews proudly reported that one Mrs. Bascombe, owner of a blue Mercury, TAM 704, had decided to become the latest member of his household. Itchy called in to say that, while his lead hadn't panned out, he had, however, met the most adorable young man, and he was leaving the hunt for a couple of hours. And a pair of fourteen-year-old girls with leather jackets and pink hair had tried to mug one of our old ladies. Unfortunately for them, they picked a graduate of the self-defense class and found themselves being used to mop up the sidewalk.

Even prim, professorial Leo Kessler joined the search. I happened to be home when he called in one time, very excited because he had executed some elementary scam in order to get the info we needed. He said he'd had no idea this could be so much fun. It sounded like his bow tie must've been askew. I figured it was only a matter of time before Leo would be wanting to borrow sleazy paperbacks from me.

Jesus.

What had I unleashed upon an unsuspecting city?

After four days, we were down to a short list of eighteen possibilities. All that meant, though, was that on the surface we hadn't been able to eliminate them. The cars were all dark, and the drivers were roughly the right age and size, but beyond that, there was no reason to think any of them was the one I wanted. There were also still over thirty of the original two hundred eleven that we hadn't been able to locate, a circumstance that did nothing to bolster my confidence.

As time went on, and with no positive results, the less likely I thought it was that my approach would work out. Hell, I had absolutely no reason to think that it would. However, I had decided to play the hand this way, and I knew I had to keep on with it, however small my chances. Without a better alternative, to change in the middle would only ensure defeat. That was known as having the courage of your convictions, an attitude that'd led to some pretty spectacular disasters.

Sal's nightly phone calls weren't helping much, either. He was getting increasingly panicked, needlessly reminding me that time was running out, that the kidnappers' deadline was getting closer.

Thanks a lot, Sal. That was just what I needed. Otherwise, I might have forgotten. Shit.

He was right, though, and I did have to start moving. I decided to let the crew from the Tar Pits run down the remaining thirty cars while I concentrated on our short list. These were spread over a big hunk of Southern California. Since there was no way to choose between them, I was going to start with the closest ones and work my way out.

Meanwhile, I put O'Brien to work trying to get a line on our possibles. Even though he'd been retired for a long time, he still knew a fair number of people on the force. Some through the lieutenant, but more from when O'Brien had broken them in as rookies.

O'Brien also knew—naturally—every bar where cops hung out off-duty. If he could be casual and quiet about it—as if that were his style—maybe he could see if anyone recognized any of the names on our list. Even if they did, it wouldn't necessarily mean anything, but we were at the point where we badly needed a break.

I supposed we could have gotten the lieutenant to run a check, but I really didn't want to involve him unless absolutely necessary. He was much too sharp. If he ever got into this, I'd never get him out. And I still figured Tommy's chances would be better if I could manage it on my own. So this had to be strictly a solo play, and I had to rely on the sense of fraternity, the old-boy network, that exists between all cops. It was owing, I guessed, to the fact that the only people who could understand what it was like were those who had done it, and anyone who had done it was always accepted as a member. If anyone could play the network, it'd be O'Brien.

I offered to give him some money so he could buy drinks, but he just wanted bus fare. He said if he couldn't get those guys to spring for an old fellow-officer, either he'd lost his touch or they were a pretty piss-poor lot.

"Well," I said, "don't get so looped you forget what you're doing"

He held up his big hands, all innocence. "Only soda water, Jake. I'm on duty."

"If I remember right, that never used to slow you down much."

"Well, maybe a little something to give the soda some color, just to be sociable, you know."

"Yeah, sure."

I dropped him off at Manny's Jailhouse Bar, thinking this could be the last time I'd ever see him and wondering how I'd explain to the lieutenant that his old man ended up in the drunk tank in the line of duty.

The first possibility I checked out was FAM 714, belonging to a guy named Gregory Dupont. He was the right age and size. He was also a clerk in a fancy Wilshire Boulevard shoe store. He wore cute little patent leather pumps and walked without bending his knees. One look at his hands, small, soft, and white, like fluttering sea anemones, and I knew he never did anything more violent than toss a salad. Scratch little Gregory. Though, if I correctly remembered their taste, he might be of interest to Itchy and Bitchy.

BAM 784, a huge dark-brown Mercedes, looked a lot better. Its owner was named Lance Silver. That was enough to arouse suspicion. So was the fact that he billed himself as a producer. Of what, he didn't say. Probably mischief. I'd seen guys like Lance in L.A. for as long as I'd been there, and in fifty years only the clothes had changed. He was a fast-talking, fast-moving hustler who knew everybody well enough to say hello, and who gave the impression of being at the center of fantastic action, a juggler with invisible balls.

It took me a while to run him down. His "office," which I suspected was only an answering service, kept giving me new addresses where he could be found as he worked his way down Sunset, but he'd always moved on by the time I got there. Guys like Lance always had to keep going, afraid that if they stopped too long it'd all catch up with them.

When I finally spotted him—going around saying hello to everyone at an outdoor café—I recognized what he was as fast as I'd recognized Gregory Dupont. Only he couldn't be dismissed so easily. At best his kind was borderline legit, and it never took much to push types like him over to the wrong side. Maybe they started off straight, but since their whole existence was predicated on making the big, easy score, they often grabbed at anything that came along, especially if the Benz was about to be repossessed.

Yeah, as soon as I saw old Lance tooting around among the beautiful people, I thought he looked real good for my boy. And I hoped he was, because I'd dealt with a couple of dozen other Lances over the years, and I knew, no matter what, I'd never be so old and feeble that I couldn't get the better of someone like that. He was all flash and glitter on the surface, all loud confidence, but there was nothing inside. One good tap and he'd shatter like a sucked egg.

The more I saw of him as he went from place to place like a hungry bee, the better I liked him for the part, but he never settled long enough in one spot for me to get close. Finally, at the fourth little chi-chi café, a place now called Sebastian's, which I remembered from the forties, when it hadn't had a name but had served decent hot dogs, he sat down for the first time.

Luck stayed with me as a parking space opened up just past the café, and I pulled in. I slicked myself down a little and strolled into Sebastian's, trying to look like I hadn't made a mistake. This was a little tough, since I was at least as old as the combined ages of any three people there. Hell, my shirt was older than most of them. My clothes weren't skintight; then again, neither was my skin. And I didn't have on a neat little gold earring. My entrance caused a silence like what must've occurred when Red Death revealed himself at the masked ball.

As I sat down two tables away from Lance, I heard someone say, "Jesus, look at that."

"I hope I die before I get that old," said a female refugee of anorexia nervosa who didn't look like she'd last the month.

"Gives me the fucking creeps." This from a three-

hundred-pound guy covered with thick black hair and little else.

"Maybe he's someone important."

"No fucking way. He's too old."

"Yeah."

"Shee-it!"

As usual they assumed I couldn't hear. I sat there smiling like I knew something they didn't. Which I did: it
was that I was their future. Ah, to be young, stupid, and
blind.

Not surprisingly, no waiter approached my table. Just
as well. The menu seemed to consist solely of Perrier, at
three-fifty a pop. Price aside, that stuff always played
havoc with my guts, like I'd swallowed an inflated bal-
loon.

After a couple of minutes, conversations started back
up again. Other than profanity, they seemed to consist of
few words except "percent," "gross," "net," "package,"
"tie-in," "deal," and a lot of big numbers. I realized that
everyone in the place was just like Lance. There wasn't a
real proposition in the bunch, only hustle, but no one
seemed to notice.

Finally I got what I came for, when Lance started talking to someone at the next table about a deal he had going. Until then he'd been sipping his Perrier, but he
couldn't keep quiet any more than he could stop moving.
He sounded like a hootchy-kootchy carnival barker trying
to pass off a fat fifty-year-old stripper as the Queen of
Sheba. His harsh nasal whine was about as euphonious
as grinding gears, but unfortunately it wasn't anything
like that weird voice Sal had described. Pity. Lance Silver
was a crook, all right. He just wasn't my crook.

I stood up, glancing at my watch. I called to the waiter
and said that when—I gave the name of the current head
of Paramount—came by, he should say that I couldn't
wait any longer, but that I'd be over at Universal for the
next couple of hours. I left to a silence at least as pro-
found as that which had greeted my arrival.

I smiled. No one is easier to hustle than a hustler.

It took me twenty minutes to drive to the Bel Air
address of Dr. Harold Jackman—who I thought was probably once a Jacoby—a successful cosmetic surgeon. Jack-

man was in Aruba performing a hush-hush tuck on some sagging celebrity, but his big black Caddy was in town. So was his kid, Austin, who'd been having a good time cruising around in Daddy's Seville. I gathered from Bitchy, who was the one who'd spotted him, that the kid was about seventeen or eighteen. That was younger than what I thought I wanted, but Bitchy said the kid was strange. Considering the source, I had no idea what that could mean, but I figured I should check him out.

There was no sign of the car or the kid. I decided to give it some time and parked opposite the house.

From the little Bitchy had said, I had the idea that Austin Jackman was one of those Southern California brats who'd been given every advantage his parents never had, and who knew a good thing when he saw it. Most of the kids around looked to be pretty decent, trying—not always successfully—to cope with where and when they'd had the misfortune to grow up, and with whom. More than a few, though, were amoral, self-centered little rodents for whom the word "no" was a meaningless exhalation of sound. If Austin was one of those, virtually anything was possible.

I'd also noted that he didn't live that far away from Sal, and it was not implausible that he and Sal's grandson knew each other. It was an ugly idea, but I wondered if maybe the thing was a hoax, if Tommy had been a willing participant in his "kidnapping." I had no reason for thinking so, other than that it wouldn't be the first time for something like that. Bah! Nonsense. If that was the case, then you went through with the drop; you didn't stage a stick-up. Besides, Sal said that Tommy was a good kid. On the other hand, Dr. Jackman probably said the same thing about his.

Before I could further tie myself up in knots with my speculations, the object of them appeared, with a squeal of brakes and smoking rubber, as two tons of dark-green Caddy hurtled up the driveway, hardly damaging a pyracantha bush and stopping a good six inches short of the garage door. Hi, everybody! Austin's home!

When he got out of the car with a bunch of his yahoo friends, I saw he was a skinny little mutant in designer jeans and a T-shirt with a salacious tongue on the front.

The biggest part of him was a nose that testified to his erstwhile Jacobyness. I wondered if it could possibly have been hidden under a ski mask . . . or even a diving helmet.

They disappeared into the house before I could form any further impressions. I gave them a few minutes, then went up and rang the doorbell.

A girl opened the door. She had long, shining blond hair, a complexion like fine satin, and eyes with all the liveliness and intelligence of a pair of opaque marbles.

"Is Dr. Jackman here?" I said.

The girl looked blankly at me, and I repeated the question. She giggled, said "Dr. Jackman," and giggled again. She floated toward the living room, leaving the front door wide open. I followed. Though my appreciation was strictly academic, I did notice that her tight jeans and skimpy top in no way hid what was under them. While I sure as hell wouldn't want to be the age of these kids again, I did acknowledge there were certain compensations.

I shook my head. "J. Spanner: Salivated himself to the point that he dried up and blew away." Come on, you old fart.

Austin was lying on the floor with a set of large headphones encasing his narrow skull. A couple of his pals were sitting at a glass coffee table, sluggishly shoving around big piles of different-colored capsules.

The girl poked Austin with her foot several times before he slowly and with difficulty raised himself to a sitting position. He looked around a little, then took off the headphones. Even from ten feet away, the sound coming out of them, something like the roar of a jet engine, was uncomfortably loud.

"A patient to see you, Dr. Jackman," the girl said, giggled, then fell silent.

Austin looked at me under half-closed eyes, with his mouth hanging open.

"You're not Dr. Jackman," I said.

Austin considered this for a while before he said, "My father's away. You wan' a 'scrip? I'll wri' you a 'scrip." He blearily looked around, I supposed for his father's prescription pad. Nice to see a kid following in his dad's footsteps.

I sighed. Austin was out. Sal had said the guy's voice was high and funny, like a record being played too fast. Austin sounded like he was talking under water, with a mouthful of mashed potatoes. Besides, I doubted that anyone in what was probably a permanent barbiturate fog could have managed the stick-up.

"Wan' some reds? Yellows? 'Ludes?"

I shook my head.

"Ups? Wan' some ups? Loo' like you coul' use some ups."

I could use something, that was for sure, but I shook my head.

"Wan' fuck Serena? Serena, go fu' th' old man."

The girl smiled placidly.

I confess I considered it—for about three seconds—before I shook my head.

Austin looked at me and shrugged in defeat. Exhausted by his efforts at hospitality, he heavily fell back on the floor. Tried to get the headphones over his ears, but it was too much trouble and he gave it up.

I went to the front door and looked back. No one had spoken or moved. It was exactly like the courtyard at Sunset Grove. I left.

There was a lot going on there that I didn't understand, and I didn't even want to try. I had changed my mind about Austin. He wasn't a creep. He was just sad.

I got back in my car. I was tired. To tell about it, it doesn't sound like much, but it had been a long day, a hell of a lot longer than I was used to. I knew I couldn't do any more, and headed back to the Valley.

I had mixed feelings about the day. In a way, I'd been very lucky and accomplished a lot. To run down three suspects in one day was way better than I had any right to expect. But the results had all been negative. At this rate —and I couldn't count on continuing this fast—it would take at least five more days to cover the short list. Sal hadn't heard yet, but we had to figure we had only a few more days, at most.

I needed a break. Did I ever.

On the radio the newscaster announced that the government had determined a new poverty line. Well, it was certainly something to shoot for.

I hardly thought at all about doped-up, luscious little Serena.

Back home I found O'Brien stretched out on the couch, snoring wetly, his big belly going up and down. The television was blasting some raucous game show.

"Hi, honey, I'm home!" I said.

"Ah, Jake." O'Brien blinked a couple of times and sat up. "How'd it go?"

I told him.

"Leo called," he said. "They ran down twenty more."

"And?"

"Negative."

"Well, at least that doesn't add anything to my list. How did you make out? Or need I ask?"

"I tell you, Jake, the things my liver has done for you."

"I thought you were going to take it easy."

"I got my reputation to consider."

"Some reputation. Anyway, what'd you find out?"

"I went to three places and saw fifteen, twenty guys."

"And had a drink with each one."

"Well—"

"I know. You got your reputation to consider."

"Christ, you have to be sociable. You can't come on like an asshole."

"Okay, okay. What did you get?"

"No one's ever heard of any of the people on your list."

"Swell. It figures."

"Hold on. I said people. You've also got a car registered to a company."

"Yeah. Something called—what is it?—Trans-Global Import/Export."

"Right. Seems that this company is connected."

"Oh, really?"

"Yeah. I didn't find anyone who knew much about it, but a few of the guys knew the name, and the word seems to be that it's pretty well connected, all right."

"Hmm."

When you thought about it, it was obvious that any company with a name like that had to be a front. Only I hadn't thought about it. Automatically gave the company car the lowest priority on my list. I wouldn't have done that fifteen years ago. And just when I thought I was doing pretty well.

Trans-Global was now right at the top. I couldn't say why, but I had a strong feeling about it, like I sometimes used to get when I knew I was close to whatever it was I wanted. The whole setup felt right. The style had been neat, professional. I didn't think it was a mainline company activity, though. Shit, if the mob was involved, they didn't need to get into something as messy as kidnapping. More likely it was an independent action. Someone at Trans-Global heard something, and decided to cut himself in for a nice little score.

Damn! It smelled good to me.

"You got that look, Jake."

I nodded. "We needed a break. I sure hope this is it."

I no longer felt tired. I wanted to get on it, but I figured there was nothing to be done until the morning.

So I fixed dinner. I got a container of homemade *menudo*, Mexican tripe stew, out of the freezer and started it heating. One thing about being broke, I'd sure learned to cook up a storm using spare parts, the kind of stuff that ordinarily went into pet food. Homemade or canned, it looked like that was my future.

While the *menudo* was simmering, I got a call from Sal. I told him about Trans-Global and asked if he'd heard of it. There was a long silence before he said he hadn't. He sounded really strange and I asked him if he was all right. He said he was, but I still thought there was something different. We talked for a few more minutes and I told him what I would do. Once again he reminded me that time was running out and urged me to stay with it.

After we hung up, I tried to determine what was different about him, but I couldn't figure it. It was almost as though he sounded relaxed for the first time since this started, but unless there was something he wasn't saying, there was no reason for that. Or maybe he intuitively had the same feeling about Trans-Global that I did.

The hell with it. I went back to the *menudo*. O'Bee was looking dubiously at it.

"What's that?"

I told him.

"Christ, Spanner, I think you'd eat anything that didn't eat you first."

"It's good. It's supposed to be just the thing if you've overindulged. Mexicans swear by it."

"They can swim in the shit, for all I care. I'm not about to start eating cow's guts."

"You know, you're really a delight to have around."

"Ah, you love it."

I made him a chicken sandwich, of which he ate very little. He hardly seemed to eat these days.

We played a couple of hours' of cribbage before I went to bed. O'Bee said he'd stay up a little longer.

I woke up in the middle of the night and saw a light coming from the living room. I looked in. O'Brien was still sitting in an armchair, a lamp on low, not dozing, not reading, not watching television. Just sitting.

It didn't look like he wanted company, so I went back to bed.

CHAPTER TEN

Early the next morning I was parked off of Vermont, opposite the seedy four-story building where Trans-Global was located. Most of the other occupants seemed to be either dealers in fabric remnants or jobbers of junk products no one had ever wanted. From what I could tell, Trans-Global had a couple of small rooms on the top floor. Totally unprepossessing, it was a perfect front. If, of course, that's what it was.

It was only a few blocks from here, in '37 or '8, that I'd tangled with a phony Russian spiritualist who'd been conning wealthy widows in Pasadena. My client got her money back, I got a black eye, and Rasputin got five to ten. When he got out, I heard he married one of his former patrons and spent the rest of his days hosting social functions to raise funds for the Republican party.

At about ten-thirty the big black Olds, SAM 726, pulled up. Trans-Global certainly kept comfortable hours. Two hulking bruisers got out of the front seat. They wore dark, ill-fitting polyester suits, and it looked like their combined I.Q. wouldn't make a three-digit number. Either one of them could have been a prime candidate for the part of the sap man. One scanned the street while the other opened the rear door. The guy that got out stood about as tall as the bruisers' armpits. He had on an expensive cream-colored suit and a big-collared silk shirt open at the neck. He was in his middle twenties, I guessed, but he could have passed for fourteen. His round, unlined face displayed the total innocence of a choirboy or a psychopath. Whatever he was, he sure didn't belong in that office building, and it looked like the rumors O'Bee had picked up were correct. Also, the feeling I had last night was stronger than ever. If this wasn't my boy, I didn't think I'd ever find him.

The three of them went inside, and I stayed in the car and waited. A couple of hours later, the kid came out, accompanied by one of the bruisers. He got in the back seat again and they pulled away. I made a hasty U-turn and followed.

Aside from what must have been a lunch break at a fancy Italian restaurant, they stopped at a whole series of adult bookstores and movie parlors. Most were crummy little storefronts whose windows had been painted over. At the few where I could see in, it appeared the kid was greeted with not much pleasure but a lot of deference. He and the proprietor would then disappear into a back room and reemerge ten or twenty minutes later. The proprietors always seemed happy when the kid left. I began to get an idea of at least some of the things Trans-Global was importing and exporting.

After spending most of the afternoon parked in front of dirty bookstores, I decided I'd better do something. While the kid was looking better and better to me, I needed confirmation before I put in any more time.

When the pair went into the Marquis Pleasure Center, I gave them a couple of minutes. Then I tried to look like a degenerate, which may not have been too difficult, and shambled in after them.

Jesus! Welcome to the modern world, Jake Spanner. Holy shit!

Judging from the nifty leather outfits and curious metal implements that filled half the store, there was little doubt which marquis they had in mind. Christ! To even dream about this stuff thirty years ago would have been sufficient grounds for committal. If I'd thought I'd seen it all, I was wrong, and I had to keep reminding myself to keep my mouth closed. My life hadn't exactly been sheltered, and my imagination was pretty good, but there was a lot of stuff there whose use I couldn't even begin to guess at.

Next to the cash register a young man with a bad complexion looked up at me without interest, and then went back to the book he was reading. Oddly enough, it was Proust. In French.

The bruiser was in a corner, sitting on a folding chair,

flipping through a magazine. The kid wasn't around, but there was a door in the rear that probably belonged to a small office.

I wasn't too worried about being recognized, since I'd been face down in the dirt for most of the stick-up, but I stationed myself out of sight, near the office door, behind a rack of books and magazines. They were all wrapped in plastic and carried price tags of between five and ten dollars. I wondered what was inside them. It used to be that women were granted divorces because their husbands had merely suggested some of the acts pictured on the covers.

A few men browsed the racks, careful to avoid looking at any of their fellow shoppers. Their sad-eyed expressions held nothing of the sense of liberated delight that the book titles so boldly proclaimed, and their presence here seemed more an act of penance than a search for pleasure.

In front of me were a lot of books with names like *Love Slaves in Chains* and *Stewardesses in Bondage*. There were about twenty of them, all by someone named Rodney Whipp. It must've been a series.

A mousy little fellow with thick bifocals and a flaking scalp pushed in front of me and scanned the books, his nose about six inches away from the covers.

"Oh, a new Rodney Whipp," he said, grabbing *Manicurists in Manacles* and scurrying away.

And I thought *my* taste in literature was dubious.

Just then the rear door opened. I briefly poked my head around the book racks and saw the kid come out, followed by a bigger, older man. The second guy looked sort of green, and his forehead was covered with sickly perspiration. His lips were drawn back in the smile of someone who'd just got his sexual organ caught in a mousetrap and was trying to appear as though nothing was wrong. No expression of any kind showed on the kid's round prepubescent face, but his slightly bulging black eyes were hard, the glassy, unblinking stare of a reptile.

I heard a voice say, "Things will be better next week, won't they." It was an order, not a question, followed by a short weird sound that I supposed was meant to be a laugh.

Bingo! The voice had the high-pitched, tinny sound of a character in an animated cartoon. The wicked rat, or something. I felt the laugh run up my spine and tickle the hair on the back of my neck. There was no question. I'd found the boy. The two lines had intersected. Incredible!

The kid left the store, followed by his muscle, who'd jumped to his feet the second his boss had appeared. My heart was pounding as I stepped out and stood next to the guy whom I assumed ran the store. He looked like he wanted to howl with anguish.

"Say, was that Jackie Edwards?" I said conversationally.

The guy shook his head without looking at me, staring at the front door, which was slowly closing on its pneumatic hinge. "Anthony Novallo—Tony New. Shit," he said with considerable feeling, and then looked at me with surprise. "What do you want, old man?"

"I wanted a birthday present for my niece, but this stuff looks too tame."

"We got the heavy stuff in the back room."

Wonderful. I should've known better than to crack a joke in a place that was about as humorous as a medieval dungeon.

"Maybe later. I think my parking meter is about to expire."

I hurried out in time to stay with Tony Novallo and the Ape Man. For the next couple of hours they continued their rounds, spreading sunlight and cheer where it would do the most good. Somewhere along the way, they picked up a woman who must've been a good foot taller than Tony New. Her halo of bright-orange hair looked like one of those kitchen scrubbers, and her monumental body could have come from the prow of a sailing ship. Her heavy make-up, though, couldn't disguise her bored expression, and there was little doubt about her line of work. I didn't want to even guess about what the kid might like to do.

At about eight o'clock the car pulled up under the porte cochère of a swanky apartment building in West L.A., and Tony and the woman got out. The uniformed doorman did everything except salute the kid, but when they passed inside he stared shamelessly after the woman. Tony's hand was resting casually on her protruding rear like it was the head of a large family dog. For a minute I thought the doorman might have a coronary. He bit on his hand and stamped his feet, then regained his composure in time to greet an elderly woman whose hair was the same shade of pale magenta as her poodle's.

The kid's car pulled away. I thought about following it but couldn't figure why I'd want to. The palooka driving it could probably get lost going around the block. He was just muscle, of no significance on his own.

The kid was the one I wanted, but I couldn't see much reason to stick around there. It looked like he was going to be occupied for a good long time. And I was beat. I'd been up and out for way over twelve hours. However excited I was that the gamble had paid off, that I'd done it, actually located the guy we wanted, adrenalin was no longer enough to keep me going. Used to be, I would've sat in the car, all night, if necessary, until the kid showed again. Then, a cup of coffee and a pair of doughnuts and I would've been ready for another twenty-four. Jesus. Who was the guy who'd once been able to do that?

Besides, however pleased I was to have run the thing this far, I had no idea how to bring it home. And without that, the whole exercise would be pointless. With a sigh I started the car to take myself home.

When I got there I found O'Brien stewing like a father whose virginal daughter was out on her first date. Being caught up in the thrill of the chase, I'd forgotten to check in with him.

"Where the hell have you been, Jake Spanner? I've been sitting here waiting for hours, not knowing what was going on, and you——"

I cut him off. If I wanted stuff like that, I'd move in with Mrs. Bernstein.

I told O'Bee what had happened. He started grinning and rubbing his hands. Then I told him I was taking him back to Sunset Grove.

"What d'you mean? We're in this all the way. That was the deal."

"The deal was that you'd help me. And you have, O'Bee. Really. I couldn't have done this without you. But it's over. We're at the end now."

The one thing I had decided on the ride back was that it was solely my play from here on out. Whatever it was going to be, it would be mine alone. It had always been that way when it came to the crunch. Some things, apparently, never changed.

O'Brien started bullying and ranting, but his heart wasn't in it. He knew I'd made up my mind. After a little while, he stopped. His big body seemed smaller, and he looked older and more tired than he had for the past few days.

"Hey, O'Bee. I'm sorry. It's just—"

"Jake, forget it. I understand. I do. You're responsible."

I nodded. He was right: I was.

"You're also a fucking jerk, but I guess that's just the way you are."

I didn't know if he was right about that; probably.

"But you just be sure, Jake Spanner, that you let me know what happens."

I assured him I would.

"Okay, let's go. I got responsibilities, too. The Iron Maiden's days must've been empty without me."

He put his belongings back into the Safeway shopping bags. He looked around once more, like he would miss the place, and we went out to the car.

We didn't talk much on the trip. When I pulled into Sunset Grove, he punched me lightly on the arm and said, "See you."

He walked down the portico that ran outside the rooms. When he passed the office, I saw the Iron Maiden zip out and speak to him. He looked at her but didn't say anything, and continued on. His lack of response must have surprised her, because she stared after him, legs apart and arms akimbo. Looking at her, I had the feeling that maybe, in fact, her days had been empty without him.

Shit. Forget it, Spanner. I had enough on my mind without pondering vagaries like that.

I took my foot off the brake and eased down the drive.

Back home I picked up the adventures of Al Tracker, which I'd been too occupied to look into for the last days. Somehow or other he found himself trapped in a deep pit filled with hostile vipers. Some people sure led full lives.

CHAPTER ELEVEN

I was out early the next morning after a night mostly spent lying awake, trying to figure possible scenarios, anxious to get going. I went by the dumpy office building, just to check, and then parked across from Tony New's apartment house.

A little after ten, the two mugs showed up with the car and Tony got in the back. The lady friend wasn't around.

I followed them back to Trans-Global, where I parked and waited.

And waited.

I still had no idea what I was going to do. The best I'd come up with was to continue surveillance, in the hope that something would turn up. Al Tracker wouldn't have understood. "You make your own breaks," he was fond of saying just before he kicked in a door or assaulted an innocent bystander in order to stir things up. About all he would've approved of was that I was now, reluctantly, carrying my gun in the glove compartment. Just in case something happened.

It did. At a little after one.

I was so astounded that I almost failed to react. Just sat there gawping like a goldfish who'd finally succeeded in jumping out of his bowl.

The kid came down the front steps. For the first time since I'd picked up his trail, he was alone. But that wasn't the cause of my excitement. In his hand was Sal's attaché case, black leather, with two red stripes running around it.

Jesus Christ, Spanner, somebody must sure think they owe you something!

The kid walked to his car, casual as anything. I turned

115

the ignition. For a sickening moment the engine did nothing except sound like it was clearing its throat. I slammed the dashboard with my fist. Not now, you son of a bitch! No fucking way! Then it caught and turned over.

The kid had just started his car. I got the Chevy into gear and pulled out. I stopped alongside the kid's Olds. There were cars parked in front of and behind him, so he was locked in.

"Move the fucking heap, asshole," he said, staring ahead.

I slid across the seat, got the gun from the glove compartment, and climbed out the passenger side. I was standing next to the kid's door. He looked up at me, his snake's eyes bulging and glaring.

"I said, move the fucking heap. Don't you understand English, you old sack of shit?"

"Is it all there?" I said, motioning with my head to the attaché case on the seat next to him.

"Is what where?"

"Open the case."

"If this is a joke, you're going to be sorry. I don't find it very fucking funny." The kid's already high voice rose even higher.

I raised the gun from my side and held it so his little pop eyes were looking right down the business end. "Open it or I'll blow your fucking head open, you slimy little punk."

Jesus, who said that? It came out of my mouth, but it sounded like someone I used to be about a million years ago. Damn, it felt good, though.

"Open it!"

The kid kept his eyes on me. His right hand went down, snapped the catches, and pulled up the top of the case. It was filled with cash, all in neat bundles and rows. It looked real nice.

"Close it," I ordered. "Keep your left hand on the steering wheel. With your right hand take the case by the end and pass it out to me. Slowly."

"Do you know who I am?" The weird voice was still rising.

"I know who you are and what you are. Do it!" I jammed the barrel into his ear. Not too gently. I had to admit that felt pretty good, too. Shit. I was really becoming an incredible thug.

A noise came out of the kid's lips, an evil-sounding hiss, but he handed me the case. Without taking my eyes or the gun off of him, I tossed it through my open door.

"You've had it, old man. You're dead."

"Now, with your right hand, slowly give me your keys." He didn't move. "Do it, you deformed little piece of shit!" I jabbed him again with the gun. This could get to be habit-forming.

He handed me the keys, which I put in my pocket.

"You won't get away with this." His lips barely moved and his voice wasn't much more than a squeak.

"Look, Tony. You had your play. It was a good one, but it fell short. Now it's over. Forget it."

His mouth opened and his lips pulled back in an animal snarl. His jaw was working but no sound came out. Flecks of foam appeared at the corners of his mouth. People talk a lot about foaming at the mouth, but in fact you rarely see it. When you do, it's a good time to make an exit. Tony New was frothing like he'd brushed his teeth with Burma Shave.

I kept the gun ready as I got in my car and closed the door. I put the Chev in drive and got the hell out of there. In the rear mirror I saw Tony standing in the street, staring after me. Just before I turned a corner, I saw him start to viciously kick and hit his car. The kid had a couple of problems.

When I was a few blocks away, I tossed the keys down a storm drain.

A few blocks more and it hit me. I had done it, goddammit! I had pulled it off! Neat as anything.

It may not have been appropriate for a fellow of my years but I bounced on the seat a few times, leaned on the horn, and then whooped out the window. This being a town where certifiable lunatics offered weekend seminars that were well attended, few people noticed my outburst. One dazed young guy with hair down to the middle of his back looked at me, smiled, and gave me the V-sign.

Right on, brother! Right on!

Whoo!

CHAPTER TWELVE

As soon as I got home I called Sal's answering service and left a message that the mission had been accomplished. Within a few minutes he called me back. He could hardly believe I'd pulled it off. If I hadn't been feeling so good, I might have been annoyed at this reaction. I mean, it wasn't that surprising I'd succeeded, was it?

Who was I kidding? Of course it was.

I asked him if he wanted me to deliver the money, but he said he'd pick it up. I told him to hurry. I didn't feel real comfortable sitting on that much dough. Sal told me not to worry; he'd hurry, all right.

He must've, because a cab pulled up in front of my place in about twenty-five minutes. I figured that even though he said he trusted his driver, he wasn't taking any chances at this point. With a random taxi, he wouldn't have to worry about a leak.

Sal came in. He was wearing either the same black suit or one just like it. Considering the strain he must've been under the last week, he looked pretty good. If anything, more relaxed, less cadaverous than before.

He looked at me, shaking his head, with the same kind of shit-eating grin I'd been seeing since I got home, whenever I looked in a mirror. He saw the attaché case on the couch and hurried over to it. He opened it and gazed at the contents. He put his hand on the money, closed his eyes, slowly exhaled. I didn't think I'd ever seen anyone more relieved, like the doctor had just told him that the tumor was benign and he'd had his life handed back to him. In a way, maybe that's what I'd done.

"Jesus, Jake, I still don't believe it."

"Well, at least you're back to where you were."

"What?"

"We were pretty damn lucky to have brought this off, but it doesn't really accomplish anything, only makes you even again. You still have a long way to go."

"I do." He nodded. There was an odd smile on his face. "But I think this time it's going to work out."

"Let's hope. You heard anything yet?"

"Not yet."

"Well, when you do, I'll lend a hand if you want."

"Thanks, Jake. And thanks for this." He motioned to the case. "I knew I could count on you."

"I don't think either of us knew that. Like I said, I was lucky."

"It doesn't matter how. All that matters is that you did it. And I want to give you something for it." He took one of the packets of bills from the case. The paper wrapper was marked $10,000.

"Forget it. I've already been paid."

"Come on, Jake."

"No. Besides, you're going to need all that for Tommy."

"I'll deal with that. I want you to have this. A finder's fee."

"No."

"Jesus, you'll never change. A man of principle."

"Not really. It's just that I have so few, I figure I better stick to the ones I've got."

"You mean, like being a jerk?"

I shrugged.

"Okay, okay," he said. "If you haven't learned by now, Jake, I guess you're never going to. But I do want to give you something."

It seemed really important to him so I said he could give me a hundred bucks and I'd treat myself to a good dinner. Sal looked at me, shook his head, then pulled a bill out of the packet.

"Thanks," I said.

Sal shrugged, put the money back into the case, and shut it.

"Well, I'd better be off. The cab's waiting."

"Right. Take care of that money. I don't want to have to get it back again."

Sal smiled, the same odd grin as before. "I'll do my best." He paused, seemed about to say something more, then changed his mind. Instead, he nodded to me and left. He waved as the cab pulled away. I had the feeling he was trying not to laugh.

I could understand that. The only thing funnier than my trying to do this thing was my actually having done it.

I did laugh. God, I felt good. I knew Sal's problem still remained, but I couldn't help it. The adrenalin continued to surge. I had done it. I had fucking well done it. I had showed them—whoever they were—that Jake Spanner could still cut the mustard. That he was good for something more than sitting in a park, absorbing sunlight. Dammit! he had planned an investigation, and run it, and brought it off. The old dick was still around. Just ask Tony New.

I felt better than I could remember feeling for twenty years. Not since I'd gotten the goods on that bent congressman who'd done his best to put me out of business once I started to get too close, and damn near succeeded, permanently.

I called up O'Bee and gave him the news. He said, "You're kidding," burst into laughter, and then said he never doubted that I'd do it. Another vote of confidence. I asked if he wanted to go out and celebrate, but he said he wasn't feeling very good. Maybe just as well. Dinner with someone who thought an omelet was exotic was not my idea of a fun evening. I said I'd see him soon.

I tried to read but couldn't sit still. I was too full of energy. I kept jumping up and pacing through the house with long strides, my cheeks getting sore from smiling continually.

Finally I decided I had to do something. I had a shower and got dressed in some of my best clothes. They dated from a previous decade, but the classic elegance of tropical linen never went out of style. Well, perhaps it did, but I didn't mind. All I needed was a panama hat and I'd look like I stepped out from some colonial epic on the two A.M. movie. Jake Spanner, rubber planter. Pretty snappy.

After checking the phone book to make sure she was

still there, I drove to the nice Westwood apartment building where Phyllis Bliss lived. Phyl and I went back to the days when she was turning tricks in a fancy Hollywood watering hole right after the war. At some point our respective businesses overlapped, and we got to know each other. At first all I knew about her was that she was a hell of a hooker. With a name like Bliss, she said, she didn't have much choice. Then I found out she was also a pretty fine woman. We became friends, and soon something more than friends. It was never a big deal with us, certainly never a romance. Though we made love, we were never lovers. We did, however, like and enjoy each other, and our relationship was a kind of compensation for all the things we'd both chosen to do without. If it didn't fill the emptiness, it softened it a little.

Phyl was a really intelligent woman and knew how to look after herself, but she'd picked a high-risk occupation. What with crooked vice cops, pimps, sleazy managers of hotels and bars, nut-case clients, and other assorted urban birds of prey, things sometimes got tight. Mostly, she handled it by herself but a few times she swallowed her pride and came to me. I was always glad to help. In fact, I would've liked her to let me help more. I got her out of a few nasty situations, including a frame-up for murder involving an agent and an actor who turned out to be worth more dead than alive.

We both retired at about the same time. As I said, she was smart, and had put away a big chunk of her considerable tax-free income. She took a degree in business at UCLA and then opened something called a plant boutique, which soon expanded to a small chain. We kept in touch, but with decreasing frequency as her life got busier and mine got slower. I hadn't seen her for a long time, but this seemed like the perfect occasion to change that.

I knocked on the door of the penthouse. It was opened by a young woman in jeans and a loose-fitting man's workshirt. Her straight dark hair was parted in the middle and hung softly to just above her shoulders. She wasn't wearing any make-up. She didn't need it.

"Is Phyllis here?" I said.

"No. She's back East for a few weeks."

"Okay. Thanks." I started to go, then paused. "Are you Miranda?"

The girl nodded. She looked at me with large brown eyes that suddenly lit up. "You must be Jake."

I agreed that I must be, and she took two quick steps and threw her arms around me. I discovered that she was not as slender as she looked under that too-large shirt. Quite a day. I pull a job, and I'm hugged by a beautiful woman.

"What was that for?" I asked when she let me go.

"Mother's told me all about you. I know exactly how much we owe you."

I made a face and waved that off. Miranda pulled me into the apartment. It was simply but well furnished, with several large good canvases on the walls.

"Uncle Jake. Mother's told me so many stories about you. You were my hero when I was little." She studied me, her intelligent eyes showing pleasure and amusement. "You look just the way I pictured you."

"Then you've got a diseased imagination, young lady."

"No, you're great. Like you've got Sidney Greenstreet waiting in the car downstairs. I love it."

She looked me straight in the eye and then winked. We both laughed. Miranda had her mother's open honesty. I liked her right away.

Phyllis hadn't thought her life was a very good one for raising a kid, and so had sent her daughter away to good schools, first here, then abroad. She'd visit Miranda frequently, though, and had always been proud of her. I could see why.

"Are you still up at Berkeley?" I said.

"Yeah. Just finishing my thesis. The only reason I'm here is that Mother asked me to look after the place while she was away."

"How is Phyl?"

"Thriving. Probably working way too hard. But then" —she smiled—"I understand she always believed in doing a job right."

I coughed. "Oh, yes. She was a real professional."

Miranda grinned. "Don't be embarrassed, Jake. I've known about Mother's life since I was eight. It never bothered her and it never bothered me. If anything, it made me a celebrity at school, among all the daughters of dermatologists and plastics manufacturers. She'll be sorry she missed you."

"I'm sorry I missed her. I wanted to take her out to dinner. Kind of a celebration."

"Will I do? You want to celebrate with me?"

"You really want to? With someone who just left Sidney Greenstreet?"

"Sure."

"Okay. Where shall we go?"

"You like Thai?"

"Never had it."

"Then that's where we'll go. If you're up to it."

"Oh, I'm up to it."

"That's what I thought. Give me a minute to change."

It didn't take much more than that before she came out of the bedroom looking absolutely sensational in a clingy silk sundress.

"I tried to find something more in your period, but this is as close as I could get."

"Oh, it's just fine," I said, trying to keep from drooling down her bare back. Was it ever.

The Krung Thep Garden was on Sunset, but far enough from the Strip to be pleasant. From the front it looked like the building might have once housed a pet store.

I parked a block away. As we walked back, Miranda took my arm in both her hands. Heads, mostly belonging to young dudes, turned to follow us.

"All those guys are wondering what it is I've got."

"You've got me," Miranda said. She winked.

Inside, the place was dark and displayed the over-ornate decoration a lot of Asians seem so fond of. Whatever parts of the walls were not covered with paintings or posters or scrolls, all elaborately framed, were filled with gold mosaic tiles, plastic fruit, and colored glass balls. Turquoise green light from two large fish tanks provided most of the illumination.

"Tasteful," I said.

"You're not here to eat the decorations."

"That's true."

We ordered about a dozen dishes. That was way more than we could eat, but it all sounded so good that I wanted to try everything. After all, this was a celebration. Soon, the table was covered with little plates filled with different kinds of curries, stir-fried squid and shrimp, crisp rice noodles, sliced raw marinated beef, spicy pork and peanuts on slices of pineapple, sour salads, all smelling of cilantro and mint, garlic and ginger, chiles and lemon grass and lime. It was the best meal I'd had for years, so good I was a little pissed off that it had taken me so long to discover this kind of cooking.

Our dinner lasted for hours. We'd eat a little, then talk, then eat a little more. Miranda was like her mother in that she loved food, and it was a pleasure to see her enthusiasm for all the good stuff. I've always liked women who had good appetites. My wife, on the other hand, seemed to think there was something vaguely embarrassing, if not distasteful, about having to eat. She used to gobble up little bits of things when no one was looking, like a secret drinker who has bottles hidden all over the house.

Not only did I eat more than I could remember doing, I also talked more. Like O'Brien a few days before, when I finally had a listener, it all just poured out, anecdotes, reminiscences, stories, all kinds of shit I hadn't thought of for years. And Miranda seemed to enjoy it, not out of politeness but with real interest. At least I hoped so. If not, I was being one hell of a boring old fart.

We finally staggered out of the restaurant when they were closing up, leaving surprisingly little food behind us. I lit up a huge, fat, delicious Cuban cigar that a friend's kid had brought back from Canada. He'd given me a few, and I'd been saving them for a special occasion. This certainly seemed an appropriate time.

After we walked around a little, I took Miranda back to the apartment. She offered me a drink, which I refused. She asked if I wanted to smoke some grass and I nodded. I was feeling so good, I didn't want it to end.

"You're something else, Jake Spanner."

"Yeah, but what?"

When all the edges had gone pleasantly blurry I leaned back on the couch and sighed. "This has been one of the best days I've ever had."

Miranda moved over next to me. "That's good. Shall I make you feel even better?"

"What do you mean?"

"I want to make love to you."

"Come on. Don't be silly."

"I'm not. I really mean it."

"Well, forget it."

"Why? Don't you want to?"

"Miranda, that isn't the point. Don't you think the idea is kind of grotesque?"

She looked puzzled. "You mean, because you're old? So what? It doesn't bother me. I like you and we had a good time tonight. That's what I see, what's important. Besides, I know all that you did for my mother and me. Don't be such a shit. Let someone do something nice for you for a change."

I sighed. "Believe me, I'd like to oblige, but I'm way past it. It's been five years." Indeed, the last time had been with her mother. We tried a few times after but it hadn't worked, and I'd given up. "Whatever you may think, I am too old."

"You're never too old."

"What makes you the expert?"

"You forget who my mother is. There's nothing wrong with you. You're just out of practice. As they say, use it or lose it, Jake Spanner."

I shook my head. "I've tried, but it died."

"Bullshit."

She took my hand and placed it on her breast. I could feel the nipple beneath the fabric. She moved her shoulders. The thin straps slipped down her arms and the front of her dress fell away. Her breasts were beautiful and the brown nipples were hard. My mouth felt dry. I brought my other hand up and felt the yielding firmness. Oh God, let me die now.

She unbuttoned my shirt. I felt her cool strong fingers moving lightly on my chest, stomach. I started to say something but she put a finger on my lips.

"Don't talk. Just relax. You don't have to do anything, prove anything. Just let me make you feel good." She smiled. "Some mothers teach their daughters to cook. Phyllis couldn't boil water, but she told me some other stuff. Let's see."

Well, why not?

She leaned over. Her lips caressed my chest. I felt her tongue. Oh God, now. Please.

Her hand was at my waist. Going lower. She moved from the couch and knelt on the floor in front of me.

I leaned back and closed my eyes, feeling the dope, feeling Miranda.

After a while I heard a little-girl voice say with amusement, "Why, Uncle Jake."

Uncle Jake, indeed.

Move over, Al Tracker.

CHAPTER THIRTEEN

I staggered home at about the same time the sky was lightening to gray. It had been a long time since I'd seen five A.M. moving in this direction.

I was beat to shit, could hardly hold my head up or shuffle my feet. Muscles I hadn't thought I had any longer were sore and aching. I felt wonderful. Absolutely wonderful.

Tired as I was, I couldn't stop grinning, like some pimply adolescent who all of a sudden feels he's master of the universe. I didn't pose much of a threat to Warren Beatty, but all things considered, I had made a pretty good accounting of myself. One might say that the old dick had risen to the occasion.

Oh, Spanner, cut it out. Jesus.

But I was awfully pleased with myself, feeling really human for the first time in years. Spanner, I thought, my grin growing even wider, you might yet turn into an absolutely filthy old man. Mentally, I rubbed my hands and made obscene noises.

I got into my tatty old pajamas, then smoked another small bowl of dope. Usually I sought sleep as an escape from the day's monotony, the easiest way to fill a few hours, but this was one day I didn't want to end. I felt too good to waste it by going to sleep. Soon, though, I couldn't put it off any longer and I reluctantly crawled into bed.

I was cavorting with a bunch of sylphic maidens, running through a sunny glade, when suddenly the sky darkened. A dead tree turned into a sinister forest demon and grabbed at me with clawlike branches. Though I tried to move away, I was poked and prodded with hard, cold fingers. Had to get away. Get away . . .

I opened my eyes and looked down the barrel of a sleek blue-black pistol. A Beretta, I thought pointlessly. The 9mm circle looked as large and inviting as the Hell mouth. It jabbed me in the cheek, not at all softly. The fingernails of the hand holding the gun were chewed and slightly dirty. I changed my focus. Behind the gun and the dirty fingernails was Tony Novallo, looking considerably less friendly than the forest demon.

One of his pea-brained palookas stood on the other side of the bed; the second was at the foot. Just in case I tried to make a break, I supposed.

I glanced at the bedside clock. It was nine-twenty. Tony New had started work early. He poked me again with the gun.

"Unh," I said brightly.

"Hand it over," he squeaked.

"Look—"

"No, you look, fuckhead." He moved the gun up to about an inch from my eyeball. "You can either say goodbye to your head or you can tell me where the dough is."

Hmm. Nice choice. Being in pajamas, in one's own bed, surrounded by two hulking morons and a demented midget with a gun, having had five hours' too little sleep, and not having a clue what was happening, did tend to put one at a slight disadvantage. If I hadn't felt so sluggish, I would've been scared shitless.

"You know where it is," I said. "I gave it back to the guy you took it from."

Apparently, that was not the correct answer. The kid's face turned dead white, then a scary shade of maroon. The hand holding the gun started to jerk and twitch. His eyeballs rolled back and his cheeks puffed up. He made a guttural exploding sound and I was sprayed with spittle.

No question, I had a genuine flaming psycho here. I'd have to be very careful if I wanted to get out of my bed again.

"Take it easy," I said. "Look, I can understand that you're sore. You had a nice little play going. You thought you were clear, then it fell through. I know how you feel.

After all, you did the same thing to us. But it didn't work, and now it's over. You're not really out anything, so why don't you just leave it alone?"

Wonderful, Spanner. That was like saying, "Come on, old chap, let's be sporting" to Attila the Hun.

The kid seemed quieter. "Where's the dough?" Quieter, yeah, but as hard and as cold as the gun he was holding. His snake's eyes were the color of asphalt.

"I told you. I gave it back to Sal Piccolo. It's probably back in the bank now."

The kid exploded again. The different colors, the saliva, the whole routine. I wondered if he was going to fling himself, writhing, to the floor, but one of the bruisers sort of held onto him. The other bruiser stared down at me, looking as though he was trying to decide on what technique he'd use to crush my esophagus.

The kid eventually regained his slippery grip on coherency. "I don't know what you think you're trying to pull, you stinking bag of bones, but it don't wash. Tear it apart."

Something that might well have been a smile creased the Neanderthals' faces, and they nodded.

"That's not necessary. I told you that—" I started to protest, but the look Tony New gave me cut it short. So did the gun barrel being pushed against my Adam's apple.

My place was pretty small, but even so, it took them surprisingly little time to empty every drawer and cupboard and overturn all the furniture. My only consolation was that the insurance would cover any damage, until I remembered I had cancelled it a year ago to save on the premiums. Anyway, the policy had probably excluded depradations by lunatics.

"Nuthin'," one of the goons said, when they returned to the bedroom. It sounded like he had a sock on his tongue.

"Ah, but did you check the toothpaste?" I said.

The kid's eyes narrowed, then he motioned with his head. One of his boys left, then came back and handed him the tube. Tony New took off the cap. He smiled without opening his lips. He squeezed off a line across my forehead. Then one from the top of my head, over my nose, and down to my chin. Then a couple more on each side. Tony New giggled. His boys dutifully joined in, sounding like barking seals.

The kid put a soft little hand up to my face and smeared the paste around. Of all the ways I liked to begin my days, a facial with mint-flavored Crest was not near the top, but I seemed to have little say in the matter. For sixty years people had been telling me it didn't pay to be a wise guy. Maybe I was finally beginning to understand.

Tony New talked as he rubbed my face. "You know, old man, what I really want to do is snuff you right now." His tone was conversational, friendly. "You've made me look bad, and I don't like for people to do that." His touch on my face had been light, but suddenly he squeezed my cheekbones hard. It hurt. Remarkable that that soft little hand could contain so much strength. Then he smiled, patted my cheek, went back to rubbing gently. "But you're lucky. That money belonged to some very important people. They want it back. So right now, I want what they want. You return the money, maybe I won't off you." He paused. "Then again, maybe I will." He giggled. That high-pitched crazy sound. His boys joined in, like that was the funniest thing they'd ever heard.

Had to hand it to the kid. He really knew how to generate incentive.

"Uh, look—" I started, but the kid squeezed my lips together.

"Shut up. If I want conversation I'll put on Johnny Carson. You got nothing to say that I want to hear except 'Here's your money.' I don't know who put you up to this or what the story is, but I'm not interested in any bullshit. What do you think I am, old man, some dumb punk you can jerk around? Sal Piccolo!" He smiled, as though remembering something pleasant, like pulling legs off of lizards. "Sal Piccolo's dead." He giggled.

"Wha—"

He jammed the barrel of the gun into my mouth. The steel against my teeth sent a shiver through my body. "You will be, too, unless I have that dough in twenty-four hours." He grinned. "And it won't be quick."

Tony New stared down at me, smiling. He took the gun out of my mouth. He motioned with his head that the muscle could leave. He turned to go; then, almost as an afterthought, looked back and abruptly brought the butt of the gun down on my shin, just below the knee. Considering that my leg was under the covers and that he could've hit me a lot harder, had he wanted to, the shock of pain was nearly unbelievable. My vision turned a blurry red and there was a roaring in my ears.

I didn't hear them leave. My gasps and sobs were too loud.

CHAPTER FOURTEEN

"What the hell is going on?" I asked the bathroom mirror when I was eventually able to hobble out of bed. The image that gazed back—wispy hair standing straight out, red-rimmed, watering eyes goggling out from a face covered with pale blue muck—looked like something that had just climbed down from the New Guinea highlands. And it didn't have any answers.

I kept asking the question as I made an attempt to get my place right-side up again. I still hadn't made any sense out of it. None of it. The kid showing up, the way he acted. That bit about Sal. Nothing figured.

About all I had decided was that Tony New must've gotten a line on me the same way I got onto him—through the car and a Department of Motor Vehicles check. I hadn't thought there'd be any reason to be circumspect, had assumed the matter was over when I'd gotten the dough back. Live and learn.

I lay down on my bed. I had just about convinced myself that it had all been a hallucination when there was a pounding on my front door. It sounded like someone was battering it with a Smithfield ham.

I pulled on a green terry-cloth bathrobe, the pile of which was mostly worn down to a patchy nub, limped into the front room, and opened the door. On the other side of the screen were two big guys—mid-thirties, I guessed—with rumpled brown suits, white wash-and-wear shirts that could've used some bleach, and pulled-down neckties spotted with the remains of a month's lunches. Except for the fact that they looked meaner, they might have been related to Tony's goons.

I was close.

Simultaneously, they flipped open little cases and showed badges and I.D. cards.

"Nicholson. Narcotics," the one in front said. The other one didn't say anything.

I quickly flashed the lapel of my bathrobe. "Spanner. Geriatrics."

Nicholson looked like he'd tasted something rotten. "Can we come in?"

Before I could answer, they'd pulled open the screen door and planted themselves in the living room.

"Sure, why not?" I said.

Nicholson looked me up and down. He didn't seem delighted by what he saw. He also seemed tired, like he'd been going full out for three or four days. "Okay, Spanner," he sighed. "What kind of game are you playing?"

Huh?

I shrugged. "A little bridge. A little cribbage. Sometimes some gin."

Nicholson pulled another face. "Jesus fucking Christ! Just what I needed, a hundred-year-old asshole." He turned to his partner. "Toss the place."

"Uh, I don't suppose you have a warrant or something like that?"

"You want us to get one?"

I looked at Nicholson. He was not a happy man. I got the distinct impression that I was a major source of his discontent.

"No, don't bother," I said. "Go ahead. Be my guest."

The partner started in. He wasn't as rough as Tony's boys, but he was nearly as messy. Swell.

While his partner worked, Nicholson just stood there, glowering and tapping his wristwatch with a thick finger. The guy found my little store of smoke, held it up for Nicholson, and the two of them shook their heads. Nicholson continued to glower and tap. No question, he was acting like a pure son of a bitch, but maybe he had his reasons. Obviously, there was a lot going on that I didn't know about. I thought maybe I should try not to antagonize any more people, at least not until after lunch.

"Sergeant—it is Sergeant, isn't it?—why don't you sit down?"

He thought about it. He sat. I sat. Progress.

"What can I do for you, Sergeant? What's going on here?"

"Funny. That was my question for you."

"I really don't know. As far as I'm concerned, all this is a mystery."

"A mystery, huh? Okay, Mr. Spanner. Tell me about your connection with Anthony Novallo, otherwise known as Tony New."

"Never heard of him," I said. So much for cooperation.

"What about the guy that was here forty-five minutes ago?"

"Oh, was that this Novallo? I never got his name."

"No? What was he doing here?"

"Looking for somebody. The previous tenant."

"Yeah? The previous tenant moved out in 1948."

They'd been checking. That sure didn't look good. I shrugged, like it wasn't my fault.

"So what'd you tell him?"

"That I didn't know where the guy was."

"And that took twenty minutes?"

I shrugged again. "We had coffee."

Nicholson made a warning sound in his throat. I wasn't doing such a swell job of making friends, but I didn't want to say anything until I had a better idea about the direction things were moving. The only thing I was sure of was that Tony New hadn't called in the cops. So why were they here?

The partner came in. He handed Nicholson the computer printout and whispered in his ear. He gestured toward the backyard and whispered some more. Nicholson looked at the guy, then at me, then said, "Shit." The partner went out. Nicholson shook the paper at me.

"What're you doing with this?"

"I collect license numbers. You know, it's kind of a hobby." Great answer, Spanner. Really cogent.

The sergeant thought so, too. "Yeah, right. Where'd you get a DMV printout?"

"I can't remember. Must've picked it up someplace."

"Yeah, they're on every corner—right?—along with the sex newspapers." He closed his eyes, squeezed the bridge of his nose, sighed wearily. "Spanner, do you know how many guys I have to deal with every day who're just like you? Shit. I will say this, though. You've got to be the oldest bastard who's ever tried to feed me a line."

"What can I say?"

"How about the straight story, for a change?"

"Okay."

"Tony New?"

"I already told you, I never saw him before this morning."

"No? What about yesterday?"

"Yesterday? Not that I know of."

Nicholson's face grew dark, angry. This seemed to be my morning for raising blood pressure. He started to say something, then swallowed it. Tried again and stopped. The third time he got it out. "Okay, cut the shit, you stupid old man! You have pushed it to the limit. Over, finished, finito! Listen—I saw you knock over Tony New yesterday. About a dozen other cops saw you do it. We have it on video tape. We've got it on movie film. We've got stills. Nice, clear, and close up."

What could I say? "Hmm," I said.

"Hmm. Fucking right—hmm! Now, just keep listening, Spanner. Apparently, from what I understand, you had a pretty good rep at one time. Maybe, maybe not. I don't know or care. Whatever it was, it was a million years ago. And as far as I'm concerned, now you're just another asshole who's fucking up my life. You're in trouble, old man. You're so deep in shit you need a shovel to see nighttime. Now, I don't want you under any misapprehension about this, so I'm going to make it clear. On the off chance that you have something other than shit for a brain—that you're an asshole, but not a completely stupid asshole—I'm going to lay it out for you so you will see how things stand."

Nicholson laid it out. Did he ever. I began to see why he was mildly pissed off. I began to understand some other stuff as well. Holy shit.

According to the sergeant, I had waltzed into what was to have been the culmination of a long-term investigation. Tony Novallo was right in the middle of a huge cocaine operation. The cops had been onto him for some time, but had been moving very slowly and carefully. They didn't just want a bust; they wanted to smash the setup for good. Yesterday had been the day. The kid had been on his way to make a major pickup, and the cops had had it covered all down the line. Until I inserted myself into the scenario.

They had gotten the coke—fifteen kilos worth—and Tony's contact, a baggage handler at LAX, but that guy was only a functionary, a hired hand between the groups in Colombia and here. The kid had been the one they wanted. Generally regarded as one of the ugliest customers anyone had seen for a long time, three levels of law enforcement had been after him for several years, without success. This operation would have done it. Tony New would've been tied up good and tight, and the cops thought they might even have been able to get to the people behind him, people Nicholson described as some very serious individuals.

Now all that work had fallen way short of its goal, and Nicholson was looking at me and wondering why. Under the circumstances, that didn't strike me as being absolutely unreasonable.

So I told him the story. The kidnapping, the ransom drop, the stick-up, the license plate, the investigation and search, locating the kid, and the surveillance. I didn't need to tell him about the recovery. The problem was, hearing myself relate it, it didn't sound any more plausible than my earlier evasions. Especially since that saga of crime and detection was coming out of the mouth of an old fart in pajamas and bathrobe who looked like he probably needed to sleep on a rubber sheet. If it seemed that way to me, I could only imagine how Nicholson was taking it. Judging from the way he was looking out from under his eyebrows, not well.

"What'd you do after you got the money?" he said.

"Don't you know?"

"Why should I know?"

"You've got this elaborate operation. Didn't you put somebody on me?"

Nicholson looked away briefly, frowning. "We weren't set up for that."

"Still . . ."

"Okay, we did. He lost you."

I could see it was a sore point with him, so I didn't make any of the wise remarks that came to mind.

"What'd you do with the money?" he said.

"I came back here and returned it to its owner."

"And who might that be?" Nicholson's tone was the same that all cops adopt when they don't believe a word you're saying, like, "Come on, let's get this ritual over so we can start to cut the crap."

I hardly hesitated before saying, "Sal Piccolo." I figured I was way past the point of maintaining client confidentiality.

Nicholson wrinkled his forehead and looked disgusted. For some reason, that didn't seem to be a very good answer this time either. He got up and went into the kitchen, where I heard him using the phone. The partner had come back after tearing the house apart and was standing stolidly by the front door, just in case I tried to make a break for it in my bedroom slippers.

Nicholson came back and stood in front of me, hands on his hips, kind of hulking over me.

"This Sal Piccolo? This the gangster?"

"Yeah."

"The same one you sent up a long time ago?"

"Yeah."

"And he came to you to help him in this thing?"

"Right again."

"No, not right. You know what I think, Spanner? I think you're full of shit. I think you are, in fact, a stupid asshole. I think you are all the more stupid because you think you can run this number on me. And I think you're in this up to your eyeballs."

"Wait—"

"You wait. Somehow or other, Novallo must've gotten onto us, and decided this would be a good way of finding out what was happening. Personally, I wouldn't use an old shit like you, but maybe he thought it'd be cute. There's a few things I haven't quite put together, but at least that accounts for how you happened to show up at just the right moment. It also explains how an old guy like you could so easily take down an evil little weasel like Tony New. And also why Tony New came here this morning."

"You're not serious."

"Spanner, I most certainly am. That, at least, makes some sense of what happened, a lot more than that song and dance you handed out. In fact, about the only thing that doesn't make sense is why you'd try to pass off such a ridiculous story."

"It may be ridiculous, but it happens to be true. Instead of arguing about it, why don't you check it?"

"And how should I do that?"

"Easy. Get in touch with Sal."

"Oh? That could be a bit rough." Nicholson bent over so his face was right up against mine. He smelled of sweat and breath mints. "You dumb shit, Sal Piccolo died two years ago."

I might have made some noises, but I doubt that any of them were intelligible.

Nicholson stood up, strode to the door, then turned back to face me, pointing with his thick index finger like it was a weapon.

"I'm going to go now, Spanner. I'm not at all sure why I'm not taking you with me. Maybe because I'm too tired right now. Or maybe because no one'd ever believe an old coot had done all the things we've got you cold on. Shit. There's probably eight or ten felony charges I could make stick, up to and including a bunch of conspiracy counts, narcotics, obstruction of justice, and armed robbery. And oh, yeah, Dempster, here, tells me you got a couple of nice specimens of the genus Cannabis growing out by your back fence. That's cultivation, Spanner. Even without the other stuff, that's good for eighteen to thirty-six months. Cold."

Cold was right. A feeling of numbness had spread over my body, like I was shot full of novocaine. Nicholson was jabbing pins into me, but it was happening to someone else.

"And you better believe I'm going to pursue it," he said, pointing. "I'll be back, and I'm going to have the same questions for you. Unless you want to spend your golden years as a guest of the grateful citizens of California, old man, you had better come up with some better answers quickly."

The screen door rattled as Nicholson went out. Dempster looked at me, nodded once to indicate that what Nicholson said went double for him, then followed his sergeant.

I stared at the open door for a long time, waiting for some warmth to return to my hands and feet. I looked at the disarray Dempster had caused and thought about putting everything away again. Why bother? If I did, the way things were going, the Hell's Angels would decide to hold a picnic here.

Shit. What a swell situation. The mob was after me because they thought I stole their money. The cops were after me because they thought I either queered their bust or I was involved in the cocaine trade. I'd been smeared with toothpaste, had my shin cracked, had my place torn apart twice, been threatened with a slow death and a long imprisonment. And the only person who could straighten this out, everyone says has been dead for two years. Wonderful. Even the guy who wrote those Al Tracker fantasies—and who clearly had a lot of trouble with his plots—would've come up with something better than this. Jesus.

I looked up. There was a tapping on the frame of the screen door. What now?

"Mr. Spanner?" a female voice said.

"He's in Peru."

She must've thought I said come in, because she did.

"Mr. Spanner, my name is Monica Eustace, and I'm with the North Hollywood Senior Community Center." She was young—early twenties, I guessed—with short light-brown hair and one of the tiniest noses I'd ever seen. She had on a short-sleeve white blouse and a knee-length plaid skirt. She looked and sounded like one of those chirpy little things you see on TV commercials for feminine hygiene products. "I was given your name as one of the people in our area who would be interested in the services we have available."

"Go away."

"There's a variety of recreational and educational programs, there's Meals on Wheels, there's—My goodness! What happened here?" She broke off her prepared spiel when she registered the fact that everything in the living room was dumped on the floor

"Spring cleaning."

"Are you all right, Mr. Spanner?"

"Dandy. Now, go away."

I looked dyspeptically at her, trying to will her to leave, but she was full of that kind of young, eager sincerity that always ignores your wishes.

"Actually," I said, "I could use some help."

"Good. That's what I'm here for. I have a Master's degree in social work, you know."

"That's really encouraging."

"Now, what can I do for you?"

"You could let me have three-quarters of a million dollars."

"What?"

"Just temporarily. So I can get the mob off my back."

"What?"

"No? Then how about an armed bodyguard, maybe two?"

"What?" Her perky little smile was beginning to waver.

"I could use a really top-notch criminal lawyer."

"What?"

"And if you can't do that, how about putting me in touch with a cryogenics clinic? I might have to do ten to twenty in the slammer, and I figure I might as well be frozen. Right?"

"What?"

"You're repeating yourself."

"What? I mean, are you feeling all right?" Her expression said she was trying to figure out if my derangement was benign or if I were likely to turn violent.

"I'm fine. You look like you could use a pick-me-up, though."

"No. I mean, have you been ill? You know, Mr. Spanner, in elderly people, certain illnesses—even mild infections—often can manifest themselves as disorientation, incoherency, confusion, even hallucinations."

Of course! What a relief! This was all due to a virus.

"If diagnosed and treated promptly," she went on, "the condition can be completely cured."

Great. A shot of penicillin and all this would go away.

"But if untreated"—she held up a warning finger—"the condition becomes chronic and irreversible."

She was starting to sound like Nicholson and Tony New, both of whom were also promising me chronic and irreversible futures.

"Go away."

"Aggressiveness is another sign of this syndrome, you know." She sounded like she was reciting from a textbook. "This condition can also be caused by anemia and/

or malnutrition. Have you been eating properly, Mr. Spanner?"

Christ! I was beginning to look back fondly on the morning's first two visitors. No doubt she meant well. That was the problem.

"Go away. Please," I added, not wanting to seem aggressive.

"And just look at you! It's after eleven o'clock and you're still sitting around in your pajamas. That will never do, Mr. Spanner. Don't you know it's important for elderly people to stay active? You can't sit around feeling sorry for yourself. Whether you feel like it or not, you have to make yourself get out and do things. Use it or lose it, Mr. Spanner!"

That was the second time in twelve hours that I'd heard that. All things considered, I preferred it coming from Miranda.

I jumped to my feet, clapping my hands. The girl cringed.

"You're absolutely right, honey. I've got to get out and start doing things. That's the ticket."

I took a step toward her and she backed up, uncertainty showing in her eyes.

"Mr. Spanner, I don't think—"

"You've been a big help, toots," I said, still advancing.

"I didn't mean—"

"Now, if you'll just get out, I can get going."

"Mr. Spanner—"

She was partly facing the door and halfway toward it.

"I really appreciate what you've done. You've got me on the right track again."

I reached out and swatted her plaid-clad behind, winking monstrously.

She hurried to the doorway.

"Mr. Spanner, you don't realize it, but you're not well."

I pulled off my bathrobe and took a step forward. The girl gasped and nearly fell through the screen door. I hurried over and slammed the front door.

"I'm going to have to report this to Mr. Bemelman," I heard through the door. "You need help whether you want it or not, and I'm going to see that you get it. Don't worry, someone'll be back here."

"They'll just have to wait their turn," I called back.

Through the window I watched her bustle out to her car. It looked like my record for the morning was still intact: I'd made another enemy. It never paid to thwart people who were determined to do things for your own good.

The funny thing was, she had been just what I needed. She was right, Spanner: use it or lose it.

CHAPTER FIFTEEN

I knew Nicholson was not nearly as dumb as he looked. Had he been, I would've been down at the station instead of getting dressed. But I also knew his threats were completely serious, and I did have to agree with him that I needed some answers.

I called Sal's service to leave an urgent message.

"I'm sorry," a woman's voice said. "We do not have a Mr. Piccolo listed among our clients."

What? I gave my head a good hard shake. Nothing rattled or ran out of my ears.

"There must be some mistake. I've been leaving messages for him for a week."

I heard an annoyed "Tch" in my ear. "Just a moment."

I was put on hold, where I was treated to a lively mariachi tune until the woman came back.

"Our records show that Mr. Piccolo has canceled our service."

"Since when?"

Another "Tch"; then, grudgingly, "If you must know, it was yesterday afternoon."

"Where can I get in touch with him? It's extremely important."

"I'm sorry, I cannot give you that information. It's confidential."

We hopped around with that one for a while. After trying courtesy, common sense, and sincerity, to no avail, I took a page out of O'Brien's book and made myself abusive, threatening, and objectionable. That worked.

Another minute on hold, this time to the whining of a

hundred violins; then the woman said, "There doesn't seem to be any information."

"What do you mean?"

"We have no address or phone number for Mr. Piccolo."

"Then how'd you get in touch with him?"

"Tch. Apparently Mr. Piccolo contacted us. We did not contact him."

"What about billing him?"

"Tch . . . The account was paid by cash. In advance. Now, if there's nothing more—"

"Just one thing. If there was nothing to tell me, why'd you make such a big production out of it?"

"The fact that there is no information is as confidential as any information there might be. Tch. Tch."

"Of course. How silly of me. Have you ever worked for the government?" I said, but the line was dead.

Driving over Coldwater Canyon to Beverly Hills, I was pretty sure what I would find, but I tried not to think about it. No need to panic beforehand, I thought. Of course not. There'd be plenty of opportunity later.

Shit.

The streets there all looked pretty much alike—rich, quiet, twisting confusingly around and back on themselves —and it took me three tries to find the one where Sal lived. I parked and looked at the white Spanish house. No, there could be no mistake.

I walked up the long drive. I hesitated, took a deep breath, mentally made an offering to whoever it was who looked after old fools, and rang the doorbell.

Feet. The sound of the spy hole in the door opening and closing. Then the door opened and the space was filled with a handsome Mexican woman wearing a hair net and a white uniform.

"Is Mr. Piccolo here?"

Her eyebrows contracted. "Who?"

Okay, Spanner. Now you can panic.

I repeated the name, and the maid said that no one named Piccolo lived there. I asked if I could see her employer. She hesitated a second, then opened the door further so I could step into the entry hall. It was covered in quarry tile. The maid went off to the rear of the house and I looked into the living room. Not much consolation, but at least I'd been right about that. Dark wood floors and fine old leather furniture. A couple of good modern paintings on the wall, and a couple of even better antique carpets on the floor. No question, I thought grimly, Sal had good taste. Yeah.

The owner of the house, a classy lady named Esterly, appeared. We introduced ourselves and I asked about Sal. The name meant nothing to her.

"Tall guy, in his seventies. Thin. Looks like Death on a bad day."

She smiled but shook her head.

"What about last Monday night? Were you here?"

She thought for a minute. "Yes. My husband and I were here all evening."

Well, I'd thought, Sal had looked reluctant to go into the house after I dropped him off. Now I knew why. He didn't want to be nailed for trespassing. Wonderful, Spanner. Your perception was truly remarkable.

There didn't seem to be anything more for me to determine, so I thanked Mrs. Esterly and left. If she'd been puzzled by my visit, she was far too polite to display it.

I, on the other hand, lacked her upbringing. I kicked the door of the Chevy and let out a string of curses that could have lowered property values.

Talk about being bitched, buggered, and bewildered. Christ.

CHAPTER SIXTEEN

I'd never thought that people really pinched themselves to see if they were awake, but that's what I did, driving back to the valley. I pinched the shit out of myself. I was awake.

Had there not been some evidence to the contrary, I would've seriously entertained that little social worker's idea that this whole thing was a delusion brought on by a vitamin deficiency. As it was, that made more sense than what I was looking at. Like most people my age, I'd worried a little about becoming ga-ga. Now, senile dementia was rapidly becoming an attractive alternative.

I looked at my watch. It wasn't even twenty-four hours since I'd been on top of the world. Today it felt like it was on top of me. "J. Spanner: Run over by the wheel of fortune."

I parked in the visitor's area at Sunset Grove and spotted O'Brien sitting in his usual place, apart from the others. In the shade of the umbrella his skin looked gray, washed out. His green eyes seemed paler than usual, focused someplace far away, and he didn't notice me until I was right next to him.

"Ah, the hero of the hour," he said, motioning me to sit down.

"More like the chump of the century."

"Huh?"

"You're not going to believe what's been happening."

"Isn't that what you said a week ago?"

"Probably. But this time even I don't believe it."

He raised an eyebrow. "So go ahead."

I took a deep breath and slowly let it out. "I never said who we were running that search for."

"No, and I didn't ask."

"I know. Well, it was Sal Piccolo. You remember him?"

"Piccolo? You mean the Salami?"

"Yeah."

"Sure I remember him. But—"

O'Bee screwed up his face, thinking. I tried to will him not to say what he was going to say.

"But he's dead." He said it. Dandy.

"So I understand."

O'Bee looked question marks at me.

"What makes you think so?" I said.

"Hell, I don't know. I must've heard it or read it someplace. You know, you think 'I knew him,' and then you forget about it. Not like it was a friend or something, just one less person around who you were once acquainted with. Must've been a couple of years ago, I think. A fire, maybe."

"I had the same idea at first—that he was dead. Then, obviously, I thought I was mistaken. Now I'm not so sure."

"Huh? You're confusing me."

"You want confusion? Get a load of this."

I filled him in about Sal—or about what Sal had told me. Then in detail about taking down Tony New the day before and returning the dough. Then this morning's visitors, the answering service, and the trip to Beverly Hills.

"My, my, Jake Spanner." O'Bee chuckled thickly when I finished. "You certainly lead a full and exciting life, for an old fella. Just one damn thing after another."

"A few damn things too many, thanks. And stop laughing. This is not so fucking funny."

O'Bee stopped laughing when he started to cough, that harsh deep kind that shook his body. When he recovered, he was even paler, and a film of sweat covered his forehead.

"You okay? You want me to get you something?"

He waved it off. "You always were a shit disturber, Jake Spanner, but this . . ."

"Yeah, I know. I've outdone myself. Wonderful, isn't it? You got any thoughts on the matter?"

O'Bee rested his chin on his hand and stared at the

brownish grass for a couple of minutes, then looked up. "Well, assuming you're not crazy—"

"An assumption I wouldn't make too hastily."

"Oh, you're crazy, all right, just not in that way."

"You're most encouraging."

O'Brien grinned. "And assuming that you haven't been haunted—"

"Yeah, I'll accept that."

"—then I'd say either you made a mistake and knocked over the wrong crook—"

"Or?"

"Or you've been set up, you dumb son of a bitch."

I nodded. "That does seem to be the choice. Shit."

We talked about it for a while. A mistake was possible. Stranger things happened all the time. You started looking for one thing and you turned up something else. Thought you located the right guy, only it wasn't. I'd done it before, more than once.

But not this time. There were too many things against it. The real kicker, though, was the attaché case. No way that Sal and the kid could both have had the same kind of case. Coincidence could go only so far.

And it was just possible, I supposed, that it had been the kid who had knocked us over and grabbed the ransom. But if so, then nothing that happened afterwards made any sense.

Unless it was all some kind of setup. I didn't have it all worked out, but it did seem to answer a lot of stuff, starting with the fact that the late Sal Piccolo was very much alive. As far as O'Brien was concerned, that explained just about everything.

Forty years ago, Sal had been known as one of the slickest, most devious, most Machiavellian characters around. He'd risen to his position of supremacy in this town, partly because he was tough, but mostly because he could out-think, out-hustle the opposition, stayed three steps ahead of them, got them so wrapped up in his convoluted schemes that they went around in circles until they ran up their own assholes and disappeared. He was that most dangerous of creatures—an unscrupulous, power-mad bastard who also happened to be smart, a ruthless villain with the talent and instincts of a con man. He would've made a fine politician.

And this was the guy who asked me so sincerely if I didn't think a man could change, and even though I doubted it, got me to give him the benefit of the doubt. Christ, Spanner: you may be old, but you sure are slow.

The more I thought about it, the clearer things got. How he got me hooked, and then just reeled me in. Got me started, the sob story about the grandson, could only trust good old Spanner, solidarity among old enemies. A taste of long-past action, excitement, adventure. Pay me something, hire me, make me feel an obligation, just like when I'd been in business. Make me take my gun, just so it's more like the old days, reinforce the idea that I was working, reestablish old patterns. Then the setup, the disaster, the failure. He figured that I still had my sense of responsibility, that I'd try to put things right. And I did. I didn't know what got to me more: that he'd screwed around with me, or that I was so goddamn predictable that he'd been able to do it. They say that a good con man doesn't do anything except let the mark act naturally. That damn Piccoli didn't con me with greed, but with pride. Shit. Played me like a fucking fiddle.

Made me part of the situation, made me feel his problem was my problem as well. Then gave me just enough of a lead so that I could see the way to resolve it. Nothing too much, just enough to get me started, make it a challenge. Got me going so that old habits could take over, so that I could show that I could still do it. Pride again!

Seen in retrospect, all kinds of things made sense. I'd been pissed off at myself for not spotting the ambush, but there'd been nothing there to spot. No car, no Tony New, nothing. Just some goon that Sal had hired for a bill or two, waiting in the bushes to sap me. Not too hard, because the old dick had to recover so he could redeem himself. Just hard enough so he wouldn't know what had or hadn't happened, hard enough to give him a very real lump so he'd assume everything else was real as well.

And there were those little things Sal had said or done that I couldn't figure, that had struck me as being odd, somehow out of tune. Even the best artists occasionally slip, forget a line, play the wrong note. It's hard to sustain a performance—especially when improvising—without making mistakes. Sal had made some, but either he'd covered them or—better—he'd had me so well set up that I provided the explanations. Well, I'd told myself, he was upset, or understandably nervous, or—Jesus! Had I been his shill, I couldn't've done a better job of explaining things away for him.

I saw how I'd been maneuvered, but there was a lot I didn't understand. The connection with Tony New. How Sal had gotten onto him. The attaché case. And the whole jig the puppetmaster had made me dance. It looked like Sal had really had a lot of confidence in me after all. I supposed I should've been flattered in a way.

"Well," O'Brien said after we talked all this out, "you know the proverbial shit creek?"

"You think I could use a paddle, huh?"

"Paddle, hell! You need a life preserver. I think you've gone under for the second time."

"That cop, Nicholson, said about the same thing. . . . What do you think I should do?"

"I think you should run like hell, Jake Spanner."

I looked at him, then shook my head.

"I hope you're not going to give me any of that stuff about seeing this through to the end. Honor, that's what a man does, shit like that. That got you into this in the first place."

"No. I meant that I can't. I've got no place to run to. I've got nothing to run with. And even if I did, I don't see how I could go far enough or stay away long enough. I figure I've got people on both sides with long reaches and longer memories."

"Then you better provide some explanations they can buy."

I nodded agreement. "It looks like I've got two lines to go on—Sal, and the kid."

"And not much time."

"Not much at all."

"You could probably use some help."

I smiled and shrugged. "Probably."

"You know, Jake, I was pissed when you cut me out before."

"I know, but I figured it was my operation. I still do."

"Okay." O'Bee nodded. "But this time, I want in all the way."

"Shit. You see what's going on here. This is no joke. It's really scary."

"I see it."

I looked at him. I wanted his help, but I couldn't see it from his side. "Why?"

For a second I saw that same look that had disturbed me in the lieutenant's office; then he grinned. "Tradition. I told you, Jake, O'Brien always has to save Spanner's ass."

"You mean like some people save old tin foil or pieces of string?"

O'Bee thought a minute, then shook his head. "Nah. That stuff might be good for something one day."

He winked.

CHAPTER SEVENTEEN

Back into town.

I dropped O'Brien at one of his cop bars, where he was going to see what more he could get on Tony New. I was concerned about O'Bee. In just the two days since I'd last seen him, he looked worse—older, weaker, less healthy. He didn't say anything and brushed off the few cautious probes I made, but I didn't have a very good feeling about him. Still, the thought of doing something other than sitting around Sunset Grove collecting lint seemed to pick him up.

I went to the library on 5th Street. There'd been times when it seemed I spent a large part of my life in there, going through old telephone directories, trying to get a line on some deadbeat or other, seeing if I could figure what hole the rabbit had run into.

I was prepared for another long haul, but I got lucky. Both O'Brien and Nicholson had put Sal's death at two years ago. Using that as the starting point, I went forward and backward, a week at a time, through the microfilmed *Times*. In the fifth week I found it.

It hadn't been one of the day's big items, only four inches on page 27. "Ex-gangster, three others, die in rooming-house fire." The headline was almost as long as the story that followed, which did little except twice repeat that information, and mention that arson was suspected.

The *Examiner* had about the same information, fleshed out with a picture of a gutted house, and a mostly fictional account of Sal's criminal career, which sounded like it might have come from a pulp magazine from the time Sal was sent up. They also had a few hyperventilated quotes about the "blaze" from the rooming-house manager, one Herbert Soames, who'd been lucky enough to have a room on the ground floor and a window that opened.

Not a hell of a lot to go on. I looked through another ten days' of papers, but there were no follow-ups. The story was as dead as the guys in the rooming house.

I found a pay phone and decided to see if my luck would hold. It did. The first eleven H. Soameses said "No" when I asked if they had lived in such-and-such a rooming house two years before. My twelfth dime brought me a guy that said, "If you're from the insurance company, I already told everything I know, a hundred times. If you're anybody else, go fuck yourself." Then he hung up. Though we were a ways yet from the cocktail hour, it sounded like Herbert had decided to get a jump on things.

The address for him was pretty close to the library. After that pleasant exchange on the phone, I thought I'd have better luck if I called on him in person.

His place was another crummy rooming house, a smallish two-story wooden affair, not too far from the one that had burned. Like every other building on the block, it had needed paint and repairs for at least ten years, but the only likely renovations would be done with a bulldozer. The neighborhood had never been that swell. Now it was home to transients, welfare cases, illegal immigrants, recent parolees, and old people trying to get by on Social Security. If I got booted out of my house, I figured this kind of place might be my future.

Always assuming Tony New and Sergeant Nicholson were going to let me have a future.

A sickly, hollow sensation opened in my stomach, like I'd stepped into an elevator and found the car wasn't there. I took a couple of deep breaths. One thing at a time, Spanner, one at a time.

I noticed a pair of ancient, scared-looking eyes staring out from a crack in the curtains in the house next door. Down the street a couple of nine-year-old hoodlums were eying me speculatively, probably wondering if it would be worth their while to roll me. In a nearby backyard a cat screamed.

I stepped over a rusting tricycle that was missing a rear wheel and went up the shaky front steps. Around the foundation there were empty beer cans, brittle pieces of yellow newspaper, and other flotsam deposited by some invisible tide. A faded cardboard sign announced ROOMS. A smaller hand-lettered card thumbtacked on the jamb informed me that Herbert Soames was the manager here. Only previous experience could have gotten him such a cushy position.

The front door was open, and I went down the hallway. Like a thousand similar buildings, it smelled of sweat, rancid oil, and futility. The last door had a metal strip on it that said Manager. I knocked.

After sounds of coughing, spitting, groaning, and shuffling, the door opened. Herbert Soames was a skinny guy with a concave chest, gray skin, and a dry, flaking scalp. His eyes were bloodshot and looked nicotine-stained. The collar of his shirt was buttoned, way too large for his saggy chicken neck. In the dark room behind him, most flat surfaces were covered with empty bottles, overturned glasses, and dirty plates. He looked to be my age. I figured he was actually about fifty.

"Thirty-five a week. In advance. No cooking in the rooms." He belched. I didn't say anything. " 'Course, if you explain the situation—" he made the universal gesture, thumb and forefinger rubbing together "—exceptions can be made."

The flat edge to his voice indicated that before he came here to make his fortune he'd come from somewhere in the Midwest. Christ, how many guys like Herbert Soames had I dealt with over the years, alcoholic fleabag flunkies trying to screw a nickle wherever they could? Hundreds, probably more. I wondered if he realized he was a cliché.

"I don't want a room," I said. "I want some information."

"Did you just call?" Yellow eyes narrowed.

"Yeah."

"And what'd I tell you."

"To fuck myself."

"Good advice." He started to shut the door.

"I didn't say I wanted free information."

Both the door and his eyes opened slightly. I pulled a

sawbuck out of my pocket. A claw shot out and grabbed
the bill. He held it close to his face. I couldn't tell if he
was studying it or smelling it. Whichever, satisfied as to its
quality, he made it disappear into a deep trouser pocket.

"That don't buy a hell of a lot."

I figured it could buy every single thing he knew, and
with my change I'd have enough for a good dinner. "I
don't want much," I said.

Soames walked back into the room, leaving the door
open. I followed him in. He sat down, located an unla-
beled bottle that still had something in it, and poured
some brown stuff into a dirty jelly glass. I moved some
magazines aside, clearing a space for myself on the day-
bed. It looked like Herbert might've been a good customer of one of Tony New's establishments devoted to
adult entertainment. Maybe I was just old, but I couldn't
see what pleasure Herbert derived from pictures of
women doing things to themselves with pieces of fruit.

I started asking my questions. Not surprisingly, he had
few answers. The other rooming house had been much
like this one. Other than the fact that Sal had lived there
for about a year before the fire, Soames couldn't tell me
anything about him. Didn't know what he'd been doing,
didn't know who he'd been seeing, nothing. Big help. I
began to think I'd wasted my money.

When I asked him about the fire, he got very evasive,
defensive, and I got the idea that some people had
thought he'd had some responsibility for it, if only
through negligence. Soames said that was most unfair,
since the inspector had been nearly certain it'd been de-
liberately set. Besides, Soames said, he himself had barely
escaped. He'd been in bed because he'd been feeling
poorly that night. Yeah, I thought; a couple quarts of
cooking sherry can do that to you.

"So you were the only survivor?"

"No. There was one other." He sounded disappointed,
as though this in some way diminished his uniqueness.

"Oh? The papers didn't say anything about that."

Soames made a face, brought up some phlegm that he
hawked into a filthy handkerchief. He examined the
treasure before putting the rag away.

"Well, I say there was one, see? Five guys lived on the
second floor. Five." He held up a hand with the fingers

spread wide. "But they only found four bodies. Four." He
tucked his thumb in. "And you shoulda seen them. Bar-
bee-cued! Talk about being burned to a crisp! Ha!" That
idea seemed to cheer him up, and he took a big swallow
from his glass. "Why, there wasn't much more of them
there than you'd get from a twenty-five cent cee-gar."

Oh, yeah? The papers hadn't said anything about that
either. I began to see what might have happened.

"How'd they identify them, then?"

Soames lifted his narrow shoulders and shuddered, then
took another swig. "The fire guys had me tell them where
everybody's room was. Kind of draw a plan. Then—" He
cringed again. "Then those bastards made me walk
through the place, pointing everything out to them. There
wasn't any call for that. I was a sick man." He coughed
a couple of times. "You know, I can't go by one of those
take-out rib places without being reminded of that night.
Shee-it."

I didn't know if it was the musty smell of old corrup-
tion in Soames's apartment or his story, but I was feeling a
bit queasy myself.

"About the, uh, survivor," I said casually, "you know
what happened to him?"

Apparently, I wasn't casual enough, because Soames
went all sly on me. He coyly smiled, showing a few teeth
about the same color yellow as his eyes, and made that
gesture with his thumb and forefinger.

Hell, why bother? Was he liable to tell me anything I
wanted to know? I doubted it, but I pulled out a five.
This was the kind of game you had to play through. At
least, that was the way I'd always done it before.

Soames grabbed the bill, rubbed a greasy thumb across
Abe's whiskers, and made it disappear into the same
pocket.

"Don't know!" Soames cackled gleefully.

Shit. I was getting tired of being jerked around.
Seventy-eight or not, I was going to wring that booze-
rotted son of a bitch's scrawny neck. And enjoy doing it.

It must've showed, because Soames hastily held up his
hands. "No. I meant, that's what's so funny about it."

"What's so funny about what?"

"After the fire. This guy—Winchester was his name—"

"Winchester?"

"Yeah. Harry Winchester. Like the rifle, you know? That's how I remember it."

"Okay. Go on."

"Well, this Winchester never showed up."

"Never showed up?"

"That's right. Disappeared. Never seen again."

"Then what makes you so sure he wasn't killed in the fire?"

Soames made a face, like I was a real dumb shit. "Told you. Four rooms, four bodies. But Winchester's room was empty."

Therefore . . . Well, why not? It must've looked reasonable at the time. Besides, what difference did it make if it was one poor loser or another? Who was there to care?

I stood up.

"A good thing, too," Soames said.

"What?"

"That he never showed up."

"Oh?"

"Yeah. He probably woulda wanted some of his rent back."

"And you weren't going to give it to him."

" 'Course not! The management can't be responsible for things like that. You pay your money and you takes your chances."

Soames nodded vigorously a couple of times at the righteousness of management's stance. I left him chuckling over the recollection of this ancient—and dubious— triumph.

After the claustrophobic atmosphere of Soames's room, even the dismal street felt pretty good.

Well, I'd paid my money and it had gotten me more out of Herbert than I'd had any right to reasonably expect.

One mystery was solved. That left me with only eighty or ninety more to go.

Obviously, what's-his-name Winchester hadn't been the one who got away. He had disappeared, though. Literally up in smoke.

The problem was, my explanation raised almost as many questions as it answered. Why had Sal disappeared after the fire? Why did he not correct the mistake that'd

been made, apparently preferring to be thought dead?
What was he trying to hide or get away with? Or from?
Could it be that he'd set the fire to cover his trail?

Sal was a nasty, sinister bastard, but I thought that that
would've been too vicious, even for him. His style was
different. On the other hand, my previous assessments of
him had not been exactly dead-on. I thought I'd better
stop making assumptions.

Since I now had some idea about what had happened
two years before, I needed to find out why. Maybe that
would give me an angle on Sal's resurrection.

And the other miracles that followed.

CHAPTER EIGHTEEN

Barbara Twill lived on one of those little streets near the Hollywood Cemetery, close to where the B studios of Gower Gulch used to be. It was one of those remnants of old Hollywood, two rows of tiny stucco bungalows facing each other across a narrow flagstone courtyard. The Mexican tile fountain in the center hadn't worked since V-E Day, and it was now filled with rubbish. A headless plaster flamingo lay on its side in one of the dried-up flower beds.

A couple of lifetimes ago, Barbara had been one of those slender, bouncy little false blondes who filled up chorus lines or the background in steamy bath scenes in Roman extravaganzas. She once told me she'd been in sixteen pictures and had spoken a total of twenty-three words, most of them one syllable. Finally, she got tired of having to say yes ten or twelve times in somebody's office before she got the chance to say it on the screen.

Like a lot of girls in her situation, she'd run with the speedy crowd of demi-crooks who made up the fringes of the big time—gamblers, hustlers, and other hopefuls who were known as local color. Using those connections, she'd set herself up as a bookie, and found she was more successful giving betting lines than lines of dialogue. She'd been doing it ever since, making her maybe the oldest bookmaker in the world.

She hadn't left her bungalow for twenty years, and for the last ten, had hardly ever gotten out of her specially built armchair. Still, her telephones kept her wired to everything, and she knew more about what was going on in the twilight world of sharks and shakers than nearly anyone in the city. Sooner or later everybody, cops and clowns, talked to Barbara Twill, to tell her his troubles or to get the lowdown on someone else's.

Behind the three-quarter-closed venetian blinds of her front window, I made out a bulky shape that raised an arm in greeting. Before I could tap on the door, I heard a voice call that it was open.

I went into a nearly dark room, the only light being the few rays that got in between the slats of the blinds.

There was a short whirring sound, and an immense overstuffed chair swiveled to face me.

"My, my. Jake Spanner. What an unexpected pleasure. What brings you here? Is one of us dying?"

I laughed. "Not you, I hope. How are you, Babs?"

My eyes were becoming adjusted to the dim light and I saw her hand wigwag, meaning so-so. The hand was small and very puffy, like an inflated latex glove. Her legs were straight out on a built-in foot rest. The feet inside laceless men's tennis shoes were tiny, but the ankles ballooned out. Emerging from her tentlike pink housecoat, her legs were thick unmoving columns loosely wrapped in Ace bandages. Her little heart-shaped mouth was nearly lost among the jowls and chins. In her wild young days as a starlet she'd been known as Bubbles. Forty-five years and a hundred fifty pounds later, she looked like Orson Welles in drag.

"Take a load off, Jake."

I pulled over a folding metal chair and did. There was a muted buzzing. Barbara rotated her chair and picked up the receiver of one of the five telephones on the large L-shaped table that half enclosed her. The table also held books, snacks, medicine—anything she might need. Immobilized by her weight, asthma, edema, varicose veins, and who knew what else, her physical world had contracted to a five-foot-square area. She seemed, however, more alive, in tune, than a lot of the zombies I had observed in my recent travels around town, each riding his own hobbyhorse with monomaniacal dedication.

"Yes . . . yes," Barbara said. "A hundred across the board. Right." She hung up and tapped out something on the typewriter terminal of one of those small personal computers which sat next to her phones. "What a sucker bet. Christ, what a turkey! He could put money on the sun coming up and lose. But I guess if gamblers were smart, there'd be a lot of poor bookies. And there aren't."

"Not many, no." I pointed to the computer. "That's new, isn't it?"

"Gotta keep up with the times, Jake. Don't know how I ever got along without it. Getting too old to keep all those numbers in my head."

"Aren't you worried about having a record, in case the cops hit you?"

She waved one of those grotesque little hands. "Nah. Got it programmed so all I have to do is hit one key and the whole memory's erased. Kind of like a stroke." She chuckled. "Anyway, who's going to bust old Babs? Owed too many favors. Too many commendations, promotions, came from little hints I dropped. Besides—" she laughed again, "even if they arrested me, they couldn't get me out the door. Have to knock down a wall first."

That was an exaggeration, but not much of one. Another phone buzzed softly.

After saying "Yes?" Barbara listened awhile, concentrating, her eyes almost disappearing behind the rolls of her cheeks. "Listen, honey, it's all bluff. Just sit tight a while. He'll come around. . . . Yeah, you too." She hung up, smiling and shaking her head. "That was Teddy Margolin."

That name sounded vaguely familiar.

"Son of Wee Willie Margolin," Babs said. "You remember?"

It took a minute, but I did. He'd had a casino out at a ranch in Northridge. Until a competitor got together with one of his croupiers, reversed the house's fix, and broke the bank and Wee Willie all at the same time. He resurfaced after the war, trying to run a scam with scrap metal or surplus fighter planes or something, but it was halfhearted.

"Seems like I'm den mother to a whole new generation. It's nice, but it's not the same. The old spirit's gone. You noticed that? Teddy's nothing like his father. No sense of style. Not even bad style." She sighed. "Those were the days, weren't they, Jake? I think about them a lot now." She shook her head. "Sometimes seem clearer, more real, than stuff that happened yesterday, last month. You find that? Forget where you are, going into the past?"

"Actually, that's kind of why I'm here, only the reverse. I'm not slipping into the past, but the past does seem to be poking itself into the present."

"Old sins coming back to haunt you?"

"Something like that. You remember Sal Piccolo?"

Babs raised her eyebrows and nodded.

"You knew him?"

She hesitated, then smiled in a way that indicated what she'd been like when she was Bubbles. "Well enough to know that his nickname was deserved."

Oh, yeah? I hadn't known that. Talk about your odd couples. Then I caught myself. At the time it had occurred, there would have been nothing at all odd about it.

Barbara's eyes were closed, a soft smile on her lips. I had to say her name a couple of times.

"Sorry, Jake. I was drifting again." She pushed a finger into her doughy forearm and sadly shook her head. It was clear where she'd been. "What do you want to know?"

"What happened to Sal?"

"He died in a fire."

"No. I meant, after he got out of prison."

Barbara paused. "You sent him up, didn't you?"

"Yeah."

"Clean?"

I shrugged. "As clean as it ever is. I created a situation . . ."

Barbara nodded. "And he hung himself." She gave a brief laugh. "You know, it's amazing how some people can always be counted on to respond in a certain way."

I smiled. With some difficulty. I knew. At the moment, a little too well, thanks.

"Look," I said, "I heard that Sal was pretty well set up when he got out."

"You're kidding."

"He wasn't? Hadn't he made a lot of dough?"

"Of course. But like all the other big shots he spent it as fast as it came. Figured the tap would just keep running. So when he was nailed, there wasn't that much. After the law grabbed all they could, his wife took whatever was left."

"So he was broke when he got out?"

"Stony."

This was no surprise. After finding out that he had nothing to do with that fancy place in Beverly Hills, and that he'd lived in a crummy rooming house, I'd figured as much. Still, when you were floating around in Cloud Cuckoo Land, every little solid bit helped.

"What'd he do?"

Barbara held out her hands, pink palms up. "What's an old villain to do? He scuffled and hustled, trying to get something going. But he was an old man and he'd been away a long time. It was a different world. For a while he even tried running a three-card-monte swindle in senior-citizen centers. Can you believe it! A guy who'd owned a big piece of this town once, trying to do something like that. Sucker old fogies. And he wasn't even any good at it. Hands too stiff. Couldn't make the queen disappear. Hell, Jake, I felt like calling him up and letting him have a few bucks. Then decided that was a loser's play. . . . Maybe afraid he wouldn't remember me." Babs looked at me, curled her lower lip, and gestured at herself and the small world that surrounded her. "Maybe afraid he would."

She was silent long enough that I thought she'd drifted again, but she was only trying to get details straight. "Then I heard—and this was only talk, so I don't know what it's worth—that he'd managed to set up something. Something serious. Something that'd fix him up big again."

"What?"

"No idea. What's serious? Sex. Gambling. Dope. Politics. No matter what, those're the things that never change. But whatever it was, it was too big for him alone, and he needed help. Then I heard he got it. Some youngster who was said to be a fast riser in certain circles. That's how come there was talk. That strange combo of old tall Sal and this short baby-faced mover." Barbara screwed up her face, then shook her head. "Whose name I can't remember. Getting old, Jake. You think it's all there, then you find gaps. And they get bigger all the time. Soon, someone's going to punch my erase button. Then where'll Babs be?"

"I wouldn't worry about it for a while yet," I said, and I meant it. I thought she was miraculous. "This name—it wouldn't be Anthony Novallo, would it?"

"That's it! Tony New!" She gave me a curious look but didn't say anything. One reason people talked to Barbara was that she never pushed.

"Then what happened?"

"Nothing. Sal died."

"And Tony New?"

"Continues to rise. But I don't inquire too closely. From what I understand, he's one ugly little character. Now *he's* like some of those people who used to be around here. Like that guy who had someone's ear on his key chain. What was his name?"

"Eddie Peanuts."

"Right." Barbara looked closely at me for a while. "Jake, what's going on here? Thought you'd packed it in a long time ago."

"I thought so, too."

"Not going to tell me, huh? Okay. When you're ready. Just you be careful. There're not many of us left."

"Not many," I said, "but right now, maybe one too many."

She tilted her head to one side but stayed silent.

I got up and went over to her. I put my lips on her forehead. Up close I noticed that her wispy hair was getting thin on top.

Babs smiled up at me. "You always were a sweet man, Jake. Not always real swift, but sweet."

Yeah, and apparently I still was. Just moving along like molasses in January. Shit.

As I went out the door, Barbara was back on the phone. "Now, look, honey," I heard her say, "you're real late. I have to see something soon, or I'm afraid you're going to be seeing my boys, and I don't think you'll really enjoy that."

In the doorway across the narrow courtyard two huge black men were lounging. They wore beautifully cut pastel silk suits, matching two-tone shoes, and sinister tribal scars on their cheeks. Even in repose they exuded a potential for mayhem, like a hand grenade or a hair-trigger shotgun. I guessed they were Barbara's boys, and I could see why a welcher would not enjoy a visit from them. I suspected they rarely had to do more than whisper a suggestion that payment would be appreciated, and the wife and kids went up on the auction block. One of them

raised a forefinger to his eyebrow in a lazy salute, and
the other flashed a dazzling grin as I walked by. From
what I overheard, they appeared to be discussing Sartre.
In beautiful French. Hmm. West African existentialist
thugs. Babs always did have a certain flair.

The sky was turning a thick purple brown. My brain
felt about the same. Lack of sleep, the unaccustomed ex-
ertions of last night—last night! was that all it was?
Christ!—and the whole of last week were beginning to
settle on me very heavily. It used to be a struggle to find
enough stuff to fill up a day. Now it seemed like I'd been
running forever. There was lots more I should do, but
there was no way I could manage it. I could only hope
that I had enough to keep Tony New interested—show
him that I really was trying—when he came calling the
next day. But even if I hadn't, it would have to do. All
that was now left of the adrenalin I'd been pumping was
a sour stomach and a burning sensation behind my eyes.
I climbed in my car and pointed it toward home.

Halfway there I realized I'd forgotten O'Brien. Jesus,
I was even more beat than I thought.

I found a phone booth and called the bar. O'Bee wasn't
there, but there was a message for me to call him at another bar, where I did reach him.

He told me what he'd picked up, mostly what I'd already heard several times—and didn't need to be told
anyway—that Anthony Novallo was one dangerous little
monster, who sometimes scared even his colleagues. He
had no friends. None of the normal restraints seemed to
apply to him, he disliked being thwarted, and he had a
fondness for inflicting pain. In other words, your everyday
healthy psycho. Most encouraging.

He was suspected of a ton of stuff and was probably responsible for another ton the cops didn't know about, but
so far he'd been untouchable. "After all," O'Brien said,
"it's not that easy to find a witness to go against someone
whose career started when he was picked up at age eleven
for gutting cats with a razor blade."

I grunted acknowledgment. I thought about tomorrow,
and that feeling of deep hollowness returned to fill my
belly.

"Oh, yeah," O'Bee said with a hoarse chuckle. "There's
one more thing."

"I can hardly wait."

"Our friend Tony's full name is Thomas Anthony Novallo."

"Yeah?"

"And he's the son of Robert Novallo."

"Okay. Who's that?"

"Nobody. A small-time insurance salesman, something like that. Died of a heart attack a few years ago."

"So? I assume there's a point to this."

"Oh, yes." He chuckled again. "Seems Robert married a girl named Diana. Her mother had divorced and remarried, but the girl kept her father's name." O'Bee paused. "That name was Piccolo."

"You mean—"

"That's right. His grandson."

The can of worms had turned into snakes, and they were climbing up my legs.

CHAPTER NINETEEN

By the time I'd picked up O'Brien, taken him back to Sunset Grove, and then finally gotten back to my place, it was completely dark. Our trip had been another of those silent rides. O'Bee didn't seem to be feeling well, pale to the point of greenness. He said he'd drunk too much, but I couldn't smell it.

I sure hadn't felt like talking. The latest bit of information had been too much for my tired brain. It kept running up against the fact that Tony New was Sal's grandkid —the Tommy who supposedly had been kidnapped—and bouncing back. I couldn't contend with it. And I sure couldn't think about the next day. About as much as I could consider was a hot shower, a warm meal, and a cool bed. I thought I could sleep for a week. Maybe if I did, this would all go away.

Right. Rip Van Spanner.

I put the car in the garage and went in the back door, turning on lights. When I switched on the floor lamp in the living room, I realized my plans for the evening would most likely be delayed somewhat.

Sitting in the center of the couch, feet barely touching the floor, hands folded, quiet as a cobra on a rock, was my favorite psychopath, Thomas Anthony Novallo. Standing next to him were his two faithful companions, Unh and Duh.

"Glad you started without me," I said.

"Fucking old men," Tony whispered.

That might have been the code word, because one of the gorillas lumbered over and looked down at me. He had more hair sprouting from his nostrils than I had on my head. He breathed through his mouth with a soft sighing sound.

He wrapped a hand around my upper arm, pressing his fingers through my little bit of flesh and muscle, right to the bone. Then he hurled me into one of the wing chairs. My hip cracked hard on the arm, my neck snapped back, and my head struck the wing of the chair before I came to rest more or less in a sitting position.

The only sound in the room was the bruiser's shallow breathing.

I didn't like the way this was starting. It looked like I had every reason to be scared. And I was.

"I thought I had some more time. I'm working on it. Really," I said, hoping to defuse the situation a little.

It must've been the wrong thing to say. The kid pulled a disgusted face and nodded once. The breather stood over me, then casually walloped me on the side of my head with a giant open paw. I went numb from my jaw to the top of my skull, and a high whistling ring filled my ear.

"Let's say this is for—" the kid paused, looking for the right word. He smiled when he found it. "—incentive," he hissed.

"Hey, I don't—"

Before I got a chance to tell him my motivation was already pretty high, the guy in front of me showed that he was ambidextrous. With his other hand he belted me on the opposite side of my head, nearly knocking me out of the chair. The worst of it was that I knew he was being intentionally gentle. How much longer?

Even ten years ago I might have tried to do something, but now there was no possibility of that. I was completely helpless, completely in their power. The thought did nothing to diminish my rising fear.

Through my watering eyes I saw Tony New was talking to me, but my ears felt like they were stuffed with cotton, and I couldn't hear a thing. I pointed to my ears and made helpless gestures. The kid said something else I couldn't hear. The other piece of muscle came over and stood behind me. He grabbed my wrists, then yanked my arms behind the chair, where he held them, continuing to pull. It felt like they were going to be ripped out of their sockets. My spine arched out like a bow and my head was pressed into the chair back.

The guy with the soft touch bent down and jerked off one of my shoes, almost taking half my heel with it. I made a feeble attempt to kick him my other foot, but he easily caught my ankle and gave me a chop just above my knee with the side of his hand, which momentarily paralyzed my leg. Off came the second shoe.

My arms were pulled harder; my back arched more. The bruiser leaned over me, reached down, and unhooked my belt. I felt a hand go inside my waistband. I tried to squirm away but only managed to further hurt my shoulders. In one quick motion the hands ripped the trousers down the front and pulled them off me. With the absolute irrelevancy that can be caused by mortal terror, I thought about the detective tearing off the blonde's silk dress in that book I'd been reading at the beginning of all this, about a million years ago.

I was stretched nearly horizontal in the chair, but by looking down I could see my scrawny, fuzzy legs sticking out of pale-blue boxer shorts that had faded clock faces printed on them.

Tony New stood up and came over to our little group. He took out a long cigarette. His boy quickly whipped out a gold lighter and held the flame up to it. Tony New puffed on the cigarette, all the while staring at me, unblinking, a smile of anticipatory pleasure on his girlish little mouth.

He knelt down out of my view, and the bruiser firmly held my legs. I heard a sound like *tsst*. I hadn't felt anything yet, but the smell of burning nylon from my sock was enough to set me off.

I cried "No! Wait! Wait!" I still couldn't hear very well but it must've been loud, because the guy let go of my legs and clamped a hand over my mouth. It smelled like he'd been peeling oranges.

Tony New motioned with his head and the guy behind me let go of my arms. I pulled myself upright, rubbed my shoulders, and waited for my head to clear. I couldn't see how, but I knew I had to do something to slow them down, to break the pattern, before they got so caught up in what they were doing that my death became inevitable, part of a natural progression, even if it hadn't originally been intended. I'd seen enough of his kind to know that once someone like this kid, someone who liked dealing pain, got started, it was tough to stop him. The situation created its own imperatives. "One thing just led to another," they'd say, shrugging unconcernedly, giggling.

"Look," I said, "do you know I saved you a lot of trouble?" Tony New stared, expressionlessly, his dark bulging eyes unblinking. "I mean, you were all set up to be busted. The cops had you staked out. If I hadn't come along, you'd've been arrested. Just like your supplier."

"You think I should say thank you?" The eyes narrowed. A hard edge came into the high-pitched voice, making it sound like a rasp against rusted iron. I didn't seem to be exactly pacifying him.

I hastily waved off that idea. "I didn't say that. All I meant was that there's more than one way to look at this."

The kid blinked slowly, like his eyelids were nictating membranes. He stepped closer to me and stared down. Involuntarily, I tried to push myself further into the back of the chair. Never had I felt so much like a thing, an object. He could do anything to me, because he recognized no connection between us. Scary. Very scary.

"Listen, old man, there's only one way for you to look, and that's into a deep dark hole. Don't give me that shit about the cops. That's one thing. What you did to me is something else. And they have nothing to do with each other. Understand?"

I nodded. So much for trying to deflect his attention. I'd hoped he'd ignore that detail. The kid was crazy, but apparently not entirely stupid.

"You've already caused me more grief," he went on, "than most people who are still walking around. I've been taking heat for two days because of you. Lots of heat. And when that happens, I like to pass it along. Remind those responsible that I don't like to be made to look like an asshole."

The kid reached down to my shorts, fingered the faded material, rubbed a thumb over a clock face. I tried to move back deeper in the chair, and it felt like my genitals were trying to climb up into my body. "You know," he said with a smile, "time's running out." He giggled briefly. Nice to know Tony New had a sense of humor. Yeah, real encouraging.

He moved back a couple of steps. He smiled again, then spoke as though thinking aloud. "I've heard that old men's bones are real brittle. Snap just like that." He broke his cigarette in half and dropped it on the floor.

"I told you. I'm doing the best I can." My voice rose almost as high as the kid's, a squeal of panic. I tried to get up, but the guy behind me put his hands on my shoulders and pressed firmly down.

The kid ignored me. "Know anything about that, Rudy?" he asked the bruiser in front.

"Toes is real good, boss," Rudy said, and yucked a couple of times.

"Hey—" I squawked.

Rudy knelt down. I tried to squirm away. Hands tightened, moving closer to my windpipe. Rudy put his knee on top of one foot, pinioning it with his whole two seventy-five or so pounds. One hand tightly held my free leg, and his other gripped my toes and started to bend them back.

I desperately searched for something to say, but all I managed was another "Hey—"

Rudy looked over his shoulder at the kid, for the go-ahead.

After a moment's consideration, a connoisseur weighing alternatives, Tony New said, "Let's not start there. You never know; we may want him to be able to move around."

Rudy shrugged and stood up. Clearly, he was a craftsman used to satisfying a demanding patron. I relaxed a little, just enough so that I was unprepared when Rudy suddenly grabbed my left wrist. Without pausing he had my little finger braced against his other hand while a large thumb pressed it out and back. My body was seized in a rising spiral of pain. My mouth opened to scream, but some kind of cloth or gag was jammed into it. The pain was so bad I could almost hear it. And then I did hear it. A sharp crack. Not much. Like a twig breaking. Only, it sounded to me like a gunshot, and the crack went through me like the thrust of a spear.

Holy fucking shit! Goddamn! Sweat poured out of my forehead and colors flashed and spun behind my eyeballs. An insane howl surged, burning, up my throat, to be muffled by whatever was in my mouth. Goddamn! Goddamn! Goddamn!

I blinked to clear my eyes. I saw my finger bent at a

wrong angle at the first joint. The initial rush of pain had subsided, yielding to regular throbs that began at the end of my finger and pulsated over and through my body. My heart was pounding so hard it almost literally shook me. I felt more drained, exhausted, hollow than I could ever remember. And this was little, just the beginning, but I knew I wasn't going to be able to take a lot more. And I knew I had to stop it soon, or I'd never get out of this chair again.

To paraphrase what someone once said, there's nothing like excruciating torture to help focus the mind. Mine, at least, saw a glimmer.

I lifted my head and looked at Tony New. He was staring back, coolly interested, detached, as though comparing my response with reactions he'd elicited in the past. I doubted that I had ever hated anyone so much, had ever wanted so badly to inflict pain in return. Had ever been so powerless to do so.

I pulled the gag from my mouth. It was an old piece of toweling. They came prepared. I wondered how many other screams it had muffled.

I considered saying something like, "Thanks, I needed that," but decided these were not the fellows to appreciate a show of spunk and resistance. Instead, I tried to sound all beaten and subservient. It wasn't hard.

"You didn't need to do this." I gingerly held up my injured hand. "I always knew you were serious."

"Serious? We haven't even started, old man."

"Oh, I know you can do whatever you want to me, but believe me, I'm not going to be able to hold up to much more."

"So?"

"So killing me isn't going to do you any good."

"It's not going to do you no good, neither," the guy behind me burst out. It was the first I'd heard from him. What a sense of repartee. He didn't so much talk as bray.

"Shut up, shithead," the kid said. His tone indicated that every time Shithead opened his mouth, the kid told him to shut it.

"I mean," I went on quickly while I had the chance, "that you're getting heat. You said so. Well, it's not going to help you to go to those people and say that Spanner got the money but you got Spanner. A dead old man in exchange for three-quarters of a million? No one's going to congratulate you on making a good deal."

At first I was afraid that I'd pushed it too far; then I saw that Tony was seriously thinking about it. Maybe he was rising fast, like everyone said, but there was still a lot of weight on top of him. Screwing up with that kind of money had never yet advanced anyone in any organization.

"What do you think this is all about, old man? Hand over the dough. If you give it to me, I'll consider leaving you alone."

"I wish I could, but I don't think I'm going to be able to get it back."

"Fucking old men!" the kid said to the ceiling in what seemed to be becoming a refrain. "Why am I wasting my time with this asshole? Rudy, get on with it."

"Wait a second. I haven't finished." I took a deep breath. Here it was. If I could sell the kid, I'd see an-another day. If not . . . "I may not be able to get your dough, but I might be able to get you the cocaine."

"Shit!" The kid looked disgusted. "Rudy."

"You can kill me or you can have a chance to get your dope." I shrugged. Christ, I wished I felt as cavalier as I sounded.

"Where's an old fart like you going to come up with fifteen keys of coke?"

"The police."

"What're you trying to pull? I'm getting tired of being jerked around by an old shit like you."

"Look, I'm not guaranteeing it. I just said there's a chance."

"How?"

"You're not the only one who's getting heat. I'm taking plenty, too. From the cops. Sergeant Nicholson."

"That bastard! He's been on me a long time."

"Yeah. He wants you bad. He's pissed at me because I queered his deal. Thinks I'm somehow connected with you."

"You and me? What a dumb shit." Nicholson's mistake seemed to amuse him, though. "Go on."

"I think he wants you bad enough that maybe, just maybe, I can convince him to let me have the coke in order to set you up. So he can nail you."

"This is supposed to tempt me?"

"Suppose I double-crossed the cops? Broke the setup so that you got the dope but stayed in the clear."

There. It was all out. Would the kid buy it? Or would Rudy go back to work? At least the kid was considering it.

"Why should I think you'll play it that way, like you said?"

I looked at Tony New, trying to strike just the right note. "If you were in my place, who'd you want after you? You or the cops?"

The kid thought, then nodded. "You're right. It'd be much healthier to have the cops pissed at you." He smiled in that way that made my bowels twitch.

I'd guessed right. If there was one thing Tony New believed, it was that everyone was scared shitless of him. That was motivation he could understand—maybe all he could understand.

"This setup idea—" he said. "How can I be sure the switch'll work?"

"I don't know how we'll do it yet, but I'm pretty sure we can come up with something that'll make you feel okay. If you don't like the way it looks, then you don't do it. Either way, you're clear. What do you say? Let me see if I can get this going. What do you have to lose?"

"Boss, I—"

"Shut up, shithead."

I didn't know what advice Shithead was going to offer, but I was glad he shut up, because it looked to me as though Tony New was sold. He was nodding as he figured the angles, then said to himself as though he decided the matter, "That cocksucker Nicholson'll shit blue mud." The thought made him flash me that discomforting smile. "Okay. You got one more day to get this going. If you don't, you won't have to bother making plans for the rest of the week. Got it?"

I nodded, relaxing a little. The future wasn't exactly welcoming, but at least there *was* one, which was more than I'd had a few minutes ago. A day at a time, Spanner. That was all you could ask for. Yeah, sure.

"Rudy, why don't you repair this old gentleman's finger?"

I didn't want the ape to touch me again, but the kid

assured me Rudy had been a medic in Viet Nam and was very good. I could only guess what else he'd learned there.

Actually, Rudy was pretty good. He got my finger straight again, made a splint out of the handle of a spoon —after snapping off the top as though it were made of plastic—and taped both up against my third finger. It was a little awkward, but it would do the job.

While Rudy was working, Tony New got all warm and friendly, or as much so as that cold-blooded little reptile probably ever got.

"What made you say you were with Sal Piccolo?"

I hesitated, then: "That was the name he gave me."

"You didn't know him?"

I shook my head. "Said he was a friend of a friend. I didn't check. He told me he needed help." I decided to hold onto whatever edge I got from the knowledge that Sal was really alive. I just had to hope Tony didn't know about my old connection with his grandfather.

Apparently not, because he just nodded. "What did this guy look like?"

"About sixty, I guess. Medium height. Kind of heavy."

Tony frowned, then shook his head. "I'd like to know who that son of a bitch was."

"Believe me, so would I." I sounded very sincere.

"At least you know it wasn't Sal Piccolo."

"Now I do. I've been poking around today." Since Tony seemed so conversational, I decided to push it a little further. "Piccolo was the guy who set up your cocaine arrangement, wasn't he?"

His eyes narrowed and he stared hard at me. "You're pretty sharp for an old fart, aren't you?"

I shrugged. "I hear things. I put things together."

"Yeah, he fixed it up. Got a line of supply. Shipment. Tied in with a guy at the airport who'd see to it that every once in a while a suitcase from a South American flight never got to the baggage pick-up place. A fucking sweet arrangement. All he needed was some capital and a connection here."

"And you could get those?"

"Right."

"And then he died?"

"Right again."

"But not before everything was all set to go?" Tony New just smiled. "Too bad for him," I said.

"Yeah, wasn't it?"

"But okay for you?"

The kid gave me a look that made me think maybe I'd gone too far, but then he grinned, showing little white teeth. He was the kind who never worried about hiding anything, whose past atrocities were merely a source of pride. There was never any guilt, because, for him, there could be no crime, only expediency, only what he wanted. Everything else was unimportant, separate from him, unconnected.

"You're smart, old man." He pointed a small soft finger at me. "But don't ever start thinking you're too smart. If you get the idea of pulling anything fancy, remember that other old man. Sal Piccolo was smart. But I didn't need him anymore. He was in my way. So I got him out of the way."

"You did the fire?" Tony New smiled. "How could you be sure you'd catch him?"

"I made sure." He smiled again, then hit his palm with a fist to show he'd knocked him out.

Christ! I tried to stay cool, but this was too much. "But he was your grandfather—"

Tony New's choirboy face flushed an angry dark red. "He was a fucking old fart." His voice was a nearly inaudible squeak.

"But the other people there . . ."

He glared at me, then said, "Let's go." He paused at the door, looked back, pointed. "Tomorrow," he hissed. Then he left, followed by Rudy and Shithead.

I was okay for a couple of minutes, then I started to shake. Some kind of uncontrollable delayed reaction, a combination of fear and pain, anger and resentment, hatred and rage and almost unbelievable disgust. My bare, skinny legs knocked together; shivers made my chest and back and shoulders twitch. I thought I would be sick, but I couldn't get out of the chair to go to the bathroom. Then slowly it subsided, leaving me feeling very cold and empty. And frightened. And eager to inflict pain, to make that mutated little monster squirm on the end of a pin. And helpless to do anything about it.

Although I was in shit up to my eyebrows and Sal Piccolo was responsible, I felt a sort of perverse admiration for him. Also a sort of perverse pleasure, because I knew that Tony New was in a lot of hot water, and I was the instrument of his difficulties. It was a small and existential satisfaction, that of the martyr, but it was the only one I had.

The situation was nearly completely clear. Had I ever been right to doubt that people might change. I apparently hadn't changed, or Sal wouldn't have been able to play on me like a goddamn violin. And Sal sure hadn't. Not only was he incredibly devious; he was the same vindictive son of a bitch he'd always been. He waited a long time, but finally found a way to get back at me after all those years. And in such a way that it would settle a more recent score and make him rich at the same time. And all the while keeping him completely safe.

Despite everything, I had to laugh. It was as nice a scheme as I had ever come across. I did all the work. The puppetmaster just sat back and waited. If it failed, he was out some money—the five hundred he used to hook me, the limo rental, other props—but nothing more. And if it worked, he was home free, invisible, untouchable, unsuspected—he was dead, for Christ sake!—and there was only Jake Spanner, the fucking stupid old dick, standing alone in the spotlight saying, "Huh?"

Nice. Very, very nice.

I didn't feel much like eating, anymore, but I had a shower. It cleaned my body but there was still the stench of fear in my nostrils.

I got into bed and picked up the adventures of Al Tracker. He was hanging by his fingers from a freeway overpass. How did he get there? I didn't care. After recent events, Al's exploits seemed all too tame and plausible.

I turned off the light and studied the inside of my eyelids.

CHAPTER TWENTY

It was a long, unpleasant night, not made any easier by the fact that for most of it I was unsure what was nightmare and what was waking recollection. Didn't exactly make me greet the morning with a song on my lips, especially since I couldn't help but wonder if this was going to be my last Friday.

The hell with it, I told myself. I still had a few cards to play. Right now they looked like twos and threes, but they still could prove to be trumps.

I put on my most sober, respectable-looking clothes. For the selling job I had to do, I didn't want to come across like a decrepit old fool. Instead, I looked like Willie Loman on a bad day. Must have a word with my tailor.

I was downtown pretty early and had to wait for Sergeant Nicholson. When he finally showed, I didn't get much of a reception, but he did take me into his little cubicle. It didn't look like he'd changed his clothes, or his disposition.

I told Nicholson some of the things I'd found out, then explained my idea. His response was to the point. "You must think I'm a complete asshole," he said, but since he didn't throw me out, I went through it once more.

After the fourth time, Nicholson was chewing on it, nervously fidgeting with a yellow pencil. The pencil snapped in half. A shiver went down my spine, and my stomach did a flip. It sounded just like my finger breaking. Nicholson looked at the two pieces in his hand. "Oh, fuck." He opened a drawer in his desk and rummaged around in the back of it, finally coming out with a crumpled half-full pack of cigarettes. He took one out, lit it, inhaled deeply. "Three months," he said. "Then you come along." The nicotine didn't seem to be making him any more cheerful.

I kept talking to him. With every go-round I thought it was sounding better and better, but then, I wasn't precisely impartial. "What've you got to lose?" I finally said. I seemed to be saying that a lot lately.

Nicholson looked with equal distaste at me and the butt between his fingers which had burned down to the filter. "You mean besides three quarters of a million in coke, my job, my pension, my self-respect, and my sanity?"

Before I could say something bright, he got up and left me alone for quite a while. I figured the longer he was away, the better my hand looked. He came back, we talked some more, and he went out again. That went on for most of the morning. Every once in a while, someone poked a head in the door, stared at me without expression, then left. I could imagine the conversations that were going on. At least I didn't hear the howls of laughter.

About noon Nicholson came in and looked sourly at me. "Tell me I'm not making a mistake," he said.

"You're not making a mistake."

"What do you know? You're full of shit." He sat down, sighed heavily. "All right. We'll give it a try."

I breathed in deeply, hoping my relief wasn't too evident.

"How you going to set it up?" he said.

"I'll give him a call." Nicholson waved an inviting hand at the phone. "I think it'll be better if I call from outside."

Nicholson stuck out his lower lip, but said, "Yeah, I suppose." He pointed. "After all this, he damn well better bite."

I'll say.

"You know," he went on, "we haven't even started, and they're already calling this 'Nicholson's Folly.' "

It could be worse, I thought. It could become known as Spanner's Last Stand.

I went a couple blocks away from headquarters, found a phone, and called the kid's office. I said it was all set, but he told me to shut up. He asked where I was, then gave me the location of another phone booth that was not too far away, told me to be there in twenty minutes, and hung up. He must've had the numbers for pay phones all over the city, so he could always arrange conversations without worrying about a tap. I was starting to realize the kid was more than just a vicious mutant. He had some brains as well. It wasn't a combination that delighted me.

I found the new booth at the rear of a parking lot, completely out in the open in case anyone wanted to watch. I wasn't there long before it rang.

"What's the story?" the kid said. From the background noise, it sounded like he'd also gone to a phone booth.

"Nicholson bought it. It was hard, but I got him to agree. He's mad to get you."

That awful, high-pitched giggle filled my ear. "Go on."

"Well, I fixed up with Nicholson that I'd arrange delivery to you in some location. You're supposed to think that they'll be staking that out, and we set up to meet someplace else. I tell Nicholson. They stake out the second location and nail you when I deliver."

"Go on."

"But I never get to the second location. I hand it over to you someplace else, someplace where you can get away, safe and clean."

"Like where?"

"How about using a bridge or an overpass?" My book last night hadn't helped take my mind off of anything, but the detective hanging by his fingers had given me an idea. "We plan it so I have to cross a bridge on the way to the delivery point. It'll be over another street, or a freeway, or something. You'll be waiting down below. I'll drop the stuff over to you, and you take off. That way, even if I'm followed, you can be far away before they even get down to the lower road."

There was a long silence. I held my breath; then I heard that laugh starting again, a nasty, gleeful sound, and I knew he liked it.

"Old man, that's nice. The cops think you're double-crossing me but you're really double-crossing them. That bastard Nicholson'll shit." Again the giggle. "Now, where's this gonna happen?"

"You pick it. You're the one that has to feel comfortable."

"That's right. And don't forget it."

We talked a bit and decided where all of this—the first

drop, the second drop, the real drop —would take place, and worked out a time for that night.

"If you're thinking about shitting me," Tony New said when it was all straight, "just keep Sal Piccolo in mind. If you fuck with me, being burned alive is going to seem like a positive pleasure. Remember."

"I'll remember," I said, but the phone was dead.

I hung up, then held onto the receiver as my knees suddenly turned weak with relief. It was all falling into place. If I hadn't been worried about being watched, I might've done a little jig. My hand of twos and threes was starting to seem pretty potent. Pretty damn potent.

Everything would go just like I told Tony New. The stake-out, the drop from the bridge, everything. Except, besides fifteen kilos of cocaine, the bag would also contain a tiny transmitter. If Tony New didn't make the pickup himself, the cops'd follow the coke until it got to him. Then that would be that. Nicholson's problems would be solved. Mine would be solved. And Tony New wouldn't have to worry about anything for a good long time.

I wasn't going to double-cross the cops, but triple-cross Tony New. Ah, Spanner, I thought; Sal Piccolo wasn't the only devious son of a bitch.

I walked around a bit, trying to see if I was being tailed, but didn't spot anyone. From another phone booth I called Nicholson and told him everything was perfect.

"Wonderful," he said, sounding like he just found out he had gonorrhea. He told me to come back to the station later in the afternoon.

Except for this last week, I hadn't been downtown more than a handful of times since I retired. I wandered the streets around Pershing Square, seeing more what had been there than what was there now. Where Henry Gattuso was drowned in a vat of olive oil. Where Stanley Skolnick had been machine-gunned down while carrying the day's takings in a paper bag, and ten thousand in crumpled ones, fives, and tens went blowing down Hill Street, tying up traffic for blocks. Where Farmboy Murdoch had very nearly made me part of the pavement, with a Ford pick-up loaded with cantaloupes. The landmarks were mostly gone, existing only in my memory. Soon they wouldn't even be there, any more than my first office on Spring Street, which was now a five-story parking structure. I'd gone in and out of that building thousands of times, but I realized, with an uncomfortable feeling, that I could no longer remember what color it had been.

The people that hung around the Square, though, hadn't changed. New faces, but that was all. Office workers getting a little sun, old deadbeats with nowhere else to go, small-time crooks waiting to take a bet or hustling up a customer for something stolen or illegal.

I sat on a bench in the sun, close to a statue of a soldier from the Spanish-American War, whose hat was white with pigeon shit. Hardly tasting it, I ate a red-hot burrito from a nearby stand that was scheduled for demolition soon. I felt better than I had when I woke up, but I tried to keep from thinking about the rest of the day, about the craziness I was in the middle of, just wanting it to be over. There were too goddamn many things to go wrong.

An old coot wearing better clothes than mine came over to bum a handout. Even though I figured he had more annual income than I did, I gave him a quarter. Maybe I was trying to build up points someplace. "Look, Spanner's a real good guy; we'll let him keep his neck on this one."

I watched an earnest young Scout try to help a hideous bag lady cross the street. She soundly cursed and beat him. I smiled. That's what was needed. More nastiness. A few more demented loners swearing to themselves.

I went back to see Nicholson. He grunted a few times, then brought out a canvas duffle bag. He opened it and I looked in. There were fifteen brick-sized, plastic-wrapped packages of shiny, translucent, white flaky powder that was worth more than three times its weight in gold.

Cocaine. It had been big in this town almost as long as there'd been a Hollywood. For no reason, I remembered a movie I saw when I was a kid back East. A silent, with Douglas Fairbanks. He played a detective named Coke Ennyday. The movie hadn't made much sense, something to do with Chinese opium smugglers, but it seemed that everyone in it had had a pretty good time.

I looked up at Nicholson. He didn't seem to be enjoying himself especially.

"If this screws up, Spanner, I'm going to pull the plug on you so fast you'll lose your dentures.

My teeth were all mine, but I got the point.

We went over things a few more times. Nicholson seemed increasingly nervous and depressed, reluctant to let so much dope out of his control. I didn't bother to try to reassure him. I had a feeling it wouldn't come out sounding very good.

I picked up the bag. It was heavy. Hell, it contained my future.

For a second, I thought about bowing out, running like hell or throwing myself at Nicholson's feet. Then it passed. I was scared, but I knew I had to go through with it. What surprised me, once it came right down to it, was finding that I wanted to. Crazy old man. I just couldn't learn.

Nicholson walked me to my car. I guessed he didn't want me mugged on the way to the parking lot. I got in.

"We'll be close," he said through the window.

"Not too close."

"Don't you have enough to worry about? Shit." He gazed up at the police building, as though expecting to see every window filled with cops looking down at him and laughing.

After I drove away, I realized he hadn't wished me luck.

CHAPTER TWENTY-ONE

On the way back home I kept going over the layout, especially how it looked from Tony New's end. I realized there were some spaces, that it was maybe not as tight as it should be, but I figured I had slid over those pretty well. I must have. The kid had bought it without much hesitation.

Well, if he wasn't at least a little bit stupid, he wouldn't be doing what he was doing. Right?

I didn't answer myself.

I parked in the garage, pulled out the bag, went in the back. In the living room the blinds were closed. I discovered that Tony New was not quite as stupid as I'd thought.

He was sitting quietly on the couch. Shithead was standing close by.

Holy fucking—

"Gee, I'm sorry," I said, trying to sound a lot calmer than I felt. "I keep forgetting to get that extra key made for you."

"Don't need no key."

"Shut up, shithead," the kid said.

"It's always a pleasure to see you," I said. "You know, *mi casa es su casa,* and all that, but what's going on? I thought—"

"I don't care what you thought. There's been a change."

"But—"

"Shut up, old man, and sit down."

It was my living room, but I accepted the invitation anyway. As I sat in the wing chair, with the bag of dope at my feet, I wished the wings would start to flap and float me out of there.

Instead, the phone rang. I started to get up, but the kid silently pointed me back down. He went into the kitchen and answered it. After a couple of minutes, he came back.

"That was Rudy. He said he couldn't spot any surveillance on you."

Mentally, I sighed. "That's good. Isn't—"

"No, it isn't. It's strange, is what it is."

"But there wasn't supposed—"

"Shut up, old man! I'd like to know why they let you walk loose out of there with fifteen keys of coke."

Tony nodded and Shithead came over, picked up the bag, and set it on the coffee table. He unzipped it, looked inside, whistled appreciatively.

"Get on with it," the kid said.

Shithead opened a small suitcase that I hadn't noticed until then and took out a black rectangular box that was about the size of a walkie-talkie unit. He flipped a switch and held it over the bag.

"It's hot."

Tony New looked at me with a smile that was anything but amused and slowly shook his head. "Find it."

One by one, the bruiser took the white bricks out of the bag and held them up to the box. It was obviously one of those gadgets that told you if there was a bug around. It figured Tony New'd have something like that. I wondered why I hadn't thought about it before. A queasy feeling was spreading through my bowels like a triple dose of a laxative.

"That Nicholson must really think I'm dumb," the kid said as he watched Shithead work. "If he let an old croaker like you go without a tight tail, then he either gave you thirty pounds of quinine or something, or he wired the coke."

Well, I clearly couldn't fault his logic. Mine, however, was looking more and more like wishful thinking, if not complete self-delusion.

With the eighth package Shithead examined, he said, "Got it!" and held it out to his boss. The kid looked disgusted and told him to open it. The bruiser got a large clear plastic bag out of his suitcase and something from his pocket that proved to be a wicked-looking switchblade when it sprang open with a swishing sound. He put the package of cocaine inside the plastic bag, carefully slit the wrapping, and let the lumps of white flakes run out. The package was half-empty when a quarter-sized object dropped out. Shithead picked it up and looked closely at it. "Homing device," he said, handing it to the kid.

Tony New held it in his palm. He wet the tip of his index finger and touched it to the film of dust that covered the transmitter. He rubbed the stuff off inside his upper lip, paused briefly, then grunted appreciatively. "Well, it ain't quinine. Though Nicholson is sure going to wish that it was." He gave a brief little laugh, then stared coldly at me, holding up the device between two fingers. "Now, suppose you tell me about this."

"I don't know anything about it," I said, hoping I sounded shaken, surprised, and completely innocent. I didn't know about the other two, but the first of those qualities came through loud and clear. With good reason.

"No?"

"No."

"You're full of shit, old man." Almost regretfully the kid said, "I guess I'll just have to get my boy to ask the questions."

Shithead yucked a couple of times, then came over and looked down at me speculatively. He still held the open knife. I felt like a Thanksgiving turkey. Now, who wants a wing?

"Really. I don't know—" Before I got to repeat my lie, there was a knock on the door.

"Who's that?" the kid said, looking hard at me.

"I don't know. I can't see through wood."

Shithead brayed a laugh, then quickly swallowed it as he glanced at Tony New. He poked me in the shoulder with his fingertips, hard enough to cause shooting pains down my arm. Why couldn't I remember not to be so damn wise all the time?

"Open it," the kid said. "But stay cool."

The bruiser pulled a gun from his pocket, which looked big enough to stop an elephant, and waved it at me. "Yeah. Be cool."

"Shut up, shithead."

The two of them moved out of the sight line from the

door but kept me covered. I wondered who it could be. The way things were going, I figured it could've been anyone, from the ghost of Christmas past to a Cuban expeditionary force come to liberate the neighborhood.

Oh, shit.

It was Mrs. Bernstein, a ruffled floral apron over a faded floral dress.

"Mr. Spanner, I haven't seen you for a while, so I just wanted to make sure you're still coming for dinner tonight, like you promised. I made your favorite." She smiled.

Shit.

"Gee, Mrs. Bernstein. I'm afraid something's come up. I was just about to call you and—"

"Who's there, Jake?" the kid said, his voice all friendly curiosity.

"Just a neighbor who—"

"Why don't you invite the lady in?"

"No, I don't—"

But Mrs. Bernstein had already walked happily past me into the living room.

"Are these your sons?" She smiled.

"Only if I'd had relations with a gila monster," I muttered.

By then Mrs. Bernstein had noticed the gun. Her smile wavered, then disappeared altogether.

"What's going on, Mr. Spanner? Are you in trouble?"

"Don't worry. It's nothing very serious."

"Lady, sit down," Tony New said, gesturing to a chair.

"Thank you, but I think I'd better—"

"Sit down!" the kid hissed.

"Mrs. Bernstein, you'd better sit down."

She looked at me, and then at them, and then bustled her plump body over to the chair.

"I'm cooking cabbage rolls, and I must get back or else they'll dry out."

"Fuck the cabbage rolls, lady, and shut up!"

"Young man! I—"

"Mrs. Bernstein," I said. "Be quiet. *Please!*"

I couldn't believe it. The nightmare was becoming more and more lunatic.

Tony New looked from me to Mrs. Bernstein. By the time he got back to me again, he was smiling in a way that made me feel like rats were walking through my intestines.

"Now," he said. "I asked you a question before we were interrupted." He held up the transmitter.

"I told you. I don't know anything about it."

The kid smiled again. "Then I guess we'll just have to ask the old lady about it."

He nodded to Shithead, who went and hulked over Mrs. Bernstein. One of his giant paws started to finger her flabby upper arm. At the touch a small yelp escaped from her, but she stifled it. Her body was rigid. She looked at me with watery brown eyes. They looked very large behind the thick lenses of her glasses.

Shit. Shit. Shit.

"All right, all right!" I said. "I'll tell you. Just get him away from her."

Tony New motioned with his head and the ape stepped away, kind of disappointed. I was beginning to hate Shithead almost as much as Rudy.

"Okay. It was a setup. After the drop, the cops were going to stick with the pickup car. If you were in the car, they'd grab you right away. If not, they'd follow it until the dope got to you."

He nodded, like it was what he'd expected. "Whose bright idea was this?"

I didn't say anything.

"Whose?" the kid hissed.

"All right. It was mine."

Tony New stared at me for a long time; then his lips drew back, revealing lots of tiny white teeth. I didn't suppose they were really pointed; they just struck me that way.

"You must've thought you were real smart. Fucking old men."

I kept quite. There wasn't much I could say.

"Dear Grandfather, that cocksucker, thought he was smart. He wasn't. What about you? You still think you are?"

"I guess not," I said with complete sincerity. "Look. The setup is queered. You've got the dope. Why not just take it and go away? Tie us up, leave the transmitter, and walk out free. Hell, by the time they catch on to what's happened, you can probably have the stuff already distributed."

For a minute I thought he was going to go along with it; then he shook his head, with that small sinister grin of his.

"Why not?"

"Because that's what you want me to do. Maybe that's part of your smart little plan."

"Oh, Jesus. I'm not that smart, for Christ sake!"

"No, you're not, old man. But maybe Rudy missed something. Maybe cops are waiting around the corner. . . . No. We'll just play things like they're scheduled. The drop'll go down, only there'll be something else in the bag, and you and I'll keep the snow and go on someplace else. And Nicholson'll be left looking up his ass, wondering what the fuck happened." He laughed in that pleasant way of his. He sure was a cheerful little son of a bitch.

"Then you'll let the lady go? You don't need to hold her."

He smiled and shook his head.

"What for? She has nothing to do with this."

"Insurance."

"What?"

"I go with you. My boy stays with the old broad. That way you don't try anything cute, like speeding or going through a red light, or something to cue the cops. If he doesn't hear from me that everything's okay, he finishes her."

I heard Mrs. Bernstein suck in some air but she didn't move or cry or say anything. I had to hand it to her; she had more spunk than I'd thought.

"Understand?" The kid smiled.

I nodded.

Shit. It was one thing to screw up when it affected you. It was something else when another person got involved. I wasn't crazy about old Mrs. Bernstein, but if nothing else, I'd do my best to see that she got out of this. However, being something that might be considered a witness, she probably didn't have much of a chance. Shit.

"Now just sit down, old man, and we'll wait."

I sat, and we waited. On the kid's instruction, Shithead got out some simple laboratory gear from his case—an alcohol burner, a flask, some glass tubes, a thermometer—

and tested samples from some of the bricks of cocaine. It looked like he was determining the melting point. Whatever he did, all the coke proved to be pure and first class. I was so glad.

At one point Mrs. Bernstein started snuffling a little.

"Don't worry," I tried to reassure her. "It'll all be all right."

She shook her head. "No, the cabbage rolls are ruined."

About three dozen snappy remarks came to mind, but I merely smiled encouragingly.

As I watched Tony New calmly sitting on the couch, feet barely touching the floor, smoking one long cigarette after another, I thought back a couple of centuries to that afternoon, when I sat in Pershing Square and just wanted all this to be over. I still wanted that. What scared me was that I found I was no longer very interested in the way it might turn out. I'd been floating at sea, hanging onto an old log, for so long that I just wanted to let go and sink. And rest. And the hell with everything else.

"J. Spanner: Sank without a trace, in the Slough of Despond."

I shook my head. My broken finger was throbbing. Tony New grinned coldly at me. Mrs. Bernstein shifted in her chair. Not yet, goddammit. Not just yet.

It finally got dark. Shithead found a suitcase of mine and put the coke into it. Then he filled up the original canvas carrier with a bunch of old paperbacks that were stacked in the spare room.

Tony New looked at the dramatic covers and the titles promising havoc, bloodshed, and mayhem, and shook his head. "Is this where you get your ideas, old man? It would've been healthier if you'd stuck to _Reader's Digest._"

For once, I had to agree with him. Hardly anybody in the _Digest_ ever got involved with kidnapping, robbery, the cops, cocaine, or the mob. Mostly they just whittled. Or carved funny faces in apples. Sounded good to me.

The kid dropped the transmitter in with the books, zipped up the bag, and we were ready to go. But not before I had to watch Shithead tie up Mrs. Bernstein, none too gently.

There wasn't much I could say to her, but I tried to say it. She smiled.

Shit.

Tony New and I went out the back door. It was another hot, gritty night, much like the one that had started all this. Cloud cover was low, and no stars were visible.

It figured.

I had wanted to make a wish.

CHAPTER TWENTY-TWO

Tony New had me back the car out of the garage while he stayed shielded by the house. After the Chevy's usual hesitation starting, I pulled even with the back porch, got out, picked up the carrier bag, opened the rear door, and tossed the bag onto the seat. At the same time, Tony New took the suitcase of coke and hustled into the back, where he lay on the floor. He was in view for maybe two seconds, but he needn't have worried. I knew that Nicholson was sticking to the plan and had his men keeping their distance. Even if he hadn't, the sight lines were so bad that an observer would've had to be at the end of the driveway in order even to stand a chance of seeing the kid's entrance into the car.

From his place on the floor behind me, Tony New reminded me not to try anything funny. As an aid to my memory, he showed me a nasty-looking automatic.

Again, he needn't have worried. Even without considering the hostage Mrs. Bernstein, I had no more bright ideas. The cops would be staying out of sight, following from at least a couple of blocks away, and all regular units in the area would undoubtedly have been alerted and told to avoid me at all costs. Short of having an accident, there was no way I could attract attention. No, I'd just have to play it by the book and hope that somewhere along the line something would present itself.

Like maybe the kid getting carsick. Yeah, sure.

I didn't have that far to go to make the drop. Tony New had arranged for it to take place near the southwest corner of Burbank, close to where there were three or four movie and TV studios, and, more importantly, where there were five places that the city streets over-passed the Ventura Freeway.

I drove carefully, staying well within the speed limit and minding all traffic lights, and reached the drop point without incident in about fifteen minutes. I crossed to the end of the overpass and pulled up, just above the outside westbound lane. I was in exactly the right place at ex-actly the right time. Everything was going like clockwork. Wonderful.

I got out on my side. There was no other traffic. After dark there hardly ever was, except on certain main streets. I opened the rear door. Tony was propped up on an el-bow, smiling and pointing his gun at me.

"You're doing fine, old man. Just keep it up."

I got the duffle bag off the seat, shut the door, and walked over to the side of the bridge. I thought about get-ting the transmitter out of the bag and pocketing it. I glanced over my shoulder. It was dark, but I could still see the top of the kid's head through the rear window and knew he was watching me.

I looked over the guardrail. Traffic was light on the freeway. About fifty yards away, a car was pulled onto the shoulder. Its hood was up and a couple of warning flares were lit behind it. I could just make out a figure standing next to the front fender.

I hoisted the bag up to the guardrail, then pushed it over so that it fell into the low creeping plants that cov-ered the sloping sidewall of the highway. As soon as the bag hit, I saw the hood of the car come down and the figure start to move toward where it had landed. I went back to the car and got in.

"Was he there?" Tony New said.

"Yeah. Who was it? Rudy?"

"No. Just some kid. Doesn't know what this is all about. Just that he's to pick up a package and deliver it to an address in Woodland Hills." He giggled.

Woodland Hills was one of the more recently devel-oped areas, an expensive suburb of large ranch-style houses, about twenty miles away. I guessed that that was what he thought was so funny, the cops chasing clear across the Valley after nothing, after a hired punk with a load of sleazy paperbacks. Pretty hilarious, all right.

My link was cut. I was alone and on my own. I could

remember when I used to like that feeling, when that feeling was one of the reasons I had chosen my line of work. But that was a long time ago, a time when, even though I was on my own, I still had some resources to draw upon. Now all I had was a scared feeling deep in my stomach and a jaw that was starting to ache from the tension.

"What now?" I said.

The kid gave me directions. I went along a surface street that ran next to the freeway, then turned into Griffith Park. This was about six square miles of nature straddling the eastern end of the Santa Monica Mountains. Even with a golf course, zoo, planetarium, outdoor theater, thirty or so miles of road, and lots of picnic grounds, there was still plenty of wilderness there, and at night, much of the park was as deserted an area as you could find anywhere in the city. It was a good place if you wanted privacy.

After I'd been driving through the park for five minutes, Tony New sat up on the seat directly behind me and nestled the barrel of his gun in the hollow behind my right ear. We drove around for a while, taking random turns. At one point we ran next to Forest Lawn Cemetery, which bordered on part of the park. I tried hard not to see any significance in that. I didn't quite succeed.

When the kid was finally satisfied that we weren't being tailed, he directed me to one of the picnic grounds, halfway between the theater and the planetarium. If something was on at the theater, the parking area was always filled, but nothing was playing that night, and there was only one car there, way at the farthest corner, near the trees. It was a black Oldsmobile, with license number SAM 726, which had recently been of passing interest in my life. Rudy was leaning his bulk against it, smoking a cigarette.

I parked near the car and turned off the engine. The kid told me to get out, then got out himself, holding the suitcase. Rudy stood up straight, looking as alert as was possible, with the pea that served him for a brain. I noticed that his pants only just reached his ankles and his socks didn't match. Pretty dapper.

"Clear?" Tony New said.

Rudy nodded.

They both looked at me as though I wasn't really there. With a chill of recognition, I realized that I soon wouldn't be.

"Hey—" I started to say.

Tony New made a small motion with his head, like shaking off an annoying fly. "Finish him," he hissed.

That was all. It was that easy for him. A matter of no significance. Just some minor waste to dispose of.

My knees buckled momentarily and my hands and feet went cold. I knew I couldn't reason with him, and I wasn't going to beg, so I just looked at him.

He gave me his little viper's grin. "You ripped me off. And then you tried to set me up. That's two times too many, old man." He turned to Rudy. "Do it."

Rudy pulled a cannon out of his pocket and took a couple of heavy steps toward me.

"Slow or fast?" he asked.

The kid looked at me and then at the suitcase he was carrying. Prudence won out; he wasn't willing to risk three quarters of a million dollars, even for the great pleasure my slow death would have brought him. "Let's get out of here," he said, and glanced around. "Take him over there." He indicated the picnic tables that were among the trees beyond the paved parking lot.

Rudy waved his gun. I walked in front of him. He silently pointed to where he wanted me to go.

Seventy-eight years scuffling and hustling, working and struggling, and it was going to end next to a wire rubbish container with a sign on it saying, "Help keep your park clean."

No way. No fucking way. They were going to kill me, but I wasn't going to be a goddamn lamb on my way to the slaughter.

Age had taken nearly every possibility away from me, but my age was also the only advantage I had left. As far as Rudy was concerned, I was too old to try anything. Had I been twenty years younger, he would've been more cautious. As it was, he was much too casual, walking too close, probably thinking ahead to having something to eat or getting laid.

I let my ankle twist under me on the uneven ground. A cry of surprise, and I went down on my hands and knees. Rudy nearly tripped over me, then prodded me with a toe. I scrabbled with my hand and picked up some loose soil. Thank god the ground was dry and dusty. With a quickness that amazed me—not to say Rudy—I leaped to my feet, whirled around, and hurled the dirt in his eyes, all in one smooth simultaneous movement.

There was no way I was anywhere near strong enough to grapple with the brute, but I didn't need much strength to slow him down some. My foot kicked out and the toe of my shoe caught him square on the kneecap. For my visit downtown I had foregone my usual sneakers or sandals, and had on a pair of heavy brogans, left over from a time when I'd spent a lot of hours walking rain-slick winter streets. It was a good solid blow that caused him to grunt with pain, but that also almost caused me to overbalance and fall on my back. I caught myself, though, and saw him hopping on one leg, rubbing his eyes. I took careful aim and kicked again. This time right in his crotch. He said something like "Ork, ork!" I knew that I might not live out the next five minutes, but at that instant I sure as hell felt joyful. Rudy made that sound again, clutched himself, and, almost in slow motion, began to sink to the ground. My arm shot out straight ahead. The heel of my palm caught him flush on the nose. I felt a flash of pain go from my wrist to my elbow to my shoulder, and I knew that I'd jammed my arm good. I also felt his nose squish flag beneath my hand. Rudy's profile, hardly very Roman to begin with, would henceforth be even more anthropoid. I hadn't broken anyone's nose since 1937. I remembered it felt pretty good the last time as well.

Rudy continued his descent to the ground. After my dazzling exhibition I should've been able to stay around and admire my handiwork, but I knew I had to take advantage of the time I'd bought, and get going. It would've been better if I'd been able to go into the woods, but that direction was all uphill and I knew I wouldn't get more than forty or fifty yards before I'd collapse in a panting heap. Adrenalin was making me feel pretty good at that moment, but I still knew that in my case, reality equaled gravity. So I started moving toward the parking lot with a stiff-legged, ice-skating kind of stride—more a fast walk than a real run—heading back down the road in the hope that I'd run into someone before the pair caught up with me.

Out of the corner of my eye I saw Tony New, suitcase still in his hand, jumping up and down and shrieking hysterically, like a stir-crazy inhabitant of a monkey house. "Get up, motherfucker! Get up! Get that fucking bag of bones! Get him!"

I glanced back. Holy shit! Rudy was getting to his feet. If he'd had even a minimally developed nervous system, he would've been out for at least a few minutes. Christ! The son of a bitch was so goddamn primitive he could probably regenerate severed limbs.

I picked up the pace. After a couple of minutes—which seemed like a couple of hours—my old brogans, which had done such good service, suddenly felt like they were made of iron. It was harder and harder for me to lift my feet. Soon, I really was skating over the pavement, dragging-pushing my legs in a spastic shuffle, gasping in air that felt like liquid fire, molten smog.

I looked back. Rudy was gaining, getting close. Blood was gushing from his nose, dripping from his chin, splashing down on his white rayon shirt. He wasn't moving very well, limping, his heavy bulky body not designed for speed, but it wouldn't take a world-class sprinter to catch me. My shuffling strides were getting shorter and shorter, and a moderately mobile tortoise would soon be more than my match.

I didn't have to look back anymore. I heard Rudy's bubbling breath, sucked in through his mouth, louder even than the roaring waterfall inside my skull. I could sense his bulk behind me.

A clubbing blow between my shoulder blades expelled what little air had gotten to my lungs. I went sprawling, arms and legs flying out in four opposing directions. I hit ground with my hands, then my forearms, then elbows, knees, shins, chest, and then chin. I tried a kind of crawl-in motion, but my arm still hurt from hitting him, and wouldn't work.

A large foot dug in under me and roughly rolled me over. Rudy straddled me, a foot on either side of my heaving chest. I tried to grab an ankle but he kicked my hand off, then stood heavily on my wrist. I looked up into his eyes. They were expressionless, like little red marbles. A drop of crimson blood fell from his nose and splattered on my cheek.

His gun was in his hand, moving toward my head. My eyes were fastened on the bottomless dark circle of the barrel. My only thought was that I wasn't ready. Shit! Seventy-eight years and I still wasn't ready. I felt more alive at that moment that I could recall feeling for ages.

There was a tremendous clanging, whirring, roaring sound. A huge wind swept over us. A dazzling, blinding light covered us, bleaching all color. What the hell was happening? It was like the hand of God was reaching down to pluck a damned old fool from his self-inflicted fate.

Then a tinny, metallic voice boomed down from above. "This is the police. The area is surrounded. Throw down your weapon and do not move."

The light shifted slightly, and I was looking up at a black and white L.A.P.D. helicopter.

Sounds of sirens. Cars screeching to a halt. More lights. Shouts.

Rudy squinted upward, bewildered, indecisive.

With energy I didn't think I had, I reached up and grabbed the revolver from his slack fingers. He looked down, surprised, then started to run toward the trees. Three quick shots exploded from somewhere behind the blazing lights. Rudy's legs seemed to give way beneath him. He fell onto his face and lay twitching, groaning.

I fell back. My mouth dropped open. I couldn't tell what I was feeling—relief, or exhaustion, or utter disbelief. Or all three. It hardly mattered.

I laughed. It seemed there was no end to the ludicrous absurdity. Talk about a *deus ex machina!* Incredible. I'd been rescued by the goddamn cavalry.

I laughed again, so hard tears filled my eyes. I was probably in a mild state of shock, slightly hysterical.

"Hey! Are you okay?" a voice said above me.

I stopped howling and blinked my eyes clear. Nicholson was leaning over me, looking surprisingly concerned.

"Oh, yeah," I said. "Fine."

"You sure? We got an ambulance on the way."

I shook my head. "Just help me up."

Nicholson pulled me to my feet. I almost crumpled back down, but the cop caught and held me. The momentary lightheadedness passed and I waved him off.

"You sure you're okay?"

"I'm sure. Just a little shaky, a few scrapes, is all."

Nicholson smiled. I thought back. It must've been the first time I'd seen him do that. "You know, you're one tough old goat."

"Yeah. It's swell, isn't it?"

I looked around. There were half a dozen cars, marked and unmarked, doors all open, lights on, a cacophony of police radios spitting incomprehensibly. Most of the cops were in two groups, one around Rudy, the other back near my car, where I'd last seen Tony New. The helicopter was sitting in a far corner of the parking area.

"Don't misunderstand the question," I said, "but what the hell are you doing here?"

"There was another transmitter hidden in the trunk of your car. I had it put there while you were sitting around my office."

"You did? How come?"

"Hell! You don't think I was going to let enough snow to make it Christmas in July, go sailing out without some kind of back-up."

That made sense, but I knew there was something else. I raised an eyebrow at Nicholson.

He shrugged, then nodded. "I also had a feeling that Novallo might try to change the game. I wanted to be ready."

"Well, shit! If that's what you thought, why didn't you stake out my place?"

"I considered it but decided it might put you in jeopardy if something went wrong."

"You mean, as opposed to the way it turned out—where I was always entirely safe and secure and never in any danger? Wonderful!"

He looked a little sheepish. "Well, we did cut it a bit close." I made a face. "Yeah, I'm sorry. Really. We were tailing you all the way, cars moving all over, keeping close, but not too close. Then, when you came into the park, it got tough, difficult to get near without being either seen or heard. When you finally settled down here, it took a couple of minutes to get things organized."

I thought of a few bright things to say but decided against it. Nicholson knew we'd both been luckier than we had any right to expect, and I saw no point in pushing it.

"Why didn't you at least tell me about the second transmitter?"

"If it came down to it, I figured it'd be easier for you to deny something if you could do it honestly."

He was probably right about that; I might not have been able to keep it hidden. But it still annoyed me. From the beginning, I'd been a shuttlecock in a deadly and demented game of badminton, and I was getting tired of it. First Sal, then the kid, now Nicholson. Let's run Spanner up the flagpole and see if anyone shoots him down.

Oh, the hell with it. I hadn't exactly been an innocent bystander.

Throughout our conversation Nicholson and I had been walking across the parking lot toward the circle of police around Tony New. When we got there, a couple of cops moved aside and I saw the kid lying on the ground. With both arms he was tightly clutching the suitcase of coke to his chest. He was rolling around, violently flailing his legs, bouncing his head onto the blacktop, cursing, howling, growling, flecks of spittle misting around his terribly distorted face. It was nice to see him bearing up so well under adversity.

"He wasn't shot, was he?"

Nicholson shook his head. "No. Just went crazy. Christ! We're waiting for a net to arrive."

Just then the kid rolled over. He let go of the case and raised himself up on his hands and knees. The cops in the circle tensed and steadied their weapons. The kid was barely recognizable as anything human, more like a bizarre, rabid animal. His eyes were the color of dirty concrete.

"Fucking old man! I'm going to take you apart! You're dead! You're dead!" He shrieked, hissed, howled, then started rolling and foaming again.

Hmm. I was getting used to this. It seemed that every forty years a member of the Piccolo family swore vengeance on me.

"Don't worry," Nicholson said as we moved away. "With what we've got, we can get bail set so high that it'll look like the national debt. He won't get out before his trial. And he sure as hell won't get out after."

"Well, if he takes as long as Sal did to honor his pledge, I'm not too concerned."

"Huh?" Nicholson said.

"Nothing. Just thinking out loud."

Nicholson looked at me, smiled. "You've had a rough night. I think we better get you home."

Home. Oh, shit! In the excitement of the last ten minutes I'd kind of forgotten.

"I'm afraid the night's not over yet."

"What do you mean?"

I told him about the happy little get-together at my place. Nicholson swore, then said he'd send a dozen units over. They'd completely surround the house, leaving Shithead no choice but to surrender.

I shook my head. "Listen. The guy that's in there—well, I've known salads that were smarter. You back him into a corner, there's no telling what he might do."

"Then you've got an idea?"

I thought a minute. I had an idea. Nicholson didn't seem delighted by it.

"Look," I said, "it can't possibly make anything worse, and it could be the easiest solution." He looked skeptical. "Besides, I figure you owe me one, after . . ." I waved my hand at the parking lot.

Nicholson looked sourly at me. He pulled a cigarette from his pocket, lit it, inhaled, exhaled, jerked it from his mouth with his thumb and forefinger and glowered at it, threw it to the ground, savagely twisted his heel on it.

"You know something?" he said.

"What?"

"I sure as hell am glad my old man is nothing like you."

He turned and went to his car to issue instructions.

CHAPTER TWENTY-THREE

I was fading fast, almost visibly deflating, like a punctured tire. My hands were trembling slightly. My brain wouldn't focus, kept drifting off to some soft gray blankness. My tongue wouldn't obey, slurring my speech. It was like I'd had a stroke, but I knew it was only fatigue—absolute, total fatigue.

I figured I'd done pretty well for myself, but there were limits, and I'd gone way beyond them. You could kid yourself only so far, then physiology took over. Like it or not, I was too old for this kind of stuff.

I wanted to bow out, let Nicholson take it, and just sleep, sleep, sleep. But I wouldn't. I had to see it through. Sal knew I couldn't let things slide, and once again I was going to prove him right. Pump myself up again. Hold on for another ten, fifteen minutes. It was sure swell to be so consistent.

I cleaned and straightened myself up. I didn't want it to be obvious that there'd been a struggle. I wanted to look calm and quiet and self-possessed. Yeah. Fat chance.

A cop drove my car to within a block of my house and got out. I slid behind the wheel, managed to go the rest of the way, and pulled up in front of my place. As I did, I saw the other cops already in position, hidden by the bushes and shadows of the neighboring houses. I paused a minute, clutching the wheel, taking deep breaths. Hold on, Spanner; just a little longer. I put my hand in my jacket pocket and felt the smooth solidity of the blackjack Nicholson had given me.

A light blinked. Long—short—long. Everything was ready.

One more deep breath and I got out of the car, loudly slamming the door. I didn't want the goon inside to think that anyone was trying to sneak up. I hummed tunelessly going up the front walk, and made a lot of noise opening the screen door and getting my key in the lock. As I pushed the door open, I pressed the brass button on the side, which unlocked it. I stepped inside, shutting the door behind me, and was greeted by Shithead, standing five feet away, gun held out in front of him, a confused, desperate expression on his face.

I held up my hands placatingly. "Relax. Relax. It's only me. I— Who the hell is that?"

I pointed to the other armchair. The first still held Mrs. Bernstein, securely tied. The second was now occupied as well. A fiftyish man with thinning gray hair, glasses, and a small droopy mustache had his hands tied behind the back of the chair. From the whimpering sounds he made, I didn't think he was enjoying himself.

Shithead yucked a couple of times. "You got company."

I ignored him. "Who are you?" I said to the man.

He moved his mouth but nothing came out.

"This is Mr. Bemelman," Mrs. Bernstein said brightly. "He's the director of the Senior Center." She sounded like she was making introductions at an Hadassah social.

"So? What's he doing here?"

Bemelman finally found his voice. It was thin and strained. "Our Miss Eustace told me she was concerned about you. She thought you were ill, experiencing hallucinations."

"She's right. You don't have to worry. This is all a delusion. It'll soon pass and you'll be okay."

Bemelman started to whimper again. Mrs. Bernstein said, "There, there."

I rolled my eyes toward the ceiling. Was there no end to this?

"Hey!" Shithead said.

I turned to him belligerently, trying to grab the initiative. "Why are you still here? Hasn't your boss called you?"

His forehead wrinkled and he shook his head.

"He hasn't?" I said. "I don't understand it. Everything

went fine. I left him fifteen minutes ago. It's all okay. So there's no reason for you to stay any longer, is there?"

The gorilla was looking more and more confused, which was just the way I wanted him. He poked the gun in my direction. "Shut up! I gotta wait for the call."

"Why? It's plain everything's okay. I wouldn't be here if it wasn't, would I? Maybe he forgot. Or maybe he figured that you'd be smart enough to leave, once I got here."

His eyes were darting around the room, as though looking for an answer or a clear instruction. "Shut up! Shut up!"

Just then the phone rang. Thank Christ. I didn't know how much longer I could vamp.

Shithead looked at me, then in the direction of the phone, then at the two hostages, then back to me. The phone kept ringing. If I waited for the ape to reach a decision, we'd be hearing bells all night.

"That's probably him. You'd better answer it," I said. That was just enough of a push.

"No," he said, waving his gun. "You answer."

I shrugged and walked in front of him into the kitchen. I picked up the phone.

"Is everything all right?" I heard Nicholson say.

"Yeah, just fine. . . . He's right here."

I held out the receiver to Shithead. He looked relieved. I put my hand in my pocket. He said "Hello" a couple of times, then started looking confused again. He was about to say something to me, when my hand came out of my pocket and swung in a big circle. It didn't quite complete the rotation. It ended when the meaty part of the sap connected with the middle of the goon's forehead. From his hairline to the bridge of his nose, the skin split like that of an overripe plum, revealing the red-orange pulp inside. His mouth fell open and he dropped face-first to the floor.

I looked down at him. Involuntary twitches shook his arms and legs. I slapped the blackjack on my palm. Funny. I didn't feel quite so tired anymore. I smiled. There's nothing quite like clobbering an evil son of a bitch to perk you right up.

Suddenly, both the front and back doors flew open. Cops with their weapons drawn raced in. Had I not managed to put Shithead out, they would've ended it in two seconds. One plan, at least, had worked perfectly.

"All over," I said.

A young patrolman looked at the heap on the floor, then at me. He shook his head. "Chee," he said.

Nicholson appeared a couple of minutes later to direct the mop-up. An ambulance that had been waiting around the corner took Shithead away. He was starting to groan.

Mrs. Bernstein and Bemelman were untied. After a few questions, they were free to go. I saw Mrs. Bernstein looking meaningfully in my direction and I hastily engaged a puzzled cop in earnest conversation. Not very nice of me, but I didn't have a clue what I could say to her. I felt I'd rather face the kid, Rudy, and Shithead all over again than have to contend with Mrs. Bernstein just then. Besides, what could I have said that would've made any sense . . . or any difference?

Bemelman was still pretty dazed, blinking his watery eyes and soundlessly opening and closing his mouth. Mrs. Bernstein took his arm and led him away, saying what he needed was some nice hot tea and a piece of homemade coffeecake. Okay. That might not solve his problems, but it sure would give him something new to worry about.

Nicholson and I briefly went over the evening's events again. He said he'd have a statement prepared for me to sign during the next day or so, but that everything looked pretty straight ahead from that point on. For a sour son of a bitch, he seemed almost cheerful.

Finally, he chased out the remaining cops. He stood over me, looking down, wearing a kind of smiling grimace. "You know, two day ago I thought you were another pain in the ass that I didn't need . . ."

"—But?"

He grinned. "But you turned out to be a pain in the ass that I did need. Thanks."

I smiled acceptance of what, for him, was probably high praise.

He put a hand on my shoulder. "You've had a busy night. Get some rest—you deserve it." He paused at the door. "And don't worry about Novallo. His ticket's canceled."

I sat on the couch for a long time after he left, thinking over the last few days. In the whole insane, incredible situation, the most insane, incredible thing was that I was still here, thinking about it. I had made it. I had survived. I had showed that I could still pull it off, that—goddammit!—Jake Spanner still had something. I didn't know if anyone cared, but it mattered to me.

Given that, I should've been feeling better, and it didn't take me long to realize why I wasn't.

The bastard that had dropped me in the shit to begin with was still floating loose. It sure wasn't the first time I'd been played for a sucker—maybe it wouldn't even be the last—but it wasn't the kind of thing that practice made any easier to accept. No, I knew I couldn't let it lie.

One of the truths I'd learned with age was that you never regretted what you did. You only regretted what you didn't do—the chance you never took, the thing you didn't say, the woman you never made, whatever. Maybe it would come to nothing, or prove nothing, but I knew I had to at least try to locate Sal Piccolo. If I didn't, it would stick in my throat for the rest of my life, however long or short that might be, and I figured I was already carrying enough stuff around as it was.

But that was for tomorrow.

This day had gone on long enough, I realized with a start when I found I had been dozing with my chin pressed against my chest.

I dragged myself to the bedroom, dropped my clothes on the floor, and fell into bed. The last thing I saw before I turned off the light was dripping letters screaming "Red Vengeance" from the cover of the paperback on the nightstand.

Any color would do, I thought, as I tumbled into sleep.

CHAPTER TWENTY-FOUR

Twelve hours later, pale golden sunlight filling my bedroom, I woke from deep, dreamless sleep to the sound of birds chirping and neighbors arguing about how someone's business meeting could not possibly have lasted until four in the morning. Apparently, having two fights and nearly being killed was a marvelous soporific. I doubted, though, that it would replace Seconal.

I yawned, stretched, sighed, decided I felt like a million bucks. Well, maybe six ninety-five, but that was still more than the plugged nickle I would've given for my chances, twenty-four hours before.

I got up, showered, brushed my teeth, shaved, slapped on some bay rum, slicked back my fringe of hair, and flashed a big grin into the mirror. Bad idea. I looked like a happy buzzard.

I made a big pot of Mexican coffee with cinnamon and cloves, and put together a *croque monsieur,* a kind of grilled ham-and-cheese sandwich that's been a favorite of mine since my days in Paris. I gobbled down one, found I was still ravenous, and ate a second. The way I felt, I could've continued on and probably devoured my kitchen, but I figured I'd better get down to it.

I poured some more coffee, and lit another of my Cuban cigars. Being alive this morning seemed a sufficiently special occasion. I pulled the telephone over and spent the next two hours making calls.

Sal had buried himself behind so many layers and veils that he was as good as invisible, the hidden puppetmaster. But the puppeteer has to pull strings, and every once in a while you can catch a glimpse of them. If you can follow them up, you might get to the manipulator himself.

I only had two links, two lines to go on—the guy who sapped me at the phony ransom drop, and the limousine. I figured they had both been hired. If I could get onto them, maybe—just maybe—they'd point me to Sal. It was pretty tenuous—lines as fine and flimsy as spider's silk—but it was all I had.

To look into the first of these, I again contacted my favorite geriatric bookie, Barbara Twill. Babs wasn't surprised by my call; said that after my visit she asked around a little about me and heard some curious stuff. Said she was expecting I'd be in touch. That was one sharp lady. I knew there was no point trying to dance around her, so for the first time I gave her the whole story.

After finding out about her ancient connection with Sal, I had some hesitation about telling her he was still alive, but I needn't have worried. She just grunted at the news. Nor did she react much to the rest of it. Didn't laugh, or whoop with disbelief, or offer meaningless after-the-fact advice. For all of which I was very grateful. That was the mark of a real friend—someone who didn't feel it was necessary to discuss at length the foolishness of which you were already well aware. Instead, she merely asked what I wanted her to do. What a swell old dame.

I told her that I figured that the goon who had hit me had been hired for that specific task, as opposed to being a partner; that after his experience with his grandson, Sal probably wouldn't trust anyone for anything.

"You mean, except for you." She laughed.

"Yeah, right."

Babs thought about it and agreed with my assumption, but pointed out that there was tons of muscle in this town, amateur and pro, and that there was enough work to keep a lot of them busy a lot of the time. Finding the one who'd done a particular job was, at best, a long shot. Still, she'd put the word out. The one thing in our favor, she said, was that the employer and the circumstances were sufficiently unusual that there might've been some conversation about it.

Her last remark to me was to watch out. "The word is that there've been a few guys who crossed Tony New—"

"Yeah?"

"And they're now fertilizing truck farms around Fresno."

"I didn't realize the kid was into recycling."

"It's not funny, Jake."

"Yeah, I know, but don't worry. It's all taken care of." She snorted, told me to be careful, then hung up.

I stared at the phone, trying not to think of central California lettuce fields. It was all taken care of, I told myself, and got out the Yellow Pages.

In a way, the question of the limousine was less straightforward than that of the hired thug. There were four pages' of rental agencies in the phone book, but that was only a nuisance. The real problem was that in order to get the information I wanted, I figured I needed more than just a description of Sal and the date the limo was hired. To sound sufficiently plausible, I should also have a name.

I only had one name—Harry Winchester, the person unaccounted for in the rooming-house fire. No question; it was a tremendous long shot. On the other hand, Sal would've needed a new identity when he disappeared. And since Winchester's remains were found in Sal's room, it was not completely unreasonable to assume Sal knew that that identity was available. Whether he kept using it or not was another matter. In any event, however thin it was, asking after a Mr. Winchester was better than my other option, which was picking a name at random and trying to talk around it.

I started calling, attempting to sound like I was looking for a haystack rather than a needle. With every call I said that on such-and-such a date, a Mr. Harry Winchester had hired a chauffeur-driven car from their agency, and that I was trying to locate him. I then proceeded with a story about a lost wallet, or that Mr. Winchester had witnessed an accident, or that I had business dealings with the gentleman but had stupidly misplaced his address —whichever line felt best at the moment. Everyone was sorry, but they thought I must have made a mistake. I asked if they were sure, and described Mr. Winchester, but they again regretted they could be of no service. All very courteous. All dead ends.

I was beginning to have my doubts about pursuing this

line, when the eighteenth call paid off. Yes, the Royal Livery Service told me, Mr. Winchester had hired a car on the day in question. Only considerable restraint kept me from hooting victoriously. Oh, Spanner, this is your day; you are on one hell of a roll. But, the cultured voice went on, company policy prohibited releasing any information about their clients without prior consent.

We talked about it for a while but I got nowhere. Then I said I'd come down so we could discuss it in person. I was welcome to, but I was told it would make no difference.

Don't be too sure of that, I thought as I thanked him and hung up.

I paced through the house a couple of times, convincing myself that I was not abusing a friendship, then called O'Brien. I wasn't surprised that he was pissed off at me when I told him about my adventures, but I was struck by the vehemence of his reaction. He sounded genuinely hurt that I had excluded him, especially after I had promised he'd be in all the way.

"Look," I finally said, "be reasonable. Don't be upset because you were left out of a very messy situation."

"I didn't ask to be."

"I know that. Anyway, as it turned out, I had no control over it. It just happened."

"Don't shit me, Jake. Even if you'd had the choice, you would've kept me out."

I sighed. "Yeah, okay. I would've."

"Yeah, you would've. 'Cause you're selfish."

Selfish. What the hell was he thinking about? That it was so much fun playing with Tony New that I wanted to keep it all to myself? Shit. O'Bee was acting very strange.

"Listen, just because I don't think anyone else's neck should go on the block with mine is no reason to—"

"No. It's because I—" He broke off. "Aw, forget it."

There was silence for a long thirty seconds before I spoke. "You want to do something, I got something for you to do. That's why I'm calling."

There was another long pause, then he said, "You bastard," and started cursing me. I felt better. Everything was back to normal.

When he stopped for a breath, I told him to put on his most disreputable-looking clothes, and that I'd pick him up in about half an hour. He was well launched into another assault as I hung up.

I put on a starched white shirt, knit tie, and the dark blue suit that I saved for funerals. I hadn't worn it for quite a while. Not because friends had stopped dying but because a few years before, I had realized that the dominant activity in my life had become watching people get buried, and I had decided that I'd go to only one more funeral.

I was almost out the door when the phone rang and I found out that I might not have that long to wait.

"Jesus, Spanner, I thought you'd never get off the phone. I was just about to send somone over." It was Nicholson.

"What's up, Sergeant?"

My number, apparently. Luck was still running with me, but it had turned rotten. The national debt had been paid off. In short, Tony New had made bail.

"I thought it was all taken care of," I said. Yeah, and Mrs. Bernstein enrolled in a cordon bleu class.

Nicholson, to be fair, was genuinely embarrassed and apologetic and angry. He was also pretty worried. "Novallo's still acting real weird. I think he's gone around the bend so many times he's running circles. I tell you, it's kind of scary. When he was checked out, there was an old guy sitting on the bench, just sitting there, not doing anything. Tony spotted him and ran over and started screaming 'Fucking old men! Fucking old men!' His lawyer had to literally pull him away."

I made some kind of sound in acknowledgment.

I heard Nicholson sigh. "I think he's liable to come after you. There's a lot of talk about what he's done to guys that crossed him."

"So I've heard. What do you suggest?"

"We'll give you protection. Twenty-four hours. He won't get near you."

I thought about it, then thanked Nicholson but refused. If the kid wanted me and was really crazy, the cops wouldn't deter him a second. If the kid wanted me and wasn't so crazy, he'd wait until the guard was lifted, which it would be before very long. Either way, the result was the same. That's what I told Nicholson. What I didn't tell him was that full-time protection would kind of get in the way of my search for Sal.

Nicholson tried to get me to change my mind. I wouldn't. After I agreed several times that I was a damn stubborn old fool, he gave it up. "Okay, Spanner. I'll save my breath. It's your funeral. I just don't want to go to it." It sounded like he really meant it. Hell, he wasn't so tough.

I left the house, not quite as chipper as I'd been. Outside, my innocent little neighborhood suddenly seemed sinister, oppressive, an assassin in every shadow, a sniper behind every bush.

I went back inside. I got my old Browning out of the closet, checked the load, then went to my car and put it in the glove compartment.

Funny. It didn't help my uneasy feeling.

As I drove away, I remembered it never had.

CHAPTER TWENTY-FIVE

On the ride out to Sunset Grove, the Chevy seemed to be acting up more than usual, spitting, missing, nearly stalling when I accelerated. It sounded like it was ready for a complete overhaul.

Weren't we all.

I found O'Brien sitting in his usual spot, staring at the brick wall. He looked about the same as the last time I'd seen him, maybe a little paler, more sallow. Freckles, usually not especially noticeable, stood out on his forehead like some strange skin disease. Two bright-red circles decorated his cheekbones.

He had on a pair of dark-green stained polyester pants, an old striped pajama top, and mismatched canvas shoes. I'd asked for disreputable, and he'd sure delivered.

O'Bee nodded a greeting, then squinted up at me. "What's the matter? Somebody die?"

I shrugged and told him about Nicholson's phone call.

He shook his head. "As I've said before, Jake Spanner, for an old fella, you lead one hell of an interesting life." I made a face. "Now I suppose you're going to tell me that you think you're too hot a potato, and that it might not be real healthy associating with you."

"Something like that."

"Well, you know what you can do with your potato. I'm coming along." The voice was gruff but his eyes were almost pleading.

I looked hard at him, shrugged. "Then let's go."

He slapped his hands, flashed a smile, and stood up. He pivoted in a circle. "How do I look?"

I made a show of studying him. I pulled out part of the

pajama shirt so it hung over his pants in the rear, and opened the two bottom buttons, exposing his white belly. He looked like an ad for a Salvation Army soup kitchen. "Perfect," I said.

In the car, going over the freeway to West L.A., O'Brien questioned me in detail about the previous evening. I couldn't tell which gave him more vicarious pleasure, what I did to the two goons or what was nearly done to me.

"You know what your problem was, Jake Spanner? You didn't have me along to look out for you." He punched me in the arm, almost causing me to slip into the next lane of traffic.

The Royal Livery Service was in a street-level store front in a small office building that housed mostly lawyers, accountants, and management services, whatever they are. I cruised slowly by so we could look in. Then I parked and we discussed how we'd play it.

"Give me about three minutes," I said as I got out.

I went into the office. It was small and decorated to look like a manor-house study or library, rather than a place of business. Sheets of some synthetic board designed to resemble oak paneling covered two of the walls, and the third was floor-to-ceiling shelves filled with books purchased by the yard. A simulated wood desk and two leatherette armchairs that might've come from a hotel lobby took care of the furniture. I couldn't figure out what kind of impression they thought they were making. Unassuming shoddiness?

Whatever it was, the guy behind the desk fit right in. He wore tweeds, had longish straw-colored hair, and was undoubtedly a good decade older than he tried to appear. He looked oddly familiar, and it took me a few seconds to realize I'd seen him in a TV commercial. That happened a lot in this town.

He greeted me and inquired how he could be of service. In person, I detected a twinge of something underneath his carefully cultivated mid-Atlantic accent. New Jersey, I thought.

I told him I was the one who'd called about Mr. Winchester, and he got a lot less friendly. As I talked to him, he fingered a five-by-eight card on his desk, glancing at it every once in a while, and I was sure that was the rental application for old Winchester.

In another ten minutes he might have told me what I wanted, simply to get rid of me, but it wasn't necessary. The door flew open and O'Bee staggered in. He was growling and cursing at nothing in particular, acting like one of those poor harmless loonies who've been deprived of their thorazine and spent their time raging at phantom antagonists. In a paper bag was a bottle of cheap wine that we'd picked up on the way, and O'Bee proceeded to pour it down his front and onto the floor in an attempt to get some into his mouth. It was a great performance, and it worked like a charm.

The mere presence of old people is usually enough to generate discomfort—if not hostility—but the appearance of a demented old drunk is something else again, especially when he's making a scene and messing up the office.

The blond guy leaped to his feet, shouting at O'Brien, telling him to get the fuck out of there. His cultured accent disappeared, and he sounded remarkably like a Newark longshoreman. O'Bee shouted back, held his ground, and it wasn't long before the guy came around the desk to shove O'Brien out onto the sidewalk.

I grinned at O'Bee, then reached across the desk and grabbed the card. I saw "Winchester" written at the top, and signaled to O'Brien. If necessary, he'd been prepared to roll around on the sidewalk with the guy, in order to give me sufficient time to locate it. I was glad he wouldn't have to.

I looked at the card.

Shit.

As they say, the operation was a success, but the patient died. The address was that of the house in Beverly Hills where I'd dropped Sal. The phone number was for the answering service.

Another goddamn dead end. For a second I'd thought my luck had swung back, but I'd forgotten the law that says if things go according to plan, there's a reason.

Shit, shit, shit.

I passed the rental agent in the doorway. He gave me a funny look, but I had nothing bright to say to him.

Back at the car O'Brien was chuckling to himself, but one look at me and he stopped. "No good?"

"Nothing."

"Damn. What are you going to do now?"

I shook my head.

"If you'll take some good advice, you should clear out for a while, give this Tony New a chance to settle down."

I nodded. "Yeah. I've got one more possibility going. If that doesn't pan out soon, I'll probably do it. Not that I can afford to."

"You can always stay with me."

"Thanks a lot. I've always wanted a roommate who smelled like he used muscatel after-shave. Open the window, would you."

He laughed and fingered his wine-soaked pajama top. "I guess I am a bit aromatic."

"You were also great. Thanks, O'Bee . . . for everything."

He smiled, then punched my leg.

CHAPTER TWENTY-SIX

When we got back to the Valley, neither of us felt much like going to our respective places, so I kept driving. The car was making protesting noises, but I told it to shut up.

It was one of those wonderfully clear days that were now pretty rare, days when you could see all the hills and mountains that ringed the San Fernando Valley. Nearly every day had been like this when I first came here, the hills in their summer colors of a hundred shades of brown, seemingly so close, you could make out every boulder and dried bit of chaparral. But even then it was changing. I could remember when they first started talking about smog, back in the early forties. That had been news in those days. Now there was something called the Pollution Standard Index, and a rating under a hundred made the front page, kind of in the man-bites-dog category.

Today, though, was one of the exceptions, and it was pretty enough to make me momentarily forget my disappointment with the limo agency, and Tony New, and Sal, and all the other shit. The hills—those that hadn't yet been graded and flattened and subdivided—still looked like they must've when the Gabrielino Indians lived in the Valley, and when the Spanish missionaries and Mexican rancheros arrived, and when the first American traders came from the East, six months around Cape Horn.

I headed into the low range of hills that straddled the county line between L.A. and Ventura. I didn't know if the hills even had a name, but they'd been used as the setting for a lot of westerns over the years. They still could be, for they seemed to have changed very little, one of the last reminders that the Valley had once been nothing but little farms and ranches and open land. The road was old, winding and narrow, but there was no traffic. Indeed, the only signs of life were the rough white fence posts and strands of barbed wire that ran along either side of the road.

O'Brien clicked his tongue. "Nice, isn't it?"

"It really is. It's easy to forget that it was all like this once."

"Yeah. Up here, you hardly know any of that even exists." He waved his hand through his open window, where, down below and in the distance, straight lines of streets and rows of houses stretched as far as the next range of hills, twenty-something miles to the east.

"Of course," I said, "we'd both go crazy up here."

"That's true, too." He laughed.

I was driving slowly, enjoying the scene and not wanting to push it too hard around the curves, when a big wide maroon car came up behind me. At a clear stretch, I slowed even further, moved to the right, and gestured with my hand that the car should go by. It stayed behind me. I honked the horn and waved again, but the car didn't pass. I shrugged and sped up a little. Suddenly, my car was jolted, bumped from behind.

"What the hell!"

I looked in the rear-view mirror and O'Bee turned around, but we couldn't see anything except glare reflecting off the tinted windshield.

I started going faster and was hit again; harder, this time.

O'Brien put a hand on the dashboard to brace himself. "That son of a bitch is fucking crazy."

"I think you hit it right on the head."

I held my speed steady, prepared for another bump, but this time the car pulled out from behind and steadily, easily, drew even with mine. I quickly glanced to my left, knowing beforehand what I was going to see. With his head barely clearing the top of the steering wheel, looking like a twelve-year-old who'd taken Dad's car for a joy ride, was my favorite psychopath, little Anthony Novallo. He was bouncing excitedly on the seat, grinning across at me.

"Is that who I think it is?" O'Bee said.

"Yeah."

"You still got the knack, Jake Spanner."

Didn't I, though. I didn't have a clue how the kid got there, whether he somehow picked me up in town, or had someone tailing me, or had himself been with me since I left my house, just waiting for a good opportunity. It hardly mattered. All of a sudden Nicholson's police protection looked awfully good.

Tony New's car moved over and hit mine just in front of the door. I had to fight hard to hold the road. He hit again. My right tires hit gravel.

"Oh, shit!" O'Bee said.

I managed to get back on the road. A split second before I was about to slam on my brakes in an attempt to get behind the kid, he got the same idea and beat me to it, eliminating my options. Now I could only go forward.

And faster. Every time I tried to slow down, either to keep control of the car or to try to get him to go by me, I got hit from behind. He was laying right up against me, forcing me to go faster and faster. I was hunched forward, both hands gripping the wheel, neck muscles straining, knuckles white, trying to get reflexes that were geared to turning pages of paperbacks to respond to hairpin curves.

I was going fifty, twenty miles over the road's limit. And being pushed harder. Fifty-five. Sixty. Nearly sixty-five around a curve with a warning sign to slow to twenty.

"Look out!" O'Bee shouted as a car coming downhill came around the bend.

I went up on the narrow shoulder, and the only thing that kept me from going over a two-hundred-foot drop was that my rear fender smashed another warning sign and I was bounced back onto the road.

"Whoo!" O'Bee said, and slapped the dashboard with his hand. I stole a quick glance at him. His lips were drawn back. His eyes were wide, gleaming. But he wasn't afraid. No, just another speed-crazed adolescent.

"Any idea where this road'll come out?" I shouted above the roar of the wind and the whine of my complaining engine.

My question was answered two minutes later, as I careened around a curve. We were at the top of the mountain. And the end of the line.

A tall, heavy chain-link gate and fence blocked the

way. Unspecified but official-looking signs were posted, warning everyone off. There was no indication who or what was behind the fence. The vagueness of it all made me pretty sure it was a missile site, one rib of the nuclear umbrella, buried deep in the mountain and not even disrupting the ecology or the view. Yeah, a vestige of unspoiled, unchanged Old California up here.

I considered ramming the fence, trying to break through to get help from whoever was inside, but it looked far too sturdy.

"Hold on!" I shouted.

The near-miss with that other car had slightly slowed down the kid and given me about fifteen seconds of breathing space. I was going to use it to turn around and pass the kid going down. I didn't have the time or the room to do it safely, so I kept my foot down and tried to swing as wide as I could. Too fast. I left the paved road and drifted up a hill that sloped from the right. I slammed on the brakes and twisted hard to the left. The car flew, bounced, down the hill, nearly crashed into the fence, sailed across the road, bounced on the pavement, came to rest on the opposite shoulder, pointing in the direction I wanted to go.

And stalled.

Goddamn son of a bitch!

I turned off the ignition, pumped the gas pedal, and turned it on again.

Unnhh, unnhh, unnhh.

After twenty years, I knew my car well enough to know that that sound meant I was going nowhere. It'd probably start in a couple of minutes, but not just then.

And I didn't have the time. Tony New's car hurtled around the bend.

"Don't argue," I said, turning to O'Bee. "We split up. He's going to come after me. When you've got enough room, get back to the car. Try to get it started, and go for help. I'll try to keep away from him until you get somebody up here." He looked at me. "Go!"

We opened our doors at the same time. I was almost out, when I reached back, opened the glove compartment, and took out my gun.

O'Bee shook his head, then smiled. "Good luck."

"Yeah, you, too. Just do what I said."

I moved across the road just as the kid's car squealed, shuddered, to a stop. His door was open even before the car had stopped bouncing. There was a gunshot, followed instantaneously by a scraping, pinging noise in front of me. I was running for all I was worth, but from the kid's position I must've looked like the slow line at a shooting gallery. "Hit the tortoise and win a plastic key-chain."

Without pausing or aiming I pulled off a shot in the kid's direction. Damn! The last time I'd done that, Eisenhower was president. I heard the bullet strike metal. Not bad. At least I could still hit the side of a car at twenty yards.

I heard Tony New cursing as he dropped out of sight, and I made it across the road, up the hill about ten strides, and dropped behind a boulder. My heart was pounding like a son of a bitch and my legs were shaking. My dark-blue suit was already covered with dust.

I stuck my head up and saw Tony New moving in a low crouch, at an angle, in front of me. I couldn't hold the gun steady so I rested it on the rock and fired again. I was way wide, but the kid still went running for cover behind a large rock close to the road. He came up firing, causing chips to fly off of my boulder and sending me down as he reached new cover, ten feet closer to me. He was getting ready to move again, but I beat him to the draw and sent him ducking as I just missed with my shot.

It was hard to believe. Right next to a hundred megatons of modern weaponry, and the kid and I were shooting it out with pistols, behind rocks. Hopalong Spanner. Swell. And where was the cavalry now?

I looked out the far side, but couldn't see O'Brien. Just as well. Tony New was still way too close to the road. If O'Bee was going to have a chance, I'd have to draw the kid farther off. That meant I'd have to move.

I fired twice, then took off. I was aiming for another rock, twenty feet higher up. In my mind, it had seemed entirely plausible, just a hop, step, and jump up the hill. I must've forgotten I wasn't thirty anymore, or even fifty. Two-thirds of the way to my next cover it started to feel like I was running through quicksand, sucked down, unable to lift my knees high enough. Then the kid started firing. As though I needed encouragement. I gritted my teeth and scrambled, desperately grabbing onto twigs, rocks, anything to pull myself up higher.

One more big step and I was there. Right leg onto that rock, then push off and I was behind cover. I moved with all my weight, all my strength. Up. Pull. Push. The rock gave way. Momentum pushed my body straight up, then backwards. I cried out in surprise. My hands shot out to the side, the gun flew behind me, and I tumbled back down the hill.

It must've looked like I'd been shot, because I heard O'Bee call my name. Then the kid giggled.

I rolled head over heels a couple of times, until I came to rest ten feet below, sprawled out on my stomach, facing downhill, my feet higher than my head. I felt stabs of pain where I'd hit the sharp edges of shale or thorny branches, but nothing bad enough to suggest a serious injury. So much for the brittleness of old bones.

Still, the shock had shaken me badly, immobilized me. My gun lay five feet away from my outstretched hand, but it might have been across a chasm. As hard as I tried, I couldn't move, make myself move, any closer to it.

I heard a sound and with difficulty raised my head to see beyond the gun. Tony New was advancing toward me, slowly climbing up the hill. His pop eyes were bulging, the color of slate. A pink tongue darted out, moistened his smiling girlish lips in anticipation of what he would do to me. He wore a dark-blue shirt, white tie, pants, and shoes, and a hideous red, white, and blue plaid jacket, all pretty dusty. The one imbecile thought in my mind was, how could I be killed by someone who looked like that?

Easily. Very easily.

He stopped close to me, grinning, giggling under his breath. He hoisted his gun and slowly took aim. From the angle, it looked like he was planning on a leg shot, to start with. He was going to enjoy this, and didn't want something like my death to prematurely terminate his pleasure.

His mouth curled into a broader smile; then suddenly he jumped back as a rock sailed over his shoulder and landed in front of him. He whirled and looked down the hill. O'Brien was slowly coming up, struggling, stopping every few feet to ineffectually lob another stone.

"O'Bee, no!" I called. "No! Run!"

But he kept coming, his face red and sweating, pushing, panting, heaving his quivering bulk up the hill. Tony New looked at him, unconcerned, just letting him come on.

"O'Bee! *O'Bee!* O'BEE!"

Then the kid seemed to get bored. "Another fucking old man," he said; then, calm as anything, fired twice.

I saw two red flowers blossom in the center of O'Bee's pajama shirt, expand, then cover his belly. He tried to throw the rock in his hand, but it only went a foot or two, and he sank to the ground.

"O'Bee!" I cried; then my voice turned to a mindless animal roar of anger and despair.

Without thinking about doing it, I suddenly found myself on my feet, moving forward, screaming, yelling. With an agility I had thought was long gone, I bent and scooped up my gun without breaking stride.

The kid turned toward me. For the first time his coolly sinister mask cracked, and there was fear. I didn't know what I looked like, but I hoped Tony New saw me as the Angel of Death descending on him, because that was how I felt.

He half-stumbled back a step and fired. My left arm exploded in pain. It felt on fire. Red, yellow, blue flames danced behind my eyeballs. But it made no difference. I pulled the trigger. Through my burning vision, wavering like a heat mirage on the highway, I saw his eyes pop ever wider in surprise; then a red circle opened in his throat and began to gush.

I tossed my gun away and closed with him. As I hit him, his gun went off again, but I had no idea whether he hit or missed me. He was knocked onto his back and I stayed on top of him, sliding down the hill, riding a giant wave of mindless hatred. When we stopped, I grabbed his pale blond hair with my left hand and began to pound his skull on a rock. I didn't know, he might have been dead when he hit the ground, but I didn't care, didn't think, just kept pounding, beating, his blood pouring over me, until I could lift my arm no more, until I was empty of the madness.

I staggered off him, stumbled over to where O'Brien lay, dropped beside him. His eyelids were still fluttering.

"O'Bee, you stupid son of a bitch," I gasped, sobbed. "Why didn't you do what I told you?"

It looked like he tried to smile. "Don't take any shit, Jake," he said. Then he died.

"O'Bee." My voice was barely audible.

I closed his eyelids. My own dropped down. Heavy, dark thunderheads rolled over me, muffling, suffocating, obliterating.

CHAPTER TWENTY-SEVEN

I woke up and found myself lying between starched, brilliantly white sheets. A muted light next to the bed revealed light-green hospital walls. It was dark outside the window.

I turned my head and saw two figures at the end of the bed. I blinked and they came into focus. One was Nicholson. Slightly behind him stood Lieutenant O'Brien.

Nicholson moved over and sat in a chair close to me. The bed was high, so our heads were nearly level.

"You goddamn foolish, stubborn old coot," he said.

"Is this some new kind of treatment? Verbal abuse?" My throat was incredibly raw, and my voice was little more than a croak.

Nicholson snorted, then shook his head. "In case you're interested—though the way you act I don't see how you could be—you're going to be okay. It was just a flesh wound. In and out. Clean. You've got lots of bruises and you'll be sore for a while, but other than that, you're fine." He shook his head again.

"How'd I get here?"

"Your little gun battle attracted the attention of the men in the . . . uh . . . installation up there, and they investigated."

"At least they didn't think they were under attack and launch a retaliation."

Nicholson looked at me, then laughed. "When they got there, they were sure they had three bodies. You were covered in blood. I guess most of it was Novallo's."

"He kind of upset me."

Nicholson sighed, stood up. "There'll be a few questions, you know."

"I figured there would be."

"But there should be no trouble." He looked down at me, sighed again. "I suppose I'm glad you're all right."

"Only suppose?"

"Do me a favor, would you, Spanner? The next time you feel the urge to pull some stunt, do it in another jurisdiction. I got enough problems."

"I'll keep it in mind."

"Sure, you will. I might as well talk to the fucking wall." He put a large hand on my shoulder, smiled. "Take care, old man."

After he went out, the lieutenant came over and took his place. He looked a little drawn, gray around the edges, but otherwise calm, in control.

"I thought I told you to stay out of trouble." He smiled weakly.

"I'm so sorry."

"Jake—"

"It was all my doing."

"Jake—"

"I wanted to keep him out of it."

"Jake—"

"He tried to save my life. Lieutenant, I'm so—"

"Jake, shut up a minute! Please." I shut up. "Listen, you don't have to tell me about my old man. I know what he was like."

"That still doesn't—"

"Would you wait a second! Jake, he was dying. Cancer. It was inoperable."

The news didn't really surprise me. I'd been reading the signs, and I knew he was pretty bad. I just hadn't wanted to admit it, actually confront it.

"Why didn't he tell me?"

"You know, that was his way, Jake. He only had a few more months, two–three at the most, and they were going to be bad, very, very bad. It scared him. He didn't talk much about it, but I knew he was afraid, and it really got to me. It wasn't the dying that frightened him, but the pain. And the waiting. Just watching, feeling himself going, and being unable to do anything. One last time he wanted to do something, Jake—feel alive, in control, to make a difference. You gave him that chance. And he found a way to go that he could accept—or that was at least more acceptable. This may sound strange, but for his sake, I'm grateful to you."

It all made sense. His enthusiasm at being involved, his annoyance when I cut him out. I'd tried to protect him from the one thing he wanted.

"You get some rest now, Jake. We'll talk about it all later." The lieutenant stood up. "From what Nicholson tells me, I guess your adventure is at an end."

I looked at him but didn't say anything.

He looked back, a curious expression on his face. "Not yet, huh?" I kept my gaze steady. The lieutenant broke into a broad grin, then winked, exactly like O'Bee used to. "Good. Give 'em hell."

He was partway through the door when he leaned back in. "You ever need a license-plate run, give me a shout."

I smiled at him and nodded. Remarkable. I'd subverted another O'Brien.

After the lieutenant left, I thought a lot about his father. O'Bee hadn't just tried to save my life; he'd succeeded. Seeing him gunned down so coolly, so terribly, had done something to me that fear for myself had been unable to do. What I couldn't decide was whether he'd given me a gift or I'd given him one.

A pretty, young nurse came in and gave me a shot that put me out for another twelve hours.

CHAPTER TWENTY-EIGHT

Next morning I was a lot better, though still a bit ragged. As long as I was careful moving my arm, the gunshot wound hardly hurt, but the bruises were starting to make themselves known. However, aches aside, I had to admit I felt pretty good, almost soaring. It was probably due to the medication, but I felt, if not actually youthful, certainly no longer old. Ultimately, panic, terror, and violence are probably unhealthy. They do, however, tend to break the routine.

I had just pushed aside the breakfast tray, when the phone rang. It was Barbara Twill.

"How'd you find me?" I said.

"You don't know? Jake Spanner, you're a hero. You made the morning paper."

"Oh, shit." Publicity was not what I wanted. "What did it say? 'Old Dick Rubs Out Young Punk'?"

"Words to that effect."

"Swell."

"I must say, you sound all right."

"Oh, I'm fine. Why?"

"The report made it sound like you were at death's door."

"Exaggeration. I tried, but they wouldn't let me in."

"That's good, 'cause I got something that'll make you feel even better."

"Yeah?"

"Yeah. Got a line on our mutual friend. Located the hired muscle, guy that sapped you. Ex-football player, now a collector for a shark. Does free-lance on the side. Thought the whole thing was so funny, he talked about

228

it. I picked up the chat, got in touch with him. No question that he was hired by our friend, who now calls himself—"

"Winchester?" I cut in.

"Right. Pretty good, Jake."

"Oh, I'm only slow before the fact. After it, I'm a regular whiz. Did the guy meet with Sal?"

"Yeah. You won't believe this."

"What?"

"Met him in front of the museum—the one opposite the Coliseum."

"So?"

"So, our friend Winchester was working there. Selling ice cream from one of those bicycle carts."

"Jesus."

"Isn't that something? I can remember when he very nearly ran this town. . . . Think you can get onto him?"

"I don't know. I'll try. Look, Babs, how much did you have to put out for this info?"

"A couple of bills. Don't worry about it."

"No, I'll pay you back."

"Forget it. I can afford it, and it's been more than worth it. Sal the Salami pushing popsicles! Hah!" She hung up.

I lay in bed a few minutes, then swung my legs over the side. I leaned against the bed until I was sure I could make it. I was stiff and sore, all right, but somehow the aches felt good, badges of honorable endeavor.

I shuffled over to the closet and put on the clothes that the cops had brought for me. The ones I'd worn yesterday were completely ruined. No more funerals for me. No, not even my own: "Sorry, but I don't have a thing to wear."

On the way out, the nurse at the floor station asked me where I was going.

"Out," I said, not breaking stride.

"You can't leave."

"Sure, I can."

"They said you might be difficult."

"They were right," I called over my shoulder. "So long."

I was starting to limber up a little by the time I reached the lobby. I kept going until I found a pay phone. It took half an hour for the cab to arrive after I called. This was a rotten town for taxis. It took another half hour to get to my place. My fare was bigger than a two-week grocery bill. At least I was still working on the money Sal had given me.

We drove by Mrs. Bernstein's house. I felt a twinge of guilt. What for, Spanner? I wondered. For being driven crazy by the woman? For putting her in danger? For saving her life?

Come on. "J. Spanner: Crushed beneath an overly developed sense of responsibility." Enough of that. No more.

And no more obits either.

Damn! but I was feeling good.

I paid the driver and went to the garage where my car was parked, again courtesy of the L.A.P.D. They'd even washed it and filled it up. I muttered something sarcastic as it started like a champ on the first try.

On the way into town, I tried to figure my chances, but didn't have a clue. By rights, Sal should have been long gone, enjoying himself in Rio, Nassau, Geneva, or another of those places where they don't pay much attention to people who arrive with briefcases filled with cash. There was no percentage in his sticking around, but somehow I had the feeling—almost a gut-level certainty—that that was just what he'd done. Had I been Sal and put such an elaborate mechanism in operation, I'd sure as hell be interested in seeing how it played itself out. Especially if I felt I was so well hidden, so deeply buried, that I'd never be found. It wouldn't be exactly smart, but it was just the kind of overconfident lapse that was conceivable.

However, even if I were right, I knew I wouldn't have a lot more time. The game was over, as the spread in the newspaper made all too clear. The main thing going for me was that maybe Sal thought I was still in Intensive Care, hanging by a thread, and he wouldn't be in that much of a hurry. If I could get a line on him around the museum—from the other vendors there, or maybe get onto the company he worked for—I might be able to run him down. It was a long shot, but once again it was the only shot I had.

I parked the car on one of those deteriorating streets that bordered the University of Southern California, and crossed into Exposition Park. The approach to the History Museum was dotted with groups of little kids, outings from day camps and summer schools, there to look at the reconstructed dinosaurs. Look this way, kids, I thought; here's one that's moving.

I was nearly at the main walk going up to the building when I saw him. I stopped dead, because I goddamn well couldn't believe my eyes. But there he was. Standing next to a cart decorated with pictures of laughing ice-cream cones. He was wearing one of those white uniform jackets and a Dodger baseball cap, handing out stuff to a gang of tiny black kids that clustered around. Sal Piccolo, the world's richest street vendor. As I've heard kids say: In-fucking-credible.

I started walking toward him. I saw him glance up, then freeze, and I knew he'd spotted me. I kept walking. He reached into his cart, pulled out a box of ice cream bars, and tossed it over the heads of the kids, who went scrambling for it.

He pushed the cart to get it moving, then jumped into the seat. The contraption was kind of a reverse tricycle, with the two wheels in front supporting the freezer box, and the handlebars, seat, and single wheel behind. Sal went along a walkway, cut across the grass, bounced over the curb and onto the street, moving in the direction of the Coliseum.

I went after him at an angle. For the third time in as many days, I was involved in another chase. I knew it was recommended that old people get plenty of exercise, but this was becoming ridiculous.

Sal's legs were really pumping on the pedals, but his vehicle was designed for stability, not speed; and, stiff and sore as I was, I was gaining on him. He veered off to the left, attempting to broaden the angle between us, and tried to jump a curb. The front end of the cart was too heavy, and he bounced back. He took another run at it and was stopped again. I had closed to within twenty-five feet. He hopped off the seat and opened the freezer compartment. He reached in and came out with the famous black, red-striped attaché case. Talk about your cold cash.

Sal started running toward the stadium with his long-legged stride, like an arthritic emu. He skirted the high surrounding fence, then went through an open service gate. I was right behind him. My body was starting to protest loudly, but I was not going to listen. No way was that S.O.B. going to get away from me this time.

We followed the oval of the stadium. We were both moving slower, but his long legs had opened up a little distance between us. He ran into an entrance tunnel, turned right, and was out of my sight. I went through the tunnel and came out into the stadium, row after row of empty seats stretching before me. I heard a sound above me, looked up, saw Sal going up an aisle, to the top of the stadium. I forced my legs to move. Up, up, up, climbing five, six, seven stories of stairs. My lungs were filled with iron weights. Lightning stabs of pain shot from my ankles to my knees.

As soon as I got to the top, he started back down, one aisle over. For once his long legs were a disadvantage. He couldn't get the stride right for going down, and I closed back to about twenty feet.

At the bottom, he clambered over the low wooden barrier, then across the cinder track and onto the football field. I almost didn't get over the railing, stuck straddling it, an arm and leg on either side, stomach and chest heaving, limbs trembling. A gasping, groaning effort. Rolled off the fence. Onto the track. Up on my feet. After him.

We were both hardly moving, one laborious, lunging step at a time. I crossed the goal line and he was ten yards in front. After him. After him. I no longer knew why I was doing this. Only knew there was pain, and that I couldn't stop. I crossed the twenty, thirty, forty. Midfield.

And I was gaining. It was the slowest run ever, down that field, but I was gaining. The attaché case started to get in Sal's way, hit his leg, threw off his rhythm. Thirty-five. Thirty. I could hear one of us gasping for air, but I didn't know which. Twenty. Closing. Closing. Fifteen. I was certain I was going to die.

At the ten, my foot caught a loose piece of sod. I hurtled forward, struggling to keep my balance, arms outstretched in front of me. I went down, but as I fell I caught him by the ankles and he dropped forward onto his face. A perfect saving tackle.

Sal groaned but he was going nowhere. Neither was I.

I lay there, out of time, out of space, the only reality my straining heart and lungs. I didn't know if it was a minute or an hour before I shakily struggled to my feet.

Sal was down on the two-yard line. I looked around. There were a hundred thousand empty seats, so the insane roaring I heard was not a jubilant crowd.

The attaché case rested on the goal line. I picked it up and went back to Sal. I rolled him onto his back. He made a sound like rusted hinges on a dungeon door. He opened his eyes.

"Mr. Winchester, I presume."

"Nice work, Jake."

"What the hell are you still doing here, you stupid asshole?"

He looked up at me, blinked, took some deep breaths. Eventually, his face began to lose its burning-red glow.

"I didn't think there was any hurry. Figured I'd wait until things quieted down. Besides"—he did something that almost looked like a smile—"I had to see how it turned out. You did pretty good, Jake."

"Don't give me that, you son of a bitch! You want to know what I been through? I been knocked out and I've been suckered. But you know about that. I've been in trouble with the cops and the mob. I've been threatened, tortured, beaten up, shot, and nearly killed at least twice. I've run a search and a couple of cons, though not nearly as good as yours. I committed armed robbery, fought a couple of thugs, had a high-speed car chase, saw a friend killed, and killed your fucking grandson." My voice had risen to a maddened roar.

Sal nodded, then said quietly, "It sounds like I missed all the fun."

I started to sputter, puffing up again, but found my anger rapidly deflating. To be honest, he wasn't entirely wrong. "Yeah, I was having all the fun while you were peddling your goddamn ice cream. Why, for Christ sake? You had the dough."

He shrugged. "Since I was staying around anyway, it gave me something to do. Better than sitting in my room. I kind of like it. I've been doing this since I became Harry Winchester."

"What about that? What happened? The kid tried to kill you. How'd you get away?"

"He knocked me out, but my head's pretty hard. Always has been. I came to, and the building was burning, smoke everywhere. Fire had already taken the front rooms and was moving back fast. I tried to get the guy out of the room across from mine, but he was already gone. Had bad lungs—asthma, or something—and the smoke had gotten to him."

"And that was Winchester?"

"Yeah. I moved him over to my room and took his wallet, and stuff. Hell, it didn't matter to him anymore."

"Why'd you stick with the name?"

"Why not? I needed to be someone. And Winchester had Social Security coming in. It helped keep me going until—"

"Until you were ready to get even."

"Yeah. Can you believe it? After I laid it all out for him, gave that punk the biggest break in his life. My own grandson."

"And you saw the way to settle another old score, by using me."

Sal smiled. "It worked. You were pretty impressive, Jake. I hardly had to give you anything, and you came up with the goods. Really fine."

"Save it," I growled. I shook the case. "About all I haven't figured is how you knew he'd be carrying this."

"Hell, I'd set up the whole thing originally, so it was easy to keep tabs on it, once I figured out what I was going to do. Knew how the kid made the pick-ups, when. Knew he always used a case like this for the money, knew where to buy one exactly like it."

"Another creature of habit?" Sal shrugged, smiled. "And you kept pushing me on the deadline because you knew when the coke pick-up would be made, and I had to be in place to spot the kid with the case?"

"Right."

"Jesus. What if I hadn't gotten onto the kid?"

"Then I would've remembered something else—some new bit of information—so you would have. But I didn't need to. You grabbed it and ran with it."

"And where were you going to run with it?"

"Tunisia." I looked a question at him. "When I was little, I can remember my father telling me about this village. He used to go across with fishermen. He said there was this white village on a cliff, shining in the sun, looking out over the sea. Said it was the prettiest place he'd ever seen. While I was in prison, I thought about that place a lot, and I decided that was the place I most wanted to see. It was a long time ago that my father was there. Maybe it's all changed. Maybe it's not even there anymore. But that's where I was going to start."

I nodded. It sounded nice, very nice. Not unlike my Moroccan memories, or daydreams, or whatever they were.

"We can still do it, Jake." I gave a disgusted look. "Think about it. The Mediterranean. Warm weather, spicy food, and hot women. The sun during the day, and a couple of nice girls to keep us warm at night. Not a bad old age, is it? What do you say, Jake?"

"I say you're crazy."

"Am I? What are you going to do? Give the money to the cops and get a handshake from the mayor? Maybe return it to the big boys? Say it was all a misunderstanding? Shit. Even if you gave it back, you think they're going to let you waltz away? These are very serious people. And remember—you're the one. The only one. As far as everyone is concerned, I died a couple of years ago. So it looks to me like you have to go away. With or without the money, you have no choice." He paused and looked hard at me. "For once, Jake, don't be a jerk. Take the money."

I looked down at him. "And you, too, I suppose."

"That'd be nice."

"After what you did to me?"

"Remember what you told me last week? I didn't do it to you. You did it to yourself. You did everything."

I started to say something, stopped. Again, Sal wasn't far wrong. He gave me a push, but I jumped in with both feet and went along all on my own. In a way, I had trouble blaming Sal. He'd only acted according to his nature, just like I'd acted according to mine. Only he'd understood mine a hell of a lot better than I'd understood his.

"Why shouldn't I take the money and leave you to your ice cream?"

Sal looked up at me, shook his head. "You couldn't do that, Jake."

"No?" I said, but I knew he was right about that, too.

Unfortunately. It must be nice to be without scruples. Very liberating.

"After all this—" I waved my hand at the insanity of the last week and a half, "do you feel like you're finally even with me?"

"Oh, yeah. Absolutely."

I thought he meant it. But so what? I knew I could never, ever trust him about anything. Then I realized that I didn't have to.

I held out the attaché case. "What would you say if I controlled the dough?"

"I'd say, fine." Sal smiled broadly. "I trust you, Jake."

Shit.

I looked around at the empty stadium.

Goddammit. The son of a bitch had manipulated me again.

But what of it?

Warm weather, spicy food, and hot women? Hell, I now knew—thanks to Miranda, another episode in my adventure—that even the last of those still had some meaning for me.

The mob, Mrs. Bernstein, and a losing battle against inflation?

I stared down at Sal, then extended my hand. "Don't you think this is an undignified position for two wealthy old gentlemen to be in?"

I pulled him to his feet. He smiled at me.

I shook my head, sighed. Sal Piccolo sure wasn't my first choice as companion for my last years.

On the other hand, it did beat the hell out of eating cat food.